DIFFERENT ROADS

I watch my goats grazing, head to tail, every day. They don't seem to notice that the fields are turning to golden brown in the autumn, for they are only looking for grass to sustain them. They apparently don't feel the cold bite of Winter, for they have their heavy wool coats to keep them warm. If one of their flock falls victim to a wolf, they barely miss his existence. I think that men are much like them. They think very little. They care only for the necessities of survival in their time and never recognize the choice of awakening before them.

—The Journals of Conrad King

MOUNT BELLEW

A SEASON OF HOPE

Happy Skiing!
Ron Dull

Written by
Ron Dull

Illustrations by
Justin McCarthy

Mount Bellew: A Season of Hope

Copyright © 2005 Ron Dull. All rights reserved.

Published by Hats Off Books™
610 East Delano Street, Suite 104, Tucson, Arizona 85705 U.S.A.
www.hatsoffbooks.com

International Standard Book Number: 1-58736-400-X
Library of Congress Control Number: 2004114156

"But I don't know what to write about," he complained. "Just put down what you know and all the rest will follow," she encouraged. "However, keep it simple. The use of language should not serve to be a barrier to communication."

Thank you to the family, to the friends, and to the true characters in life that have made it all so rich and worthwhile. The times we have spent in the mountains of the West and in the hills of New England have been extraordinary.
All of you, and the magnificent land around us, have inspired and enriched our lives in uncountable ways.
Seek adventure wherever you may find it, relish the beauty of every day, and stand on tiptoes to see a new horizon.
Life is the inspiration and the rest of this, well;
it is just a silly story.
We trust that you will enjoy our little tale and keep Love and Hope always in your hearts.

—Cap'n Ron

Wheel of Taranis

Author's note: Taranis is one of three major pan-celtic gods. He is the god of thunder and lightning. An interesting aspect in the worship of Taranis was his association with time. He was seen as the Lord of the Wheel of the Seasons. He is the deity of change. He is an appropriate god for all that had happened in Mount Bellew.

TABLE OF CONTENTS

Mount Bellew

DIFFERENT ROADS

I took the road less traveled by, and that has made all the difference.

—Robert Frost

There is a town in Ireland, County Galway, Province of Connacht. It is called Mount Bellew. My Grandmother immigrated from there when she was a little girl in 1898. She remembered little of it. She was very young. She is dead now.

She died as an old woman, bent arthritically with age, in a small town in Pennsylvania. She wasn't always so fragile. She was once a long-legged young girl with the speed of a gazelle. She moved with the grace and fluidity of a ballet dancer. How do I know this? She told me so.

Her personal stage was once upon a mountain in Vermont where she floated through pine scented forests and softly falling snow like a bird in winter flight. She used to remember those times to me as we rocked together on her wooden porch.

I remember that she had a red wicker rocker that sat commandingly by the front door. It would keep up a continual creaking to her movements. In rhythmic fashion, it kept time with the banging of the front screen door as grandchildren maintained an unrelenting assault upon the kitchen. In the early evening, while darkness began visiting shadows in the trees, we would sit out there enjoying the balmy summer night. She would bring us glass jars with holes punched in the tops.

We used them to catch fireflies.

I recall their ethereal lights blinking on and off, on and off, on and off. Sometimes we wanted to give up our hunt because we could never find the apparently invisible insects, but she would tell us with encouragement, "Just because you can't see them, Honey, doesn't mean that they're not there. You just have to keep on looking." And so, off we would go again in search of our elusive prey; hunter and hunted equally disguised in the dusky fading light.

Soon the jars, with their bits of grass tucked into the bottom for comfort, would be full of trapped little bugs. We pretended that we had created portable lanterns, but the manufactured light was too dim to see much by and the little insects, not knowing of their imprisonment, would fly and blink in confused protest. To her credit Grandmom always made us set them free again before we left for our own homes. She was strictly "catch and release"; a woman before her time.

I wonder where the small creatures thought they had been. Did they retreat to their burrows in the sweet warm grass and wonder, "What the hell was that all about tonight? Damn, same thing happened last week too..."

Did they tell their little bug children bedtime stories about their surreal paralyzation behind a glass, so clear, that they could not even see it?

"Oh Daddy Bug, you are just making that all up," they would sleepily buzz.

Between forages into the front yard to fill those jars with doomed lighting bugs, Grandmom would entertain us with the stories of her own youth. She remembered the people too and she told us the tales of years gone past, tales which were slowly unraveled in the fading glow of tiny prisoners incarcerated in the glass of their mayonnaise jar prisons.

Grandmom was Irish. And so, true to her lineage, her stories were always a sanguine blend of martyrs, hope, and heroes. Hope that the hero would never die. Hope that the martyr would become somebody, someday. Hope that they would all never get old or ill. Hope that they might pass on with dignity at least, and hope that the fireflies would escape the prison. At least *that* was in our power, and as we unscrewed the tops from the jars, the cool evening breeze would sweep the newly liberated insects back into the welcoming night.

It strikes me now that of all man's qualities, it is hope which is never failing. No matter how desperate the circumstances, we firmly believe that things will get better, that things have a way of changing, and that better times are just around the corner. Ironically, when things are good, and flowers fill the air around our lives, we just as firmly hope that change has finally settled down so that it may never alter our sense of well being and order. But of course it does. Change is fickle, and that is the nature of things.

However, it is hope which springs eternal and the bugs always had another night to fly.

Grandmom seemed genuinely mystified by how she grew to be so old and so frail—so suddenly. I guess that things just sneak up on you over 90 years. Maybe that is the reason that I chose to settle at Mount Bellew shortly after she died. It was another time, not hers, and it was another place, not the same; but it was an *idea*, which weaves its way through many lifetimes.

Perhaps I was trying to recapture some of her own memories. Perhaps I was trying to find and store my own remembrances when I was both young and physically able. Perhaps I was trying to reinforce the belief that all things must happen in their time and that, of all things, I wanted the hope that when I was rocking on my own porch someday, all alone, I would have stored a similar treasure chest of baubles and beads to rumble through in my mind. I would recall when I was a younger man: and...Oh, what a god I was!

There is a time to be crazy and irresponsible, a time to be serious and contemplative, and eventually a time for all of us to die. I found all of those times in Mount Bellew. I am lucky, because I would not want to die while realizing that I had indeed never taken the opportunity to yet live. I don't want to look in the mirror with regret and say, "What happened here? I should have climbed that mountain when I was young."

My own Mount Bellew is not a big town. It almost was, but not now. It is a small town which almost became a big town, but just couldn't quite manage the transition. Whether that was because of some inherent failure, or because of some insightful wisdom, I will have to leave that particular judgement up to you.

Mount Bellew, Utah was not named for my Grandmother's birthplace in Ireland. It was merely a coincidence. But I am sure that fate had something to do with my decision to turn off the road at that point and explore the territory.

The place actually had a chance once, a chance to join the magic, to become a part of the circus, to be "Somebody," or in this case—"Somewhere..

"Grow up son! Mature! Make some bucks!" seemed to be the paternal wisdom thrown directly at Mount Bellew from corporate headquarters.

Anyway, Hermann and Bobbi successfully killed all of that.

Good old Hermann, throwing moral cold water on all the burning bags of money coming his way. The man brought the place to the brink of glory once, and then Bobbi buried it back into the ground. Some people still hate Hermann around there; mostly the developers and the merchants. Others consider him a hero. Some call him a martyr.

It is probably fortunate that he actually prefers his boats and his sidekick, Conrad King, prefers his goats, since I doubt if they would be the most popular guys at local barbecues.

Mount Bellew is located about 100 miles south of Park City, Utah, hiding in the Wasatch mountain range. The population is somewhere around 350 (not including the cows). On any given day, the crowd can grow to a whopping 5,000 dedicated and fanatic skiers who have chosen to bypass the phony glitz or cattleyard mentality of the nearby giants for the more down-to-earth, back-to-basics feel of Bellew. It is like a mini-Mecca for the faithful few.

It is a physical place. There is nothing either soft or manicured in its approach, its terrain, or its people. There are "biker bars" so I guess there are "biker mountains." In either one you had better "blend," or you had better leave.

Your first impression is of cold, gray rock blasted into impenetrable walls from a cauldron in the pine filled forests below its base. Scattered and isolated boulders dot the landscape in inexplicable locations, while others have positioned themselves in teasing defiance of physical principle. They have apparently been blown into a random stack of cards fashioned by the ever present wind and it feels as though a mighty force would bring them all tumbling down in helter-skelter fashion. It seems as though such a force could never exist.

You approach the area on Route 226 while following the ice and boulder strewn drunken weavings of the Cohochee River. In the spring, hardy sportsmen brave its raging torrent in order to navigate its nearly freezing waters with their fragile kayaks. In the summer, it becomes a series of deep, dark pools full of marauding rainbow trout waiting dangerously to ambush any unsuspecting prey drifting on its mellow current.

It is an appropriate entrance to Mount Bellew.

There are a few condominiums, second homes, and hotel rooms to be found in the village, which is about two miles below the mountain base itself. It is as though the builders feared that the inevitable tumbling of large avalanche-driven boulders must someday ruin their enterprise and so they attempted to hide from the predestined carnage.

Common thought was that the place would never really amount to much since it was so far away from any major city. Its remote location was its savior, and its devil. You did not just happen to pass by the area. You either went there, or you did not, and only the most hardy and determined skiers were known to seek out its treasures. You could sit in a bar, casually mention that you had "been up to Bellew," and feel the measure of respect that came your way from the patrons that knew the sport.

There was a loyalty.

There is also a spirit in skiing which now seems lost in the whirlwind of ski industry buyouts and mega-mergers. Most ski areas come into existence for the very simple reason of making money for the parent corporation. It has become an entertainment industry full of clients and guests. Everything is too easy, too contrived and too focused on the bottom line.

There are a few real skiers left and they tend to seek out their own at enclaves like Mount Bellew, or Arapahoe Basin, or Mad River Glen.

It seems to me that the spirit resides in the hearts of people, not in the profit margin of the business.

We tap their wallets, but only on occasion do we tap their hearts.

To his personal credit, Hermann never forgot the old-time concept of what it was all about. He never succumbed to that which seems to have been outlawed by his Armani suit-wearing competitors: he never forgot to just have spontaneous *fun*.

Despite its frequently howling winter winds, its disorienting whiteouts and its sub-zero temperatures, the community which habitually assembled itself at Mount Bellew was always warm and inclusive. It was the gathering of family. It was a place where kids were looked after, even when they weren't yours; where names were shouted in derision from creaky chairlifts; where families spent every weekend together and Dad could occasionally beat the kid in a downhill race. It was a place where the injury of a fellow skier or the death of an old comrade was contemplated in the majestic silence of the towering hills.

Conrad knew where that spirit was; he always did. Hermann finally accepted it and Bobbi found it. It certainly was not displayed in any glamorous facilities; not at Mount Bellew where the biggest, proudest capital improvement in ten years was the Port-O-Pottie placed at the mid-station.

But there was always a smell of magic at Bellew which was carried on the pine laden air. Its perfume made the eyes when it mattered—to her.

She always said it with a smile that indicated that it was something positive, to be able to maintain basic values, solid and dependable in a whirlwind of change and fashion.

It is ironic to think, then, that this place, this Mount Bellew, "never really amounted to much" either since it is an accusation that most humans must suffer and eventually die with.

Rather like, "Nice guy, but he never really amounted to much" (So? I suppose that it is then better that he is just dead?). I am still confused by that statement. I'm not sure, even now, exactly "what" I am supposed to "amount to." And I am getting too old to fix it all anyway.

What do I know?

I know that we live through a brief exchange of daily emotions which somehow define our lives. We try to deal with it all in good faith, with good spirit, and in the end it is just that: a time. Even then, the times of remembrances get distorted with age. Some grow larger, some grow dimmer, and there you are: lightening bugs trapped in a jar, never knowing that they were captured.

It is too late now. Someday I will be buried with a bunch of other fellows who also amounted to "nothing."

No one will visit us.

Some will have amounted to "something." I suppose that their little bug tail lights burned brighter than everyone else's.

On, off. …On, off. …Off.

They will have the bigger headstones, casting shadows upon mine.

Nobody will visit them either.

Anyway, we will all be sharing the same plot of dark dirt, and late at night, when the spirits can rise up and stroll the quiet trees of our mutual cemetery in order to go play bocce ball (or whatever spirits do for eternity), I will whisper to the local inhabitant of #2567, "Say, pal, nice headstone. By the way, did you ever ski the tree run on the lower half of Bridger

17

Bowl after 14 inches of new freshies?"

If he doesn't answer, I will know that he is dead and probably had been most of his life.

If he calls me a "dipshit," well, it is probably Wally, and I will be happy to kick his butt in bocce ball.

THE SPIDER

Observe constantly that all things take place by change, and accustom yourself to consider that the nature of the Universe loves nothing so much as to change things which are, and to make new things like them; for everything that exists is, in a manner, the seed of that which will be.

—Meditations of Marcus Aurelius

THE SPIDER

"Will you walk into my parlor?" said the spider to the fly;
"'Tis the prettiest little parlor that ever you may spy.

The way into my parlor is up a winding stair,
And I have many curious things to show when you are
there."

"Oh no, no," said the little fly: "to ask me is in vain,
For who goes up your winding stair can ne'er come down
again."

—Mary Howitt

For a man on the run, Hermann Olsen showed no signs of being in a hurry, as he slowly sipped his beer in the dark confines of the bar. Above the head of the bartender, the silent pantomime of a hockey game was being played out on a TV screen which buzzed annoyingly like a morning-after headache. Through the fuzz and disconnected lines, the speeding puck was barely discernible and so he paid little attention to the action. Besides, it was only five in the afternoon and it was bound to be a rerun. That is not exactly primetime viewing for most NHL games.

Instead, Hermann was losing himself in the crying old country songs which wailed at him from inside the dusty jukebox and he soon found himself mesmerized by the busy workings of a solitary spider in a corner by the bathroom door.

He felt that the spider's intricate dance went well with the

21

music. *I wonder if spiders can hear?* He pondered. *Do you think he's working; or maybe playing; or perhaps even dancing to the music? Some scientist would tell me that he's just getting ready for dinner. That's pretty unimaginative.*

As though painting his own private picture, the insect slowly linked thread upon gossamer thread in apparent randomness, tiny feet creating a masterpiece meant solely for his own enjoyment.

There did not seem to be a plan.

One long thread here, a short arch there, a splat on the wall to make it all stick, and since he still felt pretty good *Well, what the hell, the spider thought,* a few whimsical circles on the right side for style. The little insect, pleasantly unaware of his own existence in the darkened bar, or the solitary audience which he had inadvertently attracted, worked seemingly more for his own self-entertainment than for any planned catch of a large fly feast.

Hermann felt that this was a friendly enough watering hole; not friendly in the roar of laughter or happily clicking pool balls, but friendly in the way of a comfortable old chair among silent companions. They pretty much left you alone here. It was quiet in the way of western cattlemen, farmers and local workers who, tired from a long day in the burning sun, came here to seek a short refuge from the heat, for a quick cold beer or reinforcing belt of liquor in their personal "club" before heading home to their families.

He snapped back from his reverie as a shot from the slamming front door entered the room and announced the arrival of two local mountain men.

"What's happening, Jimmy? How's business today?" one asked.

"Same as usual, Pete; consistently lousy," the bartender answered.

"Good. I wouldn't want this place to be discovered by any of those Hollywood types. "Hey look," the intruder smiled, almost surprised, "You got a customer. Things must be picking up," he chided. "How ya doing today young fella?"

"Just fine sir, how are you?" *Might as well be friendly,* thought Hermann.

"Doing damned good. Me and Conrad here got us a nice turkey today up on the mountain," the hunter offered openly. "One of the finest I've seen in a long time."

"Only one?" Hermann inquired, trying to help break the ice.

Although it was dark in the cool bar, the man called Conrad fixed him in the perpetual squint of his eyes. "Only wanted one, son; couldn't eat two," he growled like an ancient lawnmower whose rusty blades whirred in his throat.

There was a veiled threat in his rumbling voice. Hermann could see that he was not a physically big man. You couldn't describe the man as "big," but he had a way of pervading the space around him like a solitary rock on a beach; one that you could see coming from a long distance away. He looked as tough as an old leather boot which had been left out in the sun to dry; cracked, weathered, and disturbingly missing a few laces. He made Hermann nervous.

"But I know that I can drink two beers," he said brightly and a set of gleaming white teeth shone through the deeply tanned face.

Time to make this right, thought Hermann. "Well then, why don't you say I'll buy you the first one as a friend, and the second one will be for that gobbler who had a lucky day."

"You're all right, son," Pete laughed, "but them beers are gonna cost you more than money, because now you gotta come on down here and tell us old farts a story about what you're doing in this part of the country."

Hermann hesitated for a second, being leery of carrying this exchange too far. He was suddenly aware that he was not dressed for this place, didn't fit the part. He did not "blend." He wore the tattered old jeans and bleached-out Levi's shirt like a uniform of the '70s—a badge of non-conformity. His long hair and beard were in the fashion of the times, provided you were safely in an urban environment and not squirreled away in some cow-kicking bar in Mount Bellew. The look had

23

given him problems before.

"Is that a girl or a boy, Jethro?" he would hear it whispered rather non-discreetly behind his back. "Some sort of hippie freak I guess, Rufus. Maybe one of those "love" children, or some sort of doper."

The remarks would follow him derisively like a stink on his clothes. He had always avoided trouble by moving along slowly, knowing when he was outnumbered and being extra polite. Then he got out of town as soon as possible, and that was looking like one good solution right about now. The problem would be just getting past these two old cowboys; who did not look like they would move too easily.

"Come on down, boy. Conrad don't bite," Pete waved at him. "He just growls like an ornery old dog, especially when he misses the easiest shot I ever saw at one big-assed bird!" Pete, putting on his best turkey imitation, gobbled derisively in Conrad's reddened face.

Maybe this time it'll be all right, thought Hermann as he slid down to the end of the bar. *At least I'll be closer to the door, and if things get mean, I'll just bolt. I'm damned sure that I can outrun these two old goats.*

He smiled and nodded as he approached the two men, his plan still slowly forming in his head, when he suddenly felt a steel-vise clap him on the shoulder and bounce him easily on top of a waiting barstool. He crash landed to Pete's waiting and open grin.

"Hey partner, I'm Pete. I own this joint," and a huge mitt of a hand was thrust his way. He took it in his own.

"This is Conrad King," he nodded at his friend.

Hermann was reluctant to take the strong weathered hand now being pushed his way. He feared being caught in a mano-y-mano crushing contest which he was bound to lose easily and quickly, but not to do so would be to offend. Instead he found Conrad's firm handshake to be deliberately softened in order to match his own and he looked into eyes which were intense, questioning, and suspicious—all of which defied his welcoming grip.

"So what brings you to the thriving megalopolis of Mount Bellew, young fella?" Conrad began, "And forget about buying those beers," he added as the barkeep expertly slid the three ice cold mugs across the dark mahogany bar. "When we're with Pete, we don't pay."

"Oh thanks," Pete moaned. "With some more customers like you, Conrad, I can go broke earlier than I planned and then just go kill myself."

"Good. At least then you'll be less miserable," retorted Conrad, belting down half of his beer in a single thirsty and defiant gulp.

Hermann Olsen is not on his way home, and, at least in *his* mind, he is not even lost on the infamous Route 226. He is not running away from anything either, although that would be a matter of debate. Hermann feels that he is running *toward* something. He just doesn't know what.

So, at least in the thoughts of his father, he is "running away": running from all the responsibilities of the business in Baltimore, away from the family obligations, and away from the life that was so carefully crafted for him. That pretty much summed up the final paternal lecture which was still ringing in his ears over the last thousand miles of Interstate roads.

"Damn it, Hermann! I've busted my ass all my life to get this business to where it is and you're just going to walk away from it all?" his Father ranted at him in irritation.

"Dad, it's your business, not mine, and I'm just not interested in it like you are."

"Bullshit, boy! It is your business. It paid for the cars, the clothes, the schools and all the other crap. It pays for that fancy-assed house you and your mother live in. It is every bit your business as well as mine. But all you've done so far is take from it and now, when I need you to give back, you run."

"I'm not running from anything," Hermann countered defensively. "I just don't believe in what you do. I don't like it and don't want to be a part of it."

"So now you get morals?" his father sneered. "That never seemed to stop you from taking the money when you wanted it."

"No, I guess not," Hermann shrugged. "Your money bought you a lot of other unscrupulous characters who just kissed your butt for what you could do for them. What made you think that I would be different?"

And with that, Hermann moved cautiously out of his chair, passed the old man now trembling in anger and onto the Interstates headed west. He had walked out on Hermann Olsen Sr., the very powerful and esteemed Hermann the First. He had walked out on one of the most successful real estate developers of the ever-disappearing wetlands on the Eastern Seaboard, and nobody ever does that.

The islands and the marshlands were quickly vanishing beneath the unchecked groan of countless bulldozers. They were busily reshaping the black quagmires of his youth into gated enclaves of exclusive homes and carefully manicured golf courses for the well-endowed and nouve riche.

The result was pristine acreage of well clipped lawns and meandering fairways which absorbed enough pesticides, herbicides, and fertilizers to choke off the life around them. The bass in their retention ponds and wandering pseudo-lakes were full of cancerous sores. Hermann the Junior had seen them. The little froggies croaked once or twice and then croaked for good.

Hermann the Senior had become extremely wealthy by following the muddy paths of the monstrous earthmovers, and he had sent his only young son to the finest business schools in expectation that "Junior" would soon take up the reins of his bulging enterprise.

And now the little ingrate had "run away."

Pete listened attentively as the story of Hermann's life unfolded before him on an ever- marching line of beer mugs. He asked a few questions in order to keep the young man talking. Conrad asked no questions, but sat as quietly as a sage and watched this new intruder intently.

His eyes seldom left the face of the young man and you would have thought that he had gone to sleep, or had lost interest in the story, except for the fact that there was a constant laser blue light boring into Hermann's head—a light which was impossible to escape and made it even more impossible to embellish his tale with any sense of bravado or exaggeration.

So Hermann just told the truth, as mundane and boring as it might have seemed to him. It just seemed to be the only thing to do.

Eventually Pete banged his half-empty beer mug on top of the bar, as though, only now, it was all decided. "So, you're all screwed up. Just like me and Conrad and Jimmy here and just about all the other folks I know. Big deal," he added with finality.

"So, what are you looking for then, son?" he asked. "Salvation? Answers? Some half naked fakir hiding in the mountains up there?"

Hermann looked at him, stunned at the cynical response to his story.

"He ain't there." Pete glared at him while draining his beer. "Me and Conrad looked." He burped. "Lots of people looked," he said while grabbing at a new mug. "I think he's dead. Best you can hope for is to figure out what you need *right now* and then see if the rest of your life just falls into place. And you know the funny part to that, Hermann?" Pete cackled. "You won't know the answer until you're dead!"

That seemed to strike the old guy as extremely humorous and he roared at his own joke.

He took a few sips of beer in contemplation and then continued, "So, got any idea what you need?"

It was a direct question, to the point, with no promise of a future. Simple.

"Actually, I don't know Pete. I think that I need a place to hide for awhile," Hermann answered.

"Hiding ain't an option son; it's the same as being a coward," Pete said angrily. "Then your whole life will pass you by... and you're only going to get one crack at it, boy."

"Try again," he encouraged Hermann, "but remember, three strikes and you're out. After that Conrad here gets to cut loose. He hasn't liked hippies since Vietnam," he whispered almost as an afterthought.

Oh-my-God. Is he kidding or what? Have I been suckered into these guys? Oh shit. Hermann panicked in his mind. He began to perspire. He was embarrassed and felt as though his pants had been pulled down in front of the small clientele now in the bar. His eyes inadvertently made their way to the front door to check for his escape.

"Come on, son," Pete prompted him, "and be honest this time. By the way, you're right," he grinned. "Me and Conrad could never catch you if you bolted out that door. First of all, we're way too slow and second of all we wouldn't even try. You'd just be running scared from yourself again, boy."

"So drink your beer. And, *God damn it*, stop all that sweating. You're making me nervous," Pete demanded.

Hermann downed the beer in front of him in three long gulps and stared silently at the bleary-eyed cowboy beside him. *Oh, what the hell*, he thought.

"I need a place to carve out for me I guess, Pete," he began. "A place to do something that I can put my own signa-

ture on and say, 'Yeah, I was here.' And I'm not even envision-
ing it to be any grand success. Even if it fails, even if it turns
out to be a total mess, I want it to be mine.

I've been handed everything in my life and I guess I'm just
tired of feeling like an over-privileged beggar. I want to take a
bite out of life and to see if it bites back. If and when it does, I
want to see what I got. I want to see if I got the balls to look
the world in the eye and do the right thing: for me, Pete, for
me, and not for the completion of somebody else's dream,"
Hermann said with passion. "I don't believe in that dream. Not
anymore," he concluded quietly. "There's got to be something
better."

There was a silence then which settled in between the
verses of the song and the bustling of Jimmy behind the bar.

"Whoeee," whispered Pete.

Conrad screeched his stool away from the polished brass
rail. "Pete, sounds like Hermann here needs a nice failing
business with no hope of recovery so that he can prove his
balls and his stupidity. Sounds like he needs a good kick in the
ass too," he glared at Hermann. "Sounds like you and this kid
got a whole lot in common. Maybe you two should cry on
each other's shoulders for a spell while I take a very needed
leak."

"Yeah, that does sound like a plan, Conrad," Pete sighed.
"Well thought out in your usual manner," he hurled back at
him sarcastically.

"Hey, Conrad, since you're going that way, how 'bout
killing that damned spider up there by the door?" he asked.
"That should make you feel better."

Conrad moved catlike from the bar rail.

"The damned son of a bitch gives me the creeps," Pete
staged whispered to Hermann. "Always figure he'll jump
down my back when I'm not looking."

Hermann was not sure weather he was talking about the
spider or about Conrad; but either way, the old cowboy made
a show of grabbing a convenient broom and, while loudly
cussing the spider, headed off for his assault on the restroom.

Only Hermann noticed that once Pete wasn't looking, Conrad quietly stowed the broom away and left Mr. Spider happily alone, content on building his house of strings and dreams.

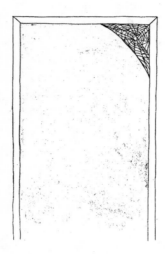

The beer soon gave way to coffee and cheeseburgers as Pete and Hermann sank deeper into conversation. Conrad patiently played the jukebox. He shot pool against himself and shot the bull with the occasional customer who entered the bar. He remained outside of the conversation and became as unobtrusive as the large yellow retriever snoring happily under the table at their feet.

Of course, Conrad certainly was not brain dead and Hermann had the feeling that, even from his remote and roving locations, the old rancher was able to absorb almost all of their talk. He was a sponge mopping the floor of their conversation and Hermann felt careful of what he wanted to spill in his path.

"Hermann," Pete continued at one point, "I'm about to offer you the worst deal in your entire life and I'll be happy and proud if you just laugh in my face and tell me to take a flying fuck at the moon. That way we can have another beer, get out of here early, and part our lives as friends."

Hermann had the sinking feeling that he had inadvertently set himself into the sights of a sly used car salesman and had no idea of how to diplomatically break off the negotiations. There was a difference here that Hermann was struggling to understand though; this salesman was actually trying to talk him out of buying a car which Pete somehow intuitively knew that the young man wanted to buy and this only served to add to Hermann's confusion.

"I got this club, son, and it doesn't make a lot of money. It makes some—just some. Enough to keep me happy, but not enough to even fix much of it up. Guess you can see that," he added with a derisive wave of his hand.

Hermann noted the deficiencies, but felt that it did not deserve a comment.

"Can't see where it would make much more, even if it looked like one of them fake Bavarian lodges," Pete said whimsically. "Just local ranchers and such come on in here. They're good people and I enjoy their company. They pay, but they don't have much money. We could do a lot better if we had a few more raving alcoholics around." He snorted.

"Anyway, there's some land out back there too," Pete continued, "1,200 acres of steep mountain, to be exact. Too radical to build much on, lots of rock, but some good turkey and mule deer hunting if you stay in shape. It used to be some sort of racing hill way back when. You can still see some of the old lift towers and, although they're pretty much overgrown, you can tell where the trails once were. That old geezer, Conrad, actually used to ski back there when he was a youngster. Heard he was pretty good, too…"

Hermann felt that it was time to bring this negotiation to a close and the best way to do that was to have a little reality check.

"Two questions, Pete," he said a bit more crisply than he had intended. "One, what is it worth? And two: what the hell would I do with it?"

"Well, son, two answers then," Pete offered sarcastically. "One: the whole shooting match is going to cost you three hundred grand. That's what it is worth and I won't take a dime less, so don't even try to knock me down. I'm one shitty bargainer so I just set a fair price for everyone and then be done with it. Don't like it, don't take it, but don't try and haggle me. It just pisses me off," he warned.

"As for two: I have no friggin' idea," he said honestly. "I suppose if you dropped a few more bucks into it you could crank up the ski area again. I don't have the time or the money for such foolishness, but you do," he encouraged. "You're young. You want a fresh opportunity, and, unless I'm reading your story wrong, you got some money behind you somewhere."

Pete mopped up the rest of his ketchup with the lone remaining french fry as the silence passed between them. Finally he said, "Looks like you're looking for more, boy, but that's it—simple as pie. You give me three hundred grand and I'm out of here. Then, if your daddy has as much confidence in your business sense as he claims, he can put his money where his mouth is: front you the cost of the improvements. I'd imagine that if you can convince anybody that your little area is worth the drive on that deathtrap of a highway out there, well, son, you just might have a business which you made all by yourself."

Hermann put his hands behind his head and settled further back into the old creaky wooden chair. He stared for a few long moments at the spider, still alive and nonchalantly going about his business.

"Pete," he finally said, "you've been damned honest with me so far. It's probably not even fair of me to ask you this question. ...Hell, you're trying to get rid of this place and I'm probably the first sucker to roll in here with enough money to make it happen. So what do you think? If you were me, what would you do?"

"Hell, I'm not you son," Pete answered almost angrily. "I got enough troubles making my own decisions. But since you asked, here's my advice: run away and run away fast. Head on back to the eastern shore and live the life that everyone else is chasing after. They're going to think you're nuts if you don't."

"I'll even buy the beers," he offered, "and the burgers. The owner always does. We'll just chalk this up to good times and be on our way."

Hermann puffed out his cheeks and blew out a long sigh.

"You need some time to think on this?" Pete asked. "Well, I don't blame you. Damn, you're more messed up in the head than I thought," he observed. "Anyway, I'll be here tomorrow, and the next day, and the next day. No place else to go. But while you're thinking on it, let me tell you a little story I read once. Something from a Kurt Vonnegut book, I think."

And Pete launched into his little tale.

"It seems this guy had a bird once. Called him Charlie or something. Can't remember what kind of bird it was…kinda like a parakeet, I guess, because he was always squawking and making noise. Reminded me of a lot of people I know," he added derisively.

"Anyway, one day the guy was just watching Charlie raise all sorts of holy hell in the cage and he got to thinking that maybe the bird really didn't like it in there so much. So he says to Charlie, 'Charlie, you know that I'm pretty much a big shot around this house and all, so I'm going to grant you three wishes. Now I can see that you don't like that cage very much, so I'll consider that wish number one.'

"And with that, the guy opened up the door to Charlie's cage, something that Charlie never could have done by himself in a million years. Well, bingo-bango out flies Charlie as quick as you please. He flew right over to the windowsill and stood there looking out. Pretty soon, he began to push his little bird head against the glass. The only thing that separated Charlie from the huge world outside was now just one thin pane of glass.

'Well Charlie,' the man beamed, 'I see your second wish, and it is about to come true.'

"And with that he opened the window for the bird. Something that little bugger never could have done in a zillion years. Well, old Charlie almost had a bird heart attack right then and there. Suddenly the whole world was opened up to him and the shock of it all almost killed him dead. He flew right back into his cage and hopped in as fast as possible.

The man closed the door and latched it again. 'Charlie,' he said, 'I see that you have made very wise decisions with your three wishes, because now you still have something to wish for: to get out of the cage.'"

Over the refuse of the dirty plates and unfinished coffee cups, Pete and Hermann locked their stares, until Pete finally broke the connection and twiddled with his fork.

"So, that little Charlie reminds me of you, Hermann," he finally said. "You can go through the rest of your life just wishing that you were out of the cage and attribute most failures on your self-imposed imprisonment. At least you'll always have hope," he smiled.

"Or, you can choose to fly out the window, right now, and maybe find true freedom with a life in the wild. Of course, you have a damned good chance of getting eaten by a cat, too, and your failures will be all your own with no one else to blame," he added.

Hermann was suddenly aware that Conrad had been sitting quietly next to him. He had silently slipped into the chair and was listening intently to Pete's tale like a child at a favorite bedtime story. He was sure that the old rancher had heard the tale before and was waiting his time to respond.

When Conrad knew that Pete had finished his story, he turned to Hermann and fixed him in the unwavering stare of his eyes. "Sounds like our little friend is all caught up in that free-will stuff."

Is he talking about me? Hermann thought.

"It's kind of unfortunate that we even have to struggle with it," Conrad continued, "but we do everyday. Free will, Hermann. It separates us from any of the other animals. Unfortunately it seems to give us a choice between taking the comfortable way out, or face down the difficult solutions."

Conrad reached over the table and quite deliberately

drained the remaining cold bitter coffee from the bottom of Pete's cup.

"Here's what I believe, son," he said as he smacked his lips. "Every man knows what is right, what is wrong, and what is true. Now those things can be different, for different men, at different times, in different circumstances. Ain't no absolutes. Ain't no guarantees," he declared. "But trying to ignore the truth just brings you pain; living in denial just digs the hole deeper. So, some people just figure they'll do nothing and maybe the problem will go away," he continued.

"In the interim, they can blame others for their own mediocrity, but doing nothing *is a choice*," he stressed. "Especially when you can elect to do *something*. Doing nothing is the same option which is given to an animal which has no free will at all. All I know is that the worse thing that you can do in this life is nothing," Conrad stated emphatically.

"You can choose to wake up and look at the truth, or you can choose to ignore the obvious and try to remain comfortable in your denial. I *know* that doesn't work," he declared. "But it makes no difference to the truth; it will still be there when you are ready to see it."

"So, what do you do?" Conrad asked quietly. It was a question apparently for Hermann, but his eyes had returned to the weathered face of his old friend and held it almost lovingly in their gaze.

"Head back to the cage," whispered Pete. "I'm tired, I'm old, and sometimes I get scared."

"Jump out the window," countered Conrad. "You're gonna die anyway."

"You see those ugly old pusses in that mirror above the bar?" Conrad then indicated with a nod of his head. "Well, someday we'll face our Maker in all of our potential, and we'll be standing there naked to the universe. The Maker, well, he's like the bartender there," he rambled on.

Jimmy acknowledged his new status as God with a smile.

"He's going to have that big old mirror behind him and in it we will see the person we could have become. We'll know the person we are, and in between the two is a personal heaven and hell, depending on how close we came. The Maker is not going to condemn us. His job is easy. He just keeps the mirror shined up. We'll simply condemn ourselves."

"And what do *you* do, son," questioned Conrad, now sad and suddenly old. "Do you jump or run?"

"What I do, Conrad, is...I think I take that bill now," Hermann said.

He motioned to Jimmy for the check.

"You leaving us, boy?" Pete looked discouraged. "Conrad and I ain't fighting," he said in hasty explanation. "We're just rehashing some old tales."

Hermann could see in Pete's reddened eyes that he now regretted telling the story and was hoping that the young man would at least stay for the evening before moving on. "You don't have to leave ya know," he offered encouragingly. "I got a room in the back where you can bed down if you want."

"No, Pete," Hermann said as he stretched himself out of the chair. "I just gotta square up with this bill and then be on my way. Got a lot of things to do tomorrow," he offered in the way of an excuse.

"I got the bill, son," Pete said as he slowly rose to take his hand. "It's on me. I enjoyed your company."

"Afraid not, Pete," Hermann smiled as he continued to search for the wallet hidden in his jeans. "See, around these parts, the owner always buys."

Conrad's hard fist came crashing down on the mahogany bar before him, sending the startled dog lumbering for safety and rattling the empty glasses. Then, like a conquering wolf, he tilted back his gray head and howled victoriously into the shocked face of his very best friend.

OCTOBER

Humans have evolved to their relatively high state by retaining the immature characteristics of their ancestors. Humans are the most advanced of mammals- although a case could be made for the dolphins- because they seldom grow up. Behavioral traits such as curiosity about the world, flexibility of response, and playfulness are common to practically all young mammals, but are rapidly lost with the onset of maturity in all but humans. Humanity has advanced, when it has advanced, not because it has been sober, responsible and cautious, but because it has been playful, rebellious and immature.

—Tom Robbins

OCTOBER

A wasted youth is better by far, than a wise and productive old age.

—Meatloaf

We rode into town in a dilapidated "one-eyed" Datsun 240Z. It was some sort of turd brown color, missing a hubcap on the left front tire and sporting a few dents from nobody remembers where. We looked good!

The "Z's" alleged "one-eye" was due to some malfunctioning electrical wiring which caused the left headlight to blink on and off, on and off in Morse Code fashion and often made approaching cars swerve erratically in self-defense. They did not know whether they were being borne down upon by either one motorcycle, or two, or perhaps even an ill-intentioned cyclops. During the more quiet moments of any given road trip we would attempt to decipher the code into secret phrases, convinced that the gods were somehow sending us an important message to be given to the world. The car was the transmitter and we were the prophets.

Hey, it worked with a "burning bush" didn't it? People bought into *that* story.

Anyway, electrical wiring is outside our realm of expertise and so I don't think it ever got fixed. I know that I did not even try. My faithful sidekick for adventure was my friend, Wally. I am more mechanical than Wally, but I know my limits. He was more practical than me and knew that we did not have a chance. So we just left it alone.

Thinking on the "faithful sidekick" thing: The Lone Ranger had that Indian, Tonto. Batman had Robin (however gay…). Hell, even little Timmy had Lassie (a *dog* for God's sake!). Each one of these intensely loyal servants had a common trait: yes, whenever the hero got into trouble, the observant sidekick would make some inane observation like, "Hey boss, I think this salad is laced with Kryptonite!"

Or maybe Tonto, now peeking over the rocks, would say, "I think we're surrounded by Indians, Kemosabe (i.e. White Boy). Looks like *you're* in deep shit."

Even Lassie, the world's smartest dog, would at least *try* to help out by going "Bark bark, woof woof" (literally translated as "Hey you assholes, that stupid kid is down a well again," or maybe that was, "Yo, if this show is named after me, why don't you all learn to speak dog?")

So, here is my beef: the goofy sidekick is supposed to help the hero get his butt out of shit. Wally never got me out of anything. He only got me into crap, and, besides that, I think he was screwing some of my girlfriends. That is another matter entirely. The point is, he was a failure as a sidekick and, although it is too late to rewrite a new faithful companion into my life, you can bet your ass that on the next go around I'm getting a big, smart dog instead!

However, I digress.

Wally and I were both in the Merchant Marine and, seeing that we had a long, extended vacation coming to us from our last stint of shipping out, we determined that a road trip (allegedly "to find damn good snow") was our only escape from impending boredom and from our parents. We loved them. We just did not want to be 22 years old and living with them.

The facts left us totally undeterred. It was the beginning of October, neither one of us really skied all that well, and there was not a single snowflake in sight, nor one expected to fall anywhere between us and Alaska. We were determined. Besides, we figured that if all else failed, we would drink ourselves across the USA and make our families proud. This was our own esthetic reason for the trip.

We could hear our dads telling stories about us as the family gathered around the communal fire, "Hey, Herb, wanna hear what my stupid kid did last week?"

About four days into the trip, the tires still grinding on dry interstate, I was getting tired of Wally. Wally was getting irritated with me. I was quietly thumbing through a recent edition of *SKI* magazine, daydreaming about buying a new "faithful companion"; perhaps a big labrador retriever. I would dress him in tights and replace Wally.

I wondered, *How long would it take to teach a retriever to drive somewhere? Or do you think that he would just drive to get something, and then come back?*

Anyway, I stumbled upon an article with some inane title like "Ski Resorts Nobody Ever Goes To," by Joe Boring and there was this obscure place mentioned called Mount Bellew.

"Hey, my grandmother was from a little place in Ireland called Mount Bellew," I pointed out to Wally.

"We're not in Ireland, you dipshit," he growled.

(See what I mean about that irritable thing?)

We traveled onward and, as far as I can recall, three major "Cosmic Forces" pulled us inexorably toward this little ski town:

#1. I was driving when we got near the exit. Wally was sleeping. I wanted to surprise him.

#2. Geographically speaking it was close by, and I had to pee.

#3. We were thirsty. Wally, even while sleeping, looked thirsty to me. This occurred a lot and probably accounted for why, after four days of driving across the U.S., we were still only in Utah but had managed to piss under fifty-four different bridges.

And so we were drawn, driven actually, by me and

Mount Bellew

"Cosmic Forces beyond our control" toward Mount Bellew: The ski area nobody ever goes to.

(They really needed a new motto or something.)

The commanding Wasatch Mountains sit as a lone sentinel on the western range of the Rocky Mountains. Stretching across Utah from the Bear River in the north to Mt. Nebo, near Nephi, in the central part of the state, they are the result of 20 million years of geologic faults, gigantic volcanic activity and the immense pressures of huge slow-moving glaciers. Most of today's elevations are generally between 9,000 and 10,000 feet. There are certainly higher peaks within the Rocky Mountains, but very few can claim to be as rugged, as inhospitable, or as beautiful as those in the Wasatch.

Initially, the mountains were a vital source of water, timber, and granite for the early settlers of the region and, although water remains an important commodity flowing from the hills for the ever-growing population of the Wasatch Front, it simply does not seem to pay all that well. So it is the recreational opportunities now provided to residents and visitors alike which have attracted the interest of modern man.

These mountains were first viewed by the white settlers in 1776 when a pair of itinerate priests, Fathers Francisco Dominguez and Silvestre Velez de Escalante, initially tra-

42

versed the range and exited near the present day Spanish Fork. It is quite likely that they might have traveled through the Mount Bellew area, had a nice Mexican dinner, gave a collective, unimpressed shrug, and moved onward.

Around the 1820s fur trappers and traders from the areas of Santa Fe and Taos were attracted to the area and such legendary men as William Ashley, Jebediah Smith, and James Bridger found their way into the cold mountains, rich and teeming with the valuable beaver. By 1840, silk had already replaced Mr. Beaver as the height of fashion and the fur trade died out.

I imagine that the Beaver family (June, Ward, and Theodore) was quite pleased with this development, as though they had finally gotten rid of Eddie Haskell and, happy to have their land back, decided to throw a huge neighborhood barbeque. The traders, their source of income now deflated, had finally departed.

By the 1870's the towns of Alta and Park City had sprung up with a flurry of mining activity. They anchored themselves in their present locations, and the settlers were there for good.

It is notable that in this most Mormon of States, Alta at one time supported twenty-six saloons and six breweries, while the major portion of Park City's municipal revenues were received from saloon licenses and fines from prostitution. I cannot even suppose what those statistics are today and really don't care to look them up, but I would think that some things don't ever change.

Perhaps this fact is something that the Reverend Brigham Young had not come to appreciate when he led his flock into the Great Salt Lake Basin in 1846. If he had known of the decadence which would soon be bubbling immediately above him in the hills, he might have chosen to merely camp overnight and keep on going through. Perhaps then somewhere like, say, San Francisco would have become a religious hotbed.

We will never know, but it boggles the imagination.

So, around 1900, Mount Bellew was all set to follow her big brothers into a millennium of prosperity and growth. They were all basking in the limelight of the Twentieth Century; but little Bellew was easily forgotten and bypassed, left languishing in her cradle of cold hard rock.

Skiing has now become one of Utah's major attractions, driving the development of significant and world-acclaimed resorts in the Wasatch Range; except for Mount Bellew that is...

The first time we drove into the constricted valley which guarded the area of Mount Bellew was, unpredictably, to be one of our last. Not that we wouldn't drive on this same road numerous times in our future, but somehow when you drive into Mount Bellew it's like entering a suspended world where you only truly enter once. You spend some time, in a time-frozen world, and then exit through the rear.

Nobody gets to enter more than once. Some never leave. Those who do, may never return.

It is a one time shot.

Oh sure, Robin Williams gets to go back to Never-Never Land, but that happens only in the movies. Try that in real life and your corporate friends will round you up with butterfly nets and have you submitted for evaluation. Captain Hook (who I happened to like) gets dead, but Peter's real problem is that after Mrs. Wendy gets her hooks into the lad, he's a condemned man and "all that boyish flying around is simply going to stop!"

There should have been a road sign reading;

Please park your life at the door

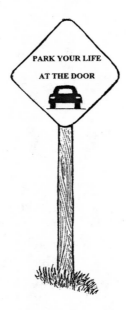

There was not. Instead, all we saw were warnings of cattle crossings, deer crossings, what to do in case of flash floods and places to buy apples. Nothing prepared us for our future, except perhaps the flash flood warnings which exhorted us to;

Climb to safety

We ignored them all. We did not see any deer and especially did not like apples. So we drove onward.

You approach the "resort" (and I'm being liberal here) along Route 226. This is a snakelike ribbon of asphalt which curls its way precariously along the Cohochee River on one side and solid ice/rock walls on the other. Perpetual frost heaves and war zone- sized potholes add to the discomfort level, providing a trip with all the fun of riding a shopping cart pulled behind a train. The access appears as though it had been bombed. Most locals need a kidney transplant by the age of 50.

The "Z's" single eye blinked merrily and soon took on the cadence of a disco strobe. That was okay by us! We had lots of disco music onboard, and although some people would rather listen to static, I wouldn't knock it. It was popular at the time.

This "road" (and now I'm *really* stretching it) acted as a sort of filter to the remote location of Mount Bellew. Only the hardy, the pure, the incurably insane, or the lost, would make the trip to the mountain. Many of these qualities were all found in the same individuals.

Many only made the drive once. No, they didn't *die*. They just vowed never to return to such a remote and facility-deprived area.

Others treated it as a hajj, a sacred trip to Mecca which is to be undertaken and conquered at least once in a lifetime. Still others accepted it as a way of life, knowing that once you have tasted totally pure water, you can stomach none other. These latter were the faithful western skiers who "flipped the bird" at other resorts along the way in order to gain access to the primeval forests, sheer cliffs and ungroomed terrain of Mount Bellew.

These were the same individuals who hung like insects from gossamer threads of line and piton on sheer rock faces in the summer and who floated tiny toy-like kayaks through the floodwaters of spring.

They were not "normal." Many of these people smoked a LOT of dope.

Warning! Warning!

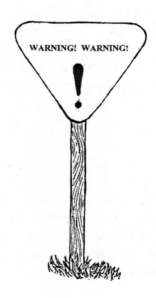

Over the course of any given winter, the shallow Cohochee River becomes a temporary home for any vehicle which strays too far from the invisible centerline. During the most severe of blizzards the route quickly resembles an arctic marina with many small craft vying for mooring space upon its icy banks. This is certainly a precarious position for the skippers of those seemingly invincible SUV's, but a source of great delight and amusement to the depraved locals.

So, I am about to give you a valuable hint on how to save yourself a hundred bucks...*IF* you ever make it to Mount Bellew.

Numero Uno...*Never* drive on your particular side of the road. Stay in the middle!

Numero Duo...Swerve only at the last moment to avoid oncoming vehicles.

Tres Amigos...Immediately regain the centerline.

There is a perfectly good reason for this apparently irresponsible technique. This is the same practice I have seen from marine pilots who move the large seagoing vessels in the Houston Ship Channel.

It is known affectionately as "Texas chicken."

Without going into the complicated physics of the matter, suffice it to say that it has worked for them for many years and with sound principle. Although a few actually understand the science involved, the others perhaps have had lobotomies and just don't care. The combination works.

It also works for the locals driving on Route 226 for much the same reasons.

Bank suction, in the case of the pilot and his ship, is created due to a decrease in pressure directly related to speed as the vessel's hull approaches the side of the channel—the Bernoulli effect. The Signore explained that a ship wants to move laterally toward a closer bank even though her heading is parallel to it. Now, we throw in the decreased pressure at the stern in combination with the pivot point of the vessel being approximately 30 percent of the length aft of the bow as she moves forward and we create a levering effect upon the ship, thus causing it to pivot in the opposite direction.

Don't mess with me. I just know this stuff.

Bank suction, in the case of the hard paved road, is created by innovative plowing techniques developed over years of winter doldrums causing unsuspecting vehicles to be sucked *toward* the waiting river.

In both cases, just the opposite of what you might expect, eh?

In practical operation, we have "The Conscientious Civil Servant" now smoking a one-ton cigar behind the wheel of a ten-ton yellow road grader. He is very bored and so he simply makes the road appear wider than it really is. This is what snow plow operators do when it is not actually snowing. It will justify his overtime hours and help assure that next year's plowing budget gets passed by the town council. Besides, it entertains him immensely.

His exploits become the subject of dinner conversations with the family:

"What did you do today, Daddy?"

"Fucked with the tourists. Eat your beans."

Anyway, pretty soon "The Unsuspecting Prey," on his way to a well-planned and prepaid holiday, comes bumbling along. His white knuckles are in a death grip upon the wheel of his rental SUV, as it fishtails its way up the black ice of Route 226. The kids in the back are singing an endless array of Christmas songs. The spirit of the season is upon them with all this snow. He only wishes that he could kill them, have a nice dozen martinis and then go to bed.

Since he can not (being restrained by guilt, legal considerations, and his fat wife), he concentrates on his task and responsibly attempts to drive on his side of the road.

This is what he has always been taught to do.

HA HA! HA HA! *Mr. Unsuspecting Prey!*

His heretofore logical driving methods are soon proven misconceived as he is forced into a life-saving response brought about by a vision of certain death suddenly invading his conscience: a large down bound logging truck!

This truck will be directly in the middle and is NOT GOING TO BUDGE!

Why?

It is driven by the grader operator's brother-in-law... and he is NUTS!

AAIEeeeee!

Poor "Mr. Unsuspecting Prey." He has made the grossly amateur move of giving way to the speeding truck *way too soon*. See?

So, our naïve citizen now suddenly finds himself skittering bodily sideways into the soft quicksand of the waiting snow exactly where the road was supposed to be. The "Invincible 4-Wheel-Drive Nuclear Powered Quadra-Track SUV" (which he paid extra for) crashes helplessly into an explosion of disintegrating snow bank and is soon securely lodged in the cold arms of white death. He must then seek immediate assistance for himself and his crying family.

Thankfully, the Christmas carols have stopped.

Of course, he could choose to stay right there and almost assuredly perish in the freezing waters, or he could take his chances on an early spring. At least he would have a good spot for the opening day of trout season. That is a plus, but I never saw anyone opt for that alternative.

Never fear, "Unsuspecting Prey!!" For this is when "The Concerned Local" (the third side of our devious triangle) shows up in a timely fashion, completely armed with some sort of massive 4x4 truck and equipped with a winch which appears to be able to move locomotives.

This fellow will look much like Arnold Schwarzenegger when he plays the hero version. He's not.

Oh sure, he might have an Austrian accent and his arms most likely will bulge massively under his tee shirt (I *know* it is winter... but he is not even cold). And he certainly looks as though he might simply lift the car back onto the road, comfort the family and happily hunt down the demented snow plow guy in order to methodically kill him and eat his evil machine to everyone's delight.

But don't be fooled! This man is a pirate! All he needs is a patch and a parrot!

Thus one might naively think that the "Concerned Local" is just being a good citizen, BUT unless a $100 tip is soon offered, the winch will fail (guaranteed), OR the truck will have a whole myriad of "truck problems" (which are much like "female problems," and you really have no chance of understanding either), OR the hapless car, though ultimately saved, will soon look like a candidate for next year's demolition derby at the VFW.

Hey, a hundred dollars is cheap! It would be a LOT more than that in some other foreign country with a highly developed capitalistic system.

Except Canada. I don't get those people. They are way too nice for their own good and would probably just tow you out for nothing. Eh?

I can not see how they will amount to anything...

Of course, politics being what they are, the entire $100 does not just belong to the local hero. A $25 donation is reasonably expected to be made to the "DOT Plowman's Spring Barbecue" or else next year the dreaded guardrail issue will be brought up again at the town meeting.

So, save yourself the hundred bucks; drive in the middle! Never give way!

...*IF* you make it to Mount Bellew...

And so Mount Bellew earned its reputation as an area that would "never amount to much": too far from major cities, too difficult to access, too gnarly to ski, too few amenities; and *far* too many strange people.

I have that "swerving thing" down pretty well. To tell you the truth, I really do it quite naturally in all road conditions. So, as planned, Wally was indeed surprised as we safely crunched into the little parking lot of the Mahogany Ridge Club. Hermann, Conrad, and Pete had left long ago, somewhere around five years before our arrival to be inexact. Five

years had passed since the three had met in the dark confines of the bar and not one damned thing had changed.

You don't mess with true success.

Jimmy had probably died or moved on, since the guy behind the bar was named Rick. And I saw a spider near the bathroom, but doubt if it would have been the same one. They really do not live that long. Hermann's bar had long ago been cleared of its refuse of cheeseburgers, cups of cold coffee, and empty beer mugs. He had followed his ethereal dream of creating something for himself and had raised sufficient money from investors in order to revitalize the little area of Mount Bellew. He had formed a small corporation called the Mount Bellew Ski Club LLC and had soon set off with Conrad to clear the overgrown trails and install some second-hand lifts. A new building now sat about 50 yards behind the old Mahogany Ridge Club and it served the general purpose of combination cafeteria, administration office, ski school, and ticket office.

The two men remained dedicated to their vision: a vision which was to keep Mount Bellew as basic as possible. They were often accused of repelling as many customers as they attracted. The criticism never affected them since they merely did not care.

You didn't get much grooming of trails here at Mount Bellew since the temperamental equipment was not only mechanically unreliable, but functioned solely dependent upon the mood of Conrad on any particular morning. If the coffee was good, if it was strong enough, if there was plenty of it; you might get a few corridors of velvety corduroy to carve early turns on before he got bored and took the tank-like machine back home. If not, you could expect "frozen death cookies" everywhere and your teeth would begin to hurt with the chattering impact of these coal-sized chunks of ice underneath your skis.

You didn't get any refunds either; not for bad weather or for lousy conditions or lack of grooming. The general thinking was that if you could not ski the conditions, then you should just go home.

Make a decision.

Oh, but when that powder began to fall from the sky... Oh, that *glorious* powder! It was the driest; it was the deepest; it was the cleanest and most extraordinary gift from the gods that ever graced a mountain on earth. It simply exploded underneath your searching feet into lacy sheets of crystalline diamonds. Soft and forgiving, it seductively invited you to point your skis down the hill, let gravity do all the work and ride its silken, sexy back through fairy dust forests of snow-laden pines and fields of sparkling jewels.

To its everlasting credit, Mount Bellew was one of the very first areas in the entire United States to welcome the new sport of snowboarding to its slopes. This had nothing to do with being "progressive." It was strictly a financial decision.

As Hermann said, "I don't give a shit. If somebody can afford a ticket, they can slide down the hill on a cafeteria tray as far as I'm concerned."

Some people did.

Hermann was a man before his time. He knew that it did not pay to be snooty.

Understandably then the crowds, which habitually called Mount Bellew their home area, soon became an eclectic blend of old, graying men on long, faded skis; bubble gum blowing teenage girls, and body pierced daredevil riders. Little kids seemed to fill in all the gaps in between and, at the

Friday night socials, they would all dance.

People accepted it for what it was and if the resort ever got around to having a logo, it would have had to be that inane yellow "Happy Face" which announced to the world to quite simply…

Have a nice day!

The whole staff seemed to make the place special. People who were working for just above minimum wage would have smiles frozen upon their ice covered faces and never thought to use the phrase, "not my job."

Liftees, who spent all morning swinging chairs for customers in the below freezing temperature, would help bus tables at the cafeteria during lunch.

The "ski god" instructors would volunteer to sell tickets to the arriving neophytes, and, on any given bright, warming winter day, you would find the managers slinging burgers and bratwurst on the outside grill.

You always went to Hermann's line because he would often conveniently forget to charge you or subtract some goofy discount he made up like "40 percent off for St. Festivist Day." He just gave the stuff away.

Hermann had opened his cage. He had pushed his little head upon the glass and had flown away into a whole new world of his own idealistic creation.

As we slid onto the cracked leather stools, a disheveled and irate Wally berated me with some of his favorite epitaphs. Mumbled insults like "moron" and "wackis" seemed to entertain him. His ill humor really does not bother me all that much (anymore), so I patiently waited until somewhere on the second beer when Wally's normally genial spirit resurfaced

enough for him to inquire of the bartender, "My good man, where in the hell is this Mount Bellew place?"

When Rick responded, "You're in it, guys," well, we started all over again with the cursing and disgusted looks thrown in my general direction. It took another three beers and four games of darts to return him to his normally irresistible personality.

At that time we decided to stay and see if it snowed. It was 50 degrees. Meteorology was not our realm of expertise, either.

Besides, now we were hungry.

It did not snow, at least for awhile, and we did not leave; for a longer while. It seems that the ski area was just getting cranked up for the upcoming season and there were a few jobs available for outstanding college graduates such as ourselves.

Wally and I sank into deep conversation concerning our career paths to date and certain *Critical Factors* were carefully taken into account prior to our decision.

(I just love these lists. It serves to show how methodical our minds can work)

CRITICAL FACTORS LIST

#1. We both had degrees in Transportation. There were three shuttle buses that moved tourists from their houses or condos in the nearby town to the ski area. Buses are *transportation*. Yes. We would be working in our chosen field. Four years of college were *not* wasted after all!

#2. The Union did not care if we shipped out again any-time soon since jobs were scarce. We figured that we were doing our brother seamen a favor by giving someone else a chance to go sail around the world.

We had already seen a number of parts of it. It was not all that impressive.

#3. Wally had recently (say, within the last two hours) fallen in lust over some sweetheart that worked at the administration building and was preplanning on getting some regular (that's too conservative a word; let's say "scheduled") sex.

#4. I was broke and he would not lend me any more money to go home.

So we stayed. Transportation Engineers! Dad would be so proud!

"Hey, Otto, my kid drives a bus now! Four years of college tuition later. Remind me to kill him when he gets home, would you?"

"Of course, Jim. Sounds like a good plan."

When they had cranked this place up over five years ago, I imagine that they never envisioned the need for such specialists as ourselves (i.e. Transportation Engineers).

Sometimes you naively start out with something small, trying to make a few bucks, and it magically grows around you in spite of yourself and your failures. You start with a job, and 30 years later you look back and you had a career. Hermann Olsen buys himself a little real estate to toy around with and ends up with a resort. Another guy drives a bus, and with a little luck, buys his very own, over the same expanse of time.

Go figure…

And so it was in the fall of 1980, when Mount Bellew was a legitimate and growing business, that we first met Pieter Petroski. We soon discovered that Pieter ran a "tight ship." Or so he told us. As the business manager of the ski area, Pieter was the man that we first had to impress in order to get our new jobs.

We planned on being very impressive.

Putting on our "reliable employee" game faces, assuming our finest "responsible individual" attitudes, filling our best pants pockets full of bullshit and pulling on some clean underwear, we interviewed with the man later to become known as "The Pan."

Our first impression of Pieter was lasting and accurate. He was pretty much a pompous asshole. But he was smart.

This was evidenced by the fact that he chose to interview us separately. I guess to be sure that we were not lying to him about something important, like a criminal record.

Hint: When having a job interview never ask the guy if the company discriminates against felons; even if you're just trying to lighten things up. It always seems to go over badly.

When I first walked into Pan's office, I quickly became leery and guarded. There was an immediate respect here, me to him, obviously not him to me. This was the same kind of respect that I would have if I had encountered an unexpected snake in my path. I was aware that the snake was capable of sharp and precise strikes. (*But is this snake poisonous?*) I did not know. I could throw sticks at the snake, try to scare it off, make it slither away and show it how brave I am; but this snake showed no fear. Instead, I could see it coil as it settled into its chair. (*Will it strike?*)

"Welcome to Mount Bellew, my friend," Pieter hissed. "Have a seat and tell me something about yourself."

I later came to realize that Pieter called everyone beneath his charge "My Friend," although he had no friends, and was not necessarily interested in having anyone here at Mount Bellew as his buddy. "My friend," as in: "Well, you will just have to find a new job, my friend" or "How do these electrodes attached to your testicles feel, my friend? Comfy?"

Pieter was one of those people who could be a master of charm and persuasion. He would instantaneously judge the social status of the one he was talking to and adjust his attitude accordingly. With me he just smirked a lot.

He dominated those he had power over and would fawn over those he felt could further his career. I never thought that Pieter had a true love of Mount Bellew. It was a stepping stone on his way to better things, an opportunity to prove his worth and then move on to a higher place.

The interview with Pieter was exactly like a Catholic ritual.

Not one of the good parts, like Mass, where you get to dress up and then sneak a few cheap peeks at the great legs of the hot high school girls that you went to school with; or the incense. I liked the incense.

No, Pieter's interview was more along the lines of the confessional part, and Pieter was the priest, sequestered in the box: ominous, darkened and judgmental. You felt that he was surreptitiously taking notes to be stowed away in a hidden logbook and used against you at the impending inquisition.

For you non-Catholics, this confession thing can be rather confusing, so let me try to clarify things. I'd really like this analogy to work.

You see, you have this "milk bottle" inside of you. It's not a real milk bottle; that would hurt and you would probably know it. It's a symbolic milk bottle that supposedly represents your soul. When you go around doing bad stuff your "milk bottle" gets these little black spots in it, like mold. You go through the Agony of Confession, which is usually scheduled on a Saturday night when you should be out partying (hence the "Agony" thing), and the milk bottle gets washed, cleaned and then you are a saint again, or maybe an angel if you are young.

Now, here is the downside: if your bottle gets totally full of this black mold, that is the equivalent of a Mortal sin and you will have to spend the rest of eternity in Hell, which is not a nice place, wishing that you had some other options. I recall Sister Caliph of the Perpetual Scowl telling us, "Nobody can help you at this point; not God, not the president, not even your mother: nobody."

She made it rather apparent that you are stuck with your decision and they (i.e. The Heavenly Jury) do not accept any excuses.

As I understand it, the only way that one can get out of a Mortal sin, like being a mass murderer or something, is to be actually insane. Then God does not count it. He made you crazy, so he takes all of the responsibility. Thus proving that everyone, even The Big Guy, screws up somewhere along the line.

But here is what seems weird: if you *really appreciate* the concept of Hell for Eternity and still commit a Mortal sin, well, you just have to be NUTS! It's like a "get-out-of-jail-free" card in Monopoly with God taking all of the blame.

"The Caliph" once whacked me in grade school for that exact train of thought but I still wonder weather Hitler could be in hell (for being maliciously evil); heaven (for just being nuts) or wandering somewhere in between: maybe like Philadelphia (for just being plain mean).

Anyway, the priest, hiding in his humid little cubicle, is supposed to act like a therapist and make sure that he has harvested all the incriminating evidence out of you before you can leave the black box. He does this by asking lots of leading questions.

"So (*you slut monger*) how many times exactly did you sleep with this young (*virginal and totally innocent*) lady? What did you do? (*and I need explicit details here you sinner*). Wow, how many times did you do that? (*the boy is a machine...*). Did she seem to like it? (*how could you tell?*). What's her name? (*got a phone number?*)."

By the time you are ready to get out of there you are *both* sweating bullets and you have gotten so horny that you can not wait to get out and start getting some more black mold in your little bottle. After all, it *is* Saturday night and the opportunities abound.

The priest is so embarrassed that he can not leave the box for another half-hour. That's okay. He does not have anywhere to go anyway.

Does this help? Catechism was always one of my stronger subjects.

Needless to say, after finishing with Wally and me, Pieter was duly impressed and, recognizing the fact that nobody else even wanted the job of driving the old shuttle/school buses, he felt pretty much forced to hire us for the season. Thus it was that Pieter "The Pan" added a few more holes to his already leaky ship of business and his personal season would be spent in futile attempts to plug the inevitable deluge.

"The Pan" earned his nickname shortly after we had departed from our interview. Wally, whose reputation for insensitivity has haunted him since childhood, could not help but be suitably impressed with Pieter's style, his cutting wit, his impeccable attire, and his slight lisp.

Suffice it to say that Pieter was extremely "light in the loafers," and it was not just the altitude involved here. I think that he was making eyes at me, but then again, I am "prettier" than Wally. I am also more liberal.

I think that Wally was jealous.

It was rumored that our new boss was gay. Not the happy kind of gay, but, you know, the sexual kind of gay. This hearsay was generated from the same rumor factory that says the sun is coming up tomorrow.

I would place a bet on that one.

Pieter's physical features did nothing to belie these rumors and, if he was trying to hide his sexual persuasion, he was doing a fantastical awful job. Slight and precise in his appearance as well as his attitude, he had small and well-defined features. He probably did not even shave until he was well into his 20s. He had close-cropped, curly blond hair which seemingly never needed a haircut.

I always thought of him as some sort of well-groomed Nazi banty rooster.

He must have had his clothes shipped in from catalogues, or went into the big city for shopping sprees since you did not find these things at the local "Arties" store in Mount Bellew. Pieter was a fastidious dresser and looked like he bought each ensemble right off of a mannequin. He was referred to as "The Sears model boy," but that seemed unnecessarily cruel, especially coming from the epicureally-challenged employees of Mount Bellew. Most of them had a total ensemble consisting of four or five different sets of jeans, a few wool shirts and a change of underwear and so their opinion of fashion was stilted.

Although most people would have felt blessed not to be required to wear the suit and tie of other big businessmen, Pieter nevertheless was always attired in well-pressed slacks and starched shirts. I imagine that he dreamed of the day when he could wear a three-piece suit to work and not fear being out of place in his environment.

Of course, I could not even imagine what *that* environment would be and would not even want to visit there.

Okay then... probably it would be a bare white room, no windows. The only blast of fresh air is coming from the air conditioning vents. Hundreds of thousands of Pieter-persons would be racing about in $1,000 suits and the sounds of cell phones in constant buzz would deafen the atmosphere. Every prisoner would be required to generate ten e-mails to the next Pieter-person on the pyramid each day, thus establishing a social hierarchy, and, at noon, all the electronic mail would come falling from the ceiling like a ticker tape parade in New York City.

There would be squeals of delight, screams of anguish, and total confusion for the next twelve hours as the hierarchy changed. A polka band would play "Roll Out The Barrel" and everyone would dance. The former chiefs would have to pick up all the papers in their expensive suits and kiss everyone's ass on their way down the corporate ladder.

There, I imagined it.
The Pieter-persons think they are in heaven. It is hell.
I better check the mold in my milk bottle...

"How come you didn't like the guy?" I inquired of Wally as we left the administration building.

"All that phony bullshit and mostly that polished accent of his," Wally said. "All just phony bullshit."

I have always enjoyed an in-depth analysis from a pathologically intolerant and prejudiced person.

"Dude, of course it's polished, you dink," I educated him. "That's what he is...PETROSKI: Polish. Anything with an SKI is Polish. SKY is some sort of Russian, or Slobovian, or something."

"You're a freakin' moron," he noted while fixing me with his patented cold stare: a baleful gaze that says, "I know what you are talking about. I just still think that you are a moron."

"What? What now?" I protested. "You know, Walter, you can be a very hard person to get along with. I just hope that he doesn't decide to make you my boss. I'll have to quit." With that, I engrossed myself in the local newspaper, hoping to find somewhere to live besides the hatchback of the "one-eyed Z."

It was getting pretty rank in there.

Peter Pan. Get it? The boy-hero who flits around in his tight fitting green leotards, fighting bad pirates with his rubber sword, living in sin with some fairy named Tinkerbelle and prancing around with his little band of Boy Scouts.

This seemed to strike Walter as appropriate and quite hysterical; thus, "The Pan."

What a wit.

CONRAD

There are people in my life who sometimes worry about me when I go off into the fields and streams, not realizing that the country is a calm, gracious, forgiving place and that the real dangers are found in the civilization you have to pass through to get there.

John Gierach

CONRAD

*I do not exist to impress the world. I exist to live my life in a
way that will make me happy.*

Richard Bach

In modern society we seem to have developed a plethora of
cowboys. There are urban cowboys, hot rod cowboys,
space cowboys, the Dallas Cowboys and some guy named
"Duane" who was in *Sex Cowboys From the Planet Urgi*.

Of course there are real cowboys, too, and the term
became commonplace in the American vocabulary after the
Civil War, when ex-soldiers, fugitives, and former slaves
migrated westward in order to find employment on Texas cattle ranches. The name soon became popular during the 1870s
when the pulp fiction writers of that day made the cowboy into
a national hero and symbol. Prior to that time, those who
worked with cattle, drovers or herders, were simply called by
the Spanish term "vaqueros."

The first livestock herds in the Utah territory were established in the 1840s under the guidance of former fur trappers,
Jim Bridger and Miles Goodyear, and soon thereafter the
entire state of Utah fell under the rule of the cowboy. The vast
cattle ranches were located in virtually all parts of the state,
from the rugged canyon lands of southeast Utah to the Raft
River Mountain Ranges of the northwest, from the Arizona
strip in the southwest to Brown's Hole in the northeast. Cattle
were the commodity and the cowboy was the king.

Conrad's small ranch was a poor reflection of those grand days from years gone by; he barely scratched out a living from the few cattle which could be supported on his land and the loss of even one of his precious animals was considered by him to be a major setback.

He had found a young cow that morning down near a dry creek bed entangled in an inextricable steel webbing of barbed wire. The animal had ripped herself open in so many places that Conrad immediately knew that there was no choice; the helpless animal needed to be destroyed. Her leg had broken in an effort to free herself from the inescapable wire and it now lay at a grotesque angle away from her body. She lay weak, unstruggling, resigned to death; dying as her lifeblood ran slowly into the dust.

Whether the animal had wandered into the wire in an attempt to feed upon the fine grasses beyond it or whether she had been driven into the sharp barbs in an attempt to escape a pack of coyotes, one would never know. Conrad had watched the coyotes numerous times before with a mixture of both distaste and admiration. They were the most social of animals and hunted together with a keen sense of teamwork. It would have been odd for them to trap their prey in a hopeless web of steel wire and then to simply leave it, but he had learned never to underestimate the cunning and intelligence of the predator. Surely they understood that the cow would not escape and had perhaps gone off onto other pursuits, maybe they had even been chased off by one of the mean old bulls that roamed the range. Whatever the case, they knew full well that they held a sumptuous and assured feast in reserve and this one could wait and provide a casual dinner.

He absently thought that he must now return later in order to butcher the meat. It would not last long in the burning sun. Conrad did not have the time or energy for that now. Some of the meat would be spoiled, but he would save what he could. The coyotes would return that night. He would have to burn the remaining carcass, so he would have to tote some fuel out also. Ruining their diabolical plan gave him a certain sense of satisfaction (*I'll have to fix that damned fence, too*), but for now it was way past lunch and there was still a fifteen minute ride back to the house. Conrad swung easily from the saddle of the mare and turned toward the pathetic mess which was the remains of the weakly quivering animal.

The quick, sure movements as he alighted from the back of the horse belied the appearance of a creaky old man and he landed softly on his feet. The weathered face mirrored the very land on which he rode, the land on which he had spent his life. It was now set sorrowfully in anticipation of his intended task. Deep creases, running like dry rivulets through a parched plain, etched across his face; memories of spring rains scratched permanently into the landscape. The rains had not come to Conrad and his land for some time now. They brought out the hidden treasures of life, which lay barely below the hardened and sun-baked surface. He remembered that upon the first touch of moisture, the countryside would leap into a verdant carpet of bright flowers, thick grasses and new plants.

It's been awhile since a good, steady rain, thought Conrad as he pulled the .45 single action Colt revolver from its holster. Every shower brought more and more erosion to his precious land, taking soil and soul, leaving it both dried and uglier after its sporadic visit. He was not sure exactly how much he missed its life-giving, but cruel touch.

He stepped over the broken, twisted mess of barbed wire and felt his feet squish into the sucking black mire of an insect-ridden swamp. He instinctively dropped to his belly and sprawled into the muck in an attempt to make himself as small as possible: bright tracer rounds zipped through his mind and over his head in a determined staccato to seek him out, a deadly game of hide and seek. He tried to pull his legs under him, but they were wrestled back by an entanglement of roots and vines, which, in nightmarish fashion, seemed intent on holding him prey. They were live, evil things, snatching and grabbing at his knees and feet, sucking his arms helplessly into the soggy goo of their den, hold-

ing him captive until the predators could come and tear at his chest with their terrible knives.

If he did not get out of here, he would die. He knew that. He felt the panic rising in his throat as he struggled to make progress.

Where was safety? Over there? He knew that some of his squad had taken refuge over to his right. He could hear their shouts, away from the singing tracers, away from the source of the pounding mortars. Was that safe, or were they just present- ing the Cong with a larger and more inviting target? Surely they could be heard; eventually they would be found. Where the hell did they screw up? Where the hell did they go wrong? This was supposed to be a simple, routine patrol but now they were being ripped to pieces by an unseen enemy.

There was confusion crashing in the air as the bellowing of men, some in pain, some in fear, filled the spaces between the rocking explosions. His squad had inadvertently stumbled into a minefield which had carefully been laid out the night before. The Vietcong had sat silently as cats seeking a mouse, as clever as the coyotes assured of a kill.

He slithered through the slime, making progress which was measured only in miserable inches, while the ubiquitous vines and plants grabbed at him in an attempt to slowly suffocate him until he could die. His breathing was heavy, labored, while the sweat pouring from beneath his helmet blinded and stung his eyes.

With the squad, *he thought.* With the squad; there is safe- ty. *But he was being pulled inexorably to his left by a constant and sorrowful bellowing, like an animal in great pain. He crawled slowly into the dark cave of sound.*

The young boy lay on his back, his black eyes wide in fear and shock. It took only a precursory glance from Conrad before he unhesitantly pulled the morphine from his pack and stabbed it into the thigh of the downed Marine.

"Lie still," he commanded. "Lie still," he repeated.

"You have to be quiet or else they'll find us," he began cooing softly to the boy, as though they were playfully hiding from their friends in a closet. His words, though soft, carried beyond the fearful crack of light and thunderous sound around them into the fog of the boy's mind.

"It's not good Conrad, is it?" the boy questioned hopefully, wanting a different answer.

"No, son, it's not very good at all," confirmed the sergeant. "Both legs look pretty bad."

An involuntary cry escaped from the boy's lips and his body shook in an uncontrollable spasm as it absorbed the truth and the pain. Conrad immediately regretted the brusqueness of his answer. (God damn me! Give the kid something to hang on to...)

"I don't want to be a cripple, Sarge," the boy said softly. "I've seen 'em. I don't want that. Am I going to make it? Can you get me out of here?" he now asked with panic rising in his voice.

"I'm sure as hell going to try, son," Conrad promised in a whisper.

But the Sergeant already knew that there was not any need to try. He didn't have any fancy medical degree hanging on his wall, nor did it take one to recognize a leg which was ripped away at the thigh and another which was mangled beyond recognition. The boy's lower half looked like meat from a butcher; a very bad butcher. The new recruit had hope where there was none and he was losing his blood in a continuous and sticky flow to the mud bed below him.

The boy needed something from him, more than the morphine could offer. He needed the glimmer of a chance to calm his mind. He knew that this man beside him was competent and strong. He believed in him. He believed in that competence and that it could give them a chance to go home.

Conrad also knew what the boy expected him to offer, but he recognized that it was shallow and unattainable. He could not give the promise of water where there was none, he could not give a stab of sunshine on an overcast day, and he could not make the enemies and demons disappear.

71

"Hang on son," he lied to the frightened soldier. "Old Conrad is going to get you out of here. We're going to be just fine."

Conrad efficiently applied the tourniquets, all the while assuring the boy in a smooth and steady voice of how well all these were going to work, how these were "sure to do the trick" for him. He became a surgeon at the bedside of a terminally ill patient, calming and treating their mind, when all hope was gone for their body. The boy's confidence in him rose slowly as his life ebbed surely away.

"I don't want to die, Sarge," the boy whispered almost conspiratorially now. He was beginning to fade away with the morphine as his blood flowed almost unchecked by the bandages into the ground below him.

"None of us do, son," Conrad whispered back, playing the game now. "So you just rest up and let me see what I can do for us."

Conrad began to stroke the sweat-soaked head beside him with his hand and looked deeply into the dark, scared eyes. He held the gaze unwaveringly in his own. The boy trusted him completely and almost began to purr under his soothing touch. With the other hand he began to slowly ease the revolver from the holster on his hip. He moved quietly and deliberately with no sudden motion so as to startle his patient.

"It's okay, son. It's all going to be okay now," He reassured him.

Ever so gently he placed the muzzle of the pistol behind the boys' ear. The young soldier was mesmerized by the neon blue of Conrad's intent eyes and never felt the light touch of the cool steel on his skull. He looked peaceful and calm, trusting implicitly in the man who would save him. Conrad pulled the trigger and shocked himself by the loud retort.

The benzene sweet smell of napalm filled the air as the jungles around them exploded into searing light and the boy's sightless eyes stared after the fighter jets, forever retreating into the distance.

It was over.

The WHOP...WHOP...WHOP... of the helicopter gun ships beat into his chest and pounded their memory into him. It was a sound that would be quintessentially Vietnam for him. The vines loosened their death grip from his legs and slithered snake-like into their burrows leaving him free, but still unable to escape their ethereal touch.

Conrad stood unsurely onto trembling legs and surveyed the land around him, relieved to be home.

"Damn, I hate wasting good livestock," he said aloud in the event that anyone had witnessed his odd struggle with the cow and he brushed at the filth which had splattered his old jeans. His face was hot, feverish, and he felt the nausea rising in his throat. He leaned weakly over the fence post, saw that he was all alone, and puked the remains of his breakfast onto the dirt below. The young cow lay still and unseeing.

A tattered old handkerchief came out of a back pocket and mopped at the sweat lying on Conrad's cracked face. His mouth gulped clean water from the canteen.

"Shit," he muttered to no one. "Shit."

"Sometimes this work just sucks," he said to himself as he now approached his skittish horse.

He had lived the nightmare repeatedly for years now and he still was not satisfied with the answer that came slithering and ghostlike to him in the endless night. The boy was going to die. It would have been in the mud, it would have been in the E-Vac, it would have been in the hospital, but he was going to die and his only destination was the morgue. If Conrad had stayed with him, he would have died too. If he had called in help, more good boys would have died and it all would have been in a vain glory attempt to save a condemned man. He had promised the boy a chance and then he had just taken it away: judge, jury, executioner and God. Conrad was sick of glory and all of its hollowness. He was weary of the flag waving from those who saw it only as a symbol of dominance, and not responsibility. He was disgusted with the men that sent good boys to die for their own self-serving causes.

Young men were gone forever, never knowing the true reasons why they had to die: because if they had known, they would not have served.

The copters with their incessant heartbeat chant of "What if...what if ... what if..." would pound into his chest every day. They had gone around in his mind for far too long now: the WHOP wop...WHOP wop... WHOP wop of the big blades never rested, never landed, and the war was *never* over.

Conrad breathed long and deep as he stared blankly at the mare waiting for him. The animal pawed the earth nervously, unsure of what she had just witnessed. The recent execution made her apprehensive and perhaps she thought that she would be the next to die at the gnarly hands of this madman. She tentatively allowed her master to saddle up slowly and then turned her head toward home.

He wrote a letter later on, soon after the young boy had died in the firefight, and the letter said that the boy had been a good Marine, that he had died in a Vietcong minefield, that he had gone quickly and that he was indeed a hero to his country. It was not a lie.

The boy was put into a proper coffin, given an escort, given a flag and then shipped home with 58,000 others from that conflict: 304,000 would be wounded. The average age was 23.

Maybe the letter gave the family a little comfort for their great loss, but Conrad never bothered to meet them to find out. He couldn't face that. No one would bother to investigate exactly how the boy actually died. A body, that mangled, was put into its bag as quickly as possible.

And so the war went on.

They would count the casualties and hope that "our side" had less than "their side" in a titanic and deadly game of "Capture the Flag." If not, then they would do a "casualty estimate" which would tip the scales enough to claim a victory. These busy little accountants in olive green suits made sure that the war was won on a daily basis. They were as important to the effort as the front line grunts. It was a game that everyone played, but nobody could ever win. The generals would then report a successful battle to their masters in Washington and valuable defense contracts were renewed. Everyone then went home to a nice dinner, except the front line slob: he was either dead or thanking God that it wasn't him this time.

That was the war; a high stakes corporate game.

Perhaps wars have not changed all that much throughout the years.

When the Vietnam War ended, it was as vacant of meaning and as incomprehensible as when it had started. Matter of fact, it is hard to remember exactly when it all did "start." There never seemed to be a definitive date or time, certainly nothing in a big event kind of way which serves as a catalyst to the great historical moments. It was more like a creeping and pervasive cancer. Young men slowly began to flow into Southeast Asia, a little at a time, then some more, and then more.

You began one day to know some of their names. One became a neighbor's son, and you became scared. One became a high school friend, and you became sad. One tragic day it became your brother, and you became enraged. Soon they just seemed to be there in force like a tide which rolled in during the night.

It ended the same way: heroes sliding back a little at a time, absorbed by the cities and the farms of their youth, forever changed, soon forgotten, no parades. It was as though they had never left but suddenly appeared, physically and mentally wounded, in your midst.

Nobody wanted to talk about the mistakes; everyone was ashamed; history was better to be ignored. But that is not possible.

Sixteen young boys died that day of Conrad's remembrance and here is what he would later write in his journal.

LOST 16

I think I'll watch TV tonight to see who fell within the fight.
Last week 16 had to give their life.
Only 16 died, in a useless strife.

Only 16 mothers will cry this week,
for a son destroyed in a battle's heat.
She didn't know why he went to war:
He was still her Baby.
Nothing More.

Only 16 wives will bitterly weep,
for they knew the young lad had a love so deep.
And as their salted tears from while they rest:
The drops will fall,
On an infant's breast.

And together they'll cry at a grave so lonely,
Wonder "why him?" "Why was he the 'Only'"?
Then breezes will blow and sweep clean the site,
They'll scatter his flowers and hide him with night.
And like a drop of fine dew, that no one will see,
He'll soon join a river
And flow to the Sea.

Only 16 brave fathers will try and be strong,
they'll say he was good and could never go wrong.
They'll say he did right, and died as men should;
But they need to cry madly,
If only they could.

Only 16 best friends will remember his life,
they'll remember their laughter and blot out the strife.
They'll remember his hopes, and thoughts, and dreams,
They'll remember that death
Was not in his scheme.

And together they'll cry at a grave so lonely,
Wonder "why him?" "Why was he the 'Only'?"
Then breezes will blow and sweep clean the site,
They'll scatter his flowers and hide him with night.
And like a drop of fine dew, that no one will see,
He'll soon join a river,
And flow to the Sea.

I think I'll watch TV tonight to see who fell within the fight.
Last week 16 had to give their life.
Only 16 died in a useless strife.

But now the tube buzzes like a busy hive
with electric news of a brand new drive.
"It'll save some lives in future days,
and only fill a couple graves."
Only a few will feel death so near.
    Driving for What ?
        Driving to where ?

Journals of Conrad King
1970

He was a good Marine, but the questions of his duty never failed to haunt him afterward.

Conrad had been a sophomore at the University of Utah, putting himself through school on a skiing scholarship when the draft finally caught up with him. For him there were no

second thoughts of where his duty might lay. He put his college on hold, he put his skiing aside, and he headed off to the Marine Corps.

He was an exemplary soldier, a tough Marine, a regular poster boy for "Semper Fi" in all of its advertised glory: rugged, smart, loyal. If Conrad had stayed with the Corps he could have made a decent career out of soldiering, but after his tour of duty in Vietnam, the government informed him that they no longer needed his services.

Just like that. No lingering goodbye kiss.

"Thanks for a good job, pal," a nebulous face would intone. "Sorry about that wound. Didn't mean to interrupt your plans, but that's how it goes. Now go home and enjoy your life."

Yeah...go home, thought Conrad. *Go home and try to catch up with the rest of your generation: those guys who were all safely hiding in a college dormitory somewhere while the napalm was burning all around.*

The Levi-clad, long haired, "love children": they were the great protesters, and maybe they did bring the war to an early and disgraceful end, but what was it all about? Protesting, not against the ignominy of war, not against the justifications of the conflict, but protesting against a system which said that they too might have to go off and die. Conrad felt that if the body bags had been filled with the poor and uneducated, then we would not have had a peep of protest.

Unfortunately for the politicians and their business friends, its slimy, death-gripping tendrils had crept into the families of the middle and upper class. Professors had seen their brightest minds stripped of their logo-bearing button-down shirts, clad in non-descript uniforms of olive green and then taken away. The best were leaving, some never to return.

The fact was that nobody gave a rat's ass about Vietnam or the Vietnamese. Not really. Most couldn't even find the country on the map. They were howling long and loud over the indignation that they were being called to serve and perhaps die in a conflict that they little understood, found no moral basis for, or could scarcely profit from. And so the private war of Washington, the corporations and the generals came to an ignominious end.

Good.

Conrad wasn't bitter. He had made his choice himself, but he did not have a life to return to. He would never go back to college; it was too late for that. He no longer carried the body of a downhill racer. The G.I. Bill was okay, but he was never academically oriented and so never took advantage of its provisions. Besides, he needed to make some money just to exist and he could not be spending it on books.

The supple and strong ski legs which had carried him to the university were the financiers of his future and they would never power him down a mountain with the grace of the Olympic hopeful he once was.

So he had returned to the small family ranch and had taken up where his father had left off. His past was here, his present was here and here was where he would spend his future.

He had generously bought the place from "The Old Man" for a price well above what it would have been worth on the open market. It never provided a life, it merely provided a living, and that living was earned only after long hours of toil. His father had gone on to waste most of the money on booze and women, gradually drinking himself into an early death. That was probably fortunate since he had barely exited before all of the money finally gave out.

Conrad's brothers had wandered away to other parts of Utah and had found employment in various trades: welders, carpenters, heavy equipment operators. Conrad had been the only one to aspire to a college education, and now that time was well past. Unless someone in the family won big in the lottery, they would all live their lives out comfortably, but without any frivolous amenities.

They had all inherited their father's capacity to drink and mutually considered it fortunate that they did not get together too often, since those little family reunions usually turned into drunken brawls, occasional fights, and enough hard feelings to last a few years. Conrad tried to control the drink, a few beers here and there, a pull or two on the Jack Daniels, maybe the occasional two or three day bender. He never considered himself an alcoholic. He just drank like a normal Irish person.

Hell, a cigar chomping ex-Marine running a hardscrabble western ranch on the verge of poverty; he'd be considered "queer" if he did *not* drink his share.

He massaged his shoulder in order to relieve the pain and to keep it flexible as the mare found her way down the familiar path to home. Conrad's wounds ran deeper than the superficial scars which hid the shrapnel in his shoulder; those bits of leftover metal only really bothered him whenever it got too cold or too damp. That cow, damn it, that bothered him. Whenever he thought that he was leaving all the Vietnam crap behind him, something would happen like that and he would go flashing back to that shit-hole place.

When Conrad got to the house, the phone was ringing. Most times he just let it ring. When he wanted to talk to somebody, he would call them. In his mind, the phone was an implement of one-way communication. He resented the intrusion that it presented in his life. He might be tying some new trout flies. He might be making a new rifle. He might be sitting in front of the fire staring into the jungles of Vietnam, getting slowly wasted, and he sure as hell was not going to talk to some telemarketing asshole trying to sell him friggin' light bulbs or timeshares.

Aw hell, he thought. The damned thing would not stop its incessant clamoring and that was a sure sign that it was somebody that he knew, somebody who sadistically recognized that he wouldn't answer the phone, so they would just let it ring until it drove him crazy. This was the fourth phone that he had to buy and he struggled to restrain himself from tearing this one out of the wall too. The things were expensive. It gave him great momentary pleasure watching it hurtle across the room, but he always regretted it later when he had to pay for a new one.

The phone continued its annoying blare. It was probably one of his four brothers looking to borrow either money or tools, both of which he had in short supply. The thought of trying to weasel out of lending either put him in a foul mood and he grabbed at the phone like a live thing which he intended to strangle in his grip.

"Yep," he barked abruptly, hoping to prepare the caller for any further rejection and mildly surprised that the phone was still alive in his hands.

"Conrad! It's Hermann. You sound like your usual cheerful and gregarious self today. Stock market got you down? Kill anybody lately? That would cheer you up."

"Yeah, but that's none of your damned business," he growled. "Whata' want, kid? And make it quick. I'm a very busy guy."

Hermann never knew if Conrad was kidding, but was always intimidated enough not to pursue the line of questioning. He suspected that the old coot was mildly unstable, but found the blend of his cantankerous nature, fierce loyalty, and practical wisdom to be immensely appealing.

On his end of the line, a slow smile began to spread on the rancher's face. Hermann had gradually become one of Conrad's only true friends and the prospect of exchanging some lively banter with him now was raising his spirits already.

NOVEMBER

You can't interfere with people you love any more than you're supposed to interfere with people you don't even know, And that's the hard part, because you often feel like interfering; you want to be the one who makes the plans. You can't protect people. All you can do is love them.

John Irving

NOVEMBER

Whatever it is that you have inherited from your Father; you are going to have to earn it if it is to really belong to you

German Saying

Saturday morning, 9 o'clock and Conrad King squinted into the early morning sun which blossomed before him. He stared over the heads of the instructors who were forming around him, fresh and excited from their early morning warm-up runs on the mountain. The new snow, which had fallen the previous evening, now dusted some of them in its debris, leaving a testimonial to either their prowess through the snow-laden glades of trees, or perhaps a visible reminder that there was a need to continue their practice in the deep powder. Derisive comments and high-fives were being exchanged throughout the gathering group of energetic instructors and, as the crow's feet which rimmed his eyes criticized the huge western sky unfolding around him, Conrad thought, *Big sky. Damned big sky. There is an area in Montana called, BIG SKY. Wow, that is one beautiful color of blue. So deep. Never been there though. Who the heck are these people? And why are there so many?*

Conrad, more often than not, lived in a world of disconnected thoughts. If you did not know him, you would have thought that this process kept him totally addled. If you did know him, and most people did not, then you ignored it.

85

Conrad was always able to zero back onto Mind Control Central before he was actually discovered. Many times you would find yourself casually watching him and wondering if the old rancher had actually fallen asleep.

He could be as motionless as a heron hunting its dinner along the shores, watchful, deadly, barely breathing, and then you would be shocked to realize that he had been staring at you, or rather, through you, with hooded and unblinking eyes. You would turn away embarrassed, shocked that you had found this man rummaging through your personal things when you were not even home. Soon, if you were the prey, you were dead.

In this particular case, "Who the heck are all these people" seemed to be lodged in his brain. The multiple purple uniforms shuffling around him made him momentarily think that perhaps he had inadvertently called some sort of Welch's Grape Juice convention to his mountain. Conrad disliked the purple color (an innovation of Pieter's), for it clashed with his beautiful "blue" sky. Of course it was not entirely Pieter's fault. It never was. Sure, he had ordered them, but it was Pieter who had kept them.

Conrad resented the fact that he was put in charge of ordering such mundane things as ski jackets. They should have known better. He should have told them. He should have told them that he lived in a world under a purple sky. At least that is what he thought it was. He was told that it was "blue" and so he referred to it as "blue." He remembered it from years gone by, but now, in Conrad's eyes, there were shades of dark purple and some lighter purples: purples nevertheless. He dutifully called them all "blue" in order to maintain some sort of sanity and order in his mind.

The color blindness which had begun to inexplicably plague him after Vietnam was more an annoyance than a hindrance. Most of Conrad's world now existed in black or white, shades of gray, and colors not found naturally in nature. His worldview pretty much mirrored what he saw. He was not a man given to frivolous opinions, and yet some of his observations would best be described as "oddly different."

He had no need to identify anything in-between definitive right and absolute wrong. Situations which were questioned by most people in complicated shades of political or moral correctness were simply boiled down to his basic sense of fairness. He followed nobody's rule book or procedure manual except his own and the general feeling that perhaps he was on a different chapter at times than everyone else did not concern him at all.

When Conrad had purchased the uniforms he thought that they were a lovely shade of dark blue. "Just like the sky," he had offered at the weekly management meeting.

The man wisely avoided doing much shopping by himself.

Unfortunately, when they had opened up the recent shipment, the reaction was pretty much a universal groan of "Oh God, Conrad, what the hell are these?" They had just reached a unanimous decision to send the whole mess back when Pieter had slithered into the storeroom. "Oh Christ, now we're going to have to listen to his crap," mumbled Conrad to no one in particular.

Pieter fortunately (or unfortunately) loved the unusual new attire.

"They're unique, they're sharp, and they're bright. Conrad, you are a genius my friend," he bubbled. "They are just gorgeous."

And so the jackets stayed; and the crop of friendly, mobile grapes seemed to be growing at his feet.

Conrad King had taken on the position of Ski School Director at the request of Hermann. A bond had formed between them, forged from numerous camping trips into the backcountry, more than a few bottles of bourbon, and gallons of sweat which was shed in the rebuilding of the tired old ski area. Sometimes, with growling chainsaws in hand, it seemed that Hermann worked for Conrad and not the other way around. They always managed to rectify that ambiguity over a few cold beers at the end of the long day—or when the bills came due.

Trails were cleared, buildings erected, gravel shoveled, and five years passed since that day in the dark Mahogany Ridge Club when Pete had taken his money and departed for the easy life in Florida.

In Hermann's vision it was supposed to be "just a small area for the locals" and so they had cut two new beginner trails on some relatively gentle terrain and had refurbished the dilapidated lifts. They then built a small ski rental shop at the base and the only flat terrain that could be found had been bulldozed into parking.

"It wasn't much," as Grandmom would say, but then again, Conrad and Hermann had not been expecting much either. Life, however, has a way of gaining on us, of gathering a certain momentum, of assuming a course for which we never fully intended, and then it takes us for its own ride.

The name "Mount Bellew" was soon being whispered beside the quiet campfires which dotted the trout streams in summer. It was passed surreptitiously in the shaded confines of hunting stands in the autumn. It was hidden from the public eye like drug deals in the night, a forbidden pleasure, and, like all things so forbidden, its success was instantly guaranteed. The tiny area began to gain a reputation for its gnarly terrain and its back-to-basics style. Bellew was a long way from the ambiance of Park City, and that was just the way people who came here wanted it.

Like under-the-counter Viagra, it was soon attracting attention throughout the state. The people who dared the passage down Route 226 were rapidly multiplying like so many pilgrims who believed that they had found a sacred shrine.

Unprepared for success, Hermann and Conrad abruptly found themselves running an honest to god ski area, and they needed instructors, liftees, maintenance personnel and service people. The headaches grew with the area. The highway passage inexplicably became part of the overall adventure. Mount Bellew had landed on the map, and the guys still weren't so sure that they liked the whole idea.

Purple...Grapes...Big Grapes...Ivana; Conrad's continued

thoughts were inadvertent. He worked in quick, word association response to any problem.

Ivana. He had already met Ivana. Matter of fact, he had hired her personally. Not only was her resume impressive, *she* was impressive. Conrad was not necessarily scared of anything, but he wisely knew who and what to respect. His eyes inadvertently wandered in her direction.

Ivana Chomutov: what a great Slavic name! She could have been the lost love of a Russian Czar! She could have been the heroine of a heroic tale to be told to inspire the downtrodden! She could have been an arrogant princess beheaded by the revolutionary masses!

She was a former hockey queen.

While playing as a formidable defenseman for the Czechoslovakian woman's team, she was affectionately known as "The Wall." Of course, the degree of affection was entirely dependent upon which side of the puck you found yourself on since the "injury record" kept on her stick like the legendary notches on an assassin's gun, was prodigious; but she herself remained unscarred.

The team now refers to her simply as "The Defector," since she quietly slipped away from them during the exhibition games of the Women's World Hockey League in Ontario. Three years later she arrived at Mount Bellew.

I apologize in advance to the Czech Republic, but the reality remains, the team has not amounted to much since that time.

Ivana was a gorgeous woman, in a very large Amazonian way. She literally dominated any room she found herself to be in. Her demeanor and her physique did not take well to being ignored. She was every bit the professional athlete, with a solid 175 pounds distributed over her 5-foot 11-inch frame. Her thick blond hair, usually braided in ropelike knots, framed a face of Nordic perfection and her complexion was as clear as the northern skies.

During man's early Neanderthal existence, her desirability would have been legendary. She could have wrestled a bear into the cave for dinner, cleaned it, cooked it, and then chewed the hide into nice house slippers while the men grunted around the fire. She could have kept you warm in the winter and given you shade in the summer: everything the early cave-guy would have needed... before the remote was invented.

In the past, when men were men and women *still* bossed them around, great continents were settled with women like this, but since that particular challenge went out of style years ago, so did the masculine appreciation of her unique beauty.

Throughout the old mining days of the Wild West, a woman of Ivana's stature, beauty and obvious talents (not charm) would have married three or four men in the town as the poor old sods were killed off in the cold and forbidding labyrinth of mines. Her desirability as a mate would never have been overlooked; but then again, these were guys that would spend hours gazing lovingly at cattle.

We live in a modern society where becoming a slim, svelte, and beautiful woman seems to be the ultimate female goal. Why not *hugely* beautiful: Rubenesque and healthy? I once saw the ocean liner Queen Mary 2; that was nice.

Are men so insecure that large women are intimidating to the average man?

Damn! I know I was. *I* never asked her out.

No matter how big a room might be, it revolved around Ivana's presence like planets around the sun. It was as though a blimp was settling over the Superbowl.

Who cares what is happening on the field: "Hey Dad, look at the blimp!"

If Ivana had found a way to be sponsored by Goodyear, if she had found a way to attach lights to her sizeable body, if Goodyear had only known of her existence, then there she would have been, flying over important college football games, bringing us Tiger Woods at the Masters, beaming down on the Macy's Day Parade while radiating her dazzling teeth (all intact) upon the world.

Ivana could have been a very wealthy woman.

When she was created, God was definitely having a whimsical day. He decided to build her like a Viking war boat and then wrapped layers of muscle and bone around a heart as big as her body. Her volcanic eruptions of emotion—whether it be anger, frustration, competitiveness and, more devastatingly love—were titanic.

Although Conrad was careful not to encourage the obvious infatuation that she held for him, he was always glad to have her in the lineup. The tall, powerful woman with her long golden hair was rather like getting a Hummer for Christmas after you were expecting to find a zippy Mazda under the tree. At first, the sheer size of it is a complete shock. So much car. But once you get used to the steering and comfort, you begin to appreciate it. "Surprise! This thing can really move!"

Conrad's eyes passed over the anxious Ivana, who was staring back at him; unfortunately this was not to be her day. He chose his instructors as carefully as a chief of surgery chooses doctors for his patients, and this case was definitely not for her. True to her status as a professional athlete, she looked as eager to get into the lineup as a good dog waiting to go to the hunt, but he had a private client now who was going to need a decidedly more delicate touch and Ivana's innate competitiveness just did not fit that situation.

Maybe Conrad would save her for some macho men that just wanted to go jump off cliffs. *That* should make her happy as she left them sprawling in her considerable wake.

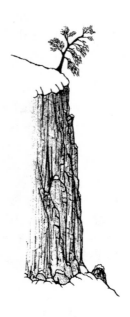

Oh, damn, thought Bobbi. Here it was, one of those glorious western days where the early morning sun was warming the thin air around her and the deep blue sky went on forever. The new six inches of fresh powder, which had fallen overnight, left an untouched carpet of soft velvet-like base silently screaming out to be carved into with huge swooping turns. She had been trying to backline it all morning and just hoped that Conrad did not catch her eye.

Don't look at him, Bobbi. Watch your ski poles. Chat with anybody. Who is this dweeb that I'm pretending to be so interested in and why has he not washed that jacket in about the last ten years? God, I hope he doesn't begin to think that I'm actually interested in his bullshit. Please, please, please... Don't look at me Conrad. Go away! Maybe I should slide behind Ivana and hide. There's plenty of room there; but then I'd have to talk to her. She's scary.

The trouble was that the entire instructor core was looking the very same way and thinking the very same collective thoughts. *Don't look at him. Watch your ski poles. Chat with anybody.* Like dumb sheep about to be slaughtered, they assumed that by staring at a distant object they could appear to be too stupid or disconnected to ever be assigned to an actual paying customer; they were all trying to appear invisible.

Dogs do this in an attempt to be clever. They will not look at you if you really want them to do something. They figure that if *they* can not see *you*, then *you* must not exist. If you do catch their eye, and then point, they stare at your finger and wonder, "Yeah right. What's the big deal with *that*? It's a finger for god's sake. So what?"

Sometimes you have to whack dogs with a magazine to get their attention. Conrad used a ski-pole on his instructors.

Mental hiding: this is a feat which is hard to accomplish when one is wearing a bright purple coat; and a feat which is impossible when you looked like Bobbi O'Donnell.

"Bobbi, you're up," barked Conrad "Come on girl, rise and shine! We got work to do."

Look at them all there, hanging their heads and pretending that the mystery of life is somehow written in the snow at their feet. As if I haven't seen this before..., he thought smugly as he walked down the line.

Conrad had killed lots of livestock. He knew their wily ways to evade the inevitable knife and he wasn't about to be deceived by mere humans. He gave a seemingly comatose instructor a playful whack on the rear just to see if he was alive.

"You're out of here Bozo," he said, "Your lucky day. Go ski and see me for afternoon lineup."

The heretofore lifeless form suddenly erupted into grins and boundless energy as he rushed for his equipment in an attempt to escape before Conrad had a change of mind, or some paying client showed up.

It did not matter how many clothes she had donned to fight off the terrible winter cold, when Bobbi O'Donnell walked, she was a Venus swimsuit model on a fashion runway, and it was your duty to watch her intently.

The sleek-looking, hip-hugging, tight ski pants which Bobbi routinely wore, were not part of the official and pre-scribed uniform. This 60's look had long ago given way to the more unisex and functional design of rugged bibs with volu-minous legroom, numerous pockets and nuclear warmth. They were not Bobbi's style and she had no intention of wear-ing them. She did not need any "legroom" since her legs roamed wherever they wanted and she did not need any pock-ets either, for people quite naturally paid her way when around her.

She might have needed some of the warmth, though.

Bobbi had violated the uniform policy every day since she had been here and Conrad should have put his foot down. Not that he was going to; it was just another passing and random thought. It was not that Conrad didn't care. He did care. He cared that it was pretty much a unanimous agreement that Bobbi could wear stretch pants whenever she wanted to and anybody who tried to stop her would be ostracized from all future male bonding functions.

Interestingly enough, a lot of the women seemed to agree.

Pieter, as a minority of one, wanted Conrad to clamp down on her choice of attire, but then again, it was thought that Pieter was just jealous of her long legs and wanted her to look frumpier.

She had made the momentary mistake of glancing in Conrad's direction and he immediately got caught in the onyx spider threads of Bobbi's eyes. *Oh, oh...now you've gone and done it girl.* ... He held them in the blaze of his own. It seemed impossible for either to let go. It was not her fault. Many a man had fallen into their subtle trap.

Bobbi's eyes were naked. They needed no clothing to make them beautiful and nothing could ever hide their intentions. She listened to you with her intent black eyes as though the words would stream into the endless pools and somehow find their way inside. When she was angry, they would darken even further and bolts of fire flashed through them like lightening thrown from black storm clouds. When she was happy, they were fireworks lighting up her face. When she was in love, they became soft and endless.

The trap was that you wanted to wander in their depths and linger there forever, but the wise man soon realized that after the fall there was only confusion looking back from the abyss.

Bobbi had gone to some of the finest private schools in the East, where learning about class was far more important than attending class and the cost for graduation could be found in a sizable donation to the library. She was not dumb, just unmotivated, and certainly smart enough to know that her family's considerable wealth would open up all the doors she would ever wish to pass through in life. Bobbi had developed a fairly pleasant personality, care of the charm schools, which brought her all the superficial friends that she needed in order to appear popular. Half were men, so half just wanted to get into bed with her. That left the other 50 percent, and most of them either secretly despised her or refused to trust her, especially around the first 50 percent (i.e. men).

Oddly enough, that was okay with Bobbi, since she really had no plans to get close to anyone anyway and found most men boring and trite. Her friendships had little depth and that was just the way she preferred it.

95

Her father, Robert, had introduced her to the sport of skiing during her childhood, when the family was frequent visitors to such places as Sun Valley and Aspen. He had always enjoyed the thrill of racing down the finely manicured slopes, the brisk air making his big Celtic face beam like a setting sun. The fine service and superb foods served afterwards added to their warmth together and, as they would sit before the massive crackling fires, she would hear his deep voice and wonder if there could ever be men like this in her future.

Robert O'Donnell did not inherit his wealth and power. He was one of three children born to a hard-working electrician in Chicago. He was obviously the brightest of the bunch and began experimenting with electronics before the word even had a meaning. When nobody knew what high-tech was (outside of a microwave oven) and how to set the clock on your VCR was the subject of cocktail conversations, Robert was designing the microchips of the future.

He was a successful self-made man who often impressed Bobbi with tales of himself and others like him who had clawed and scratched their way to the top of the business ladder. Robert had died suddenly, and in his will, he had made sure that everything Bobbi could ever want would be provided. She could never fault him for that, but she sadly did not know where to go in life in order to please and honor her father's memory.

Bobbi was proud of the fact that she had been named after her father. She had loved him dearly and missed him with a physical pain. As a child, she had shadowed him like a loyal puppy whenever and wherever she could. She felt safe in the presence of the big old Scotsman. She liked his smell; it was rugged. She liked the way his big lap felt; it was secure. She liked the way the small men scurried around in his presence; it was power.

The money that Bobbi inherited was both a curse and a blessing. Although she had many notable traits (mostly physical), her most outstanding trait was inherited directly from her father: money. Lots of it. Matter of fact, a lot more than she habitually flashed around her co-workers at Mount Bellew.

She enjoyed the things that it was able to provide, for she had gotten used to having those things. She enjoyed the control that money gave her over almost any situation, but it had robbed her of the more important things her father had held so dearly in himself and in others. Bobbi lacked the ability to negotiate, not just pay; the tenacity to stick with a project, because it was all you had; the guts to bet a thousand bucks, when you only had ten in your pocket, because you were so sure of yourself. Those were the things that made Robert great and Bobbi had yet to find them in her heart.

She had raced competitively for the small colleges that she had attended, achieved just enough success to make her feel cocky and, after graduation, had turned her sights westward to try her hand at ski instructing. "Why not?" said her father, shortly before his death. "It's as good a start as any other American Literature major is going to nail down these days."

As a new instructor, Bobbi had specialized in children. She did not necessarily enjoy children, but had a momentary and passing need to appear compassionate and motherly. She had hoped that by being close to them, it would somehow jump-start a maternal instinct that seemed altogether lacking in her hormones. She even worked at being entertaining, spending many hours at home in an attempt to develop what ultimately turned out to be an awful array of slight-of-hand tricks. Bobbi naively thought that such an art would become useful while teaching children. Not that it would help them ski better, but maybe it would stop them from whining.

As we all know, she did not have a snowball's chance in hell with that.

In the end, she was able to achieve a level of poor efficiency. Although most of the "magic" was quickly unraveled by any half-wit kid and even more easily by any avalanche dog (like the "hide the cookie" trick), on slow days she could keep the majority of instructors amused during the brief lineups and some others bewildered for hours.

Unfortunately, the steely edge of her personality often surfaced at the brink of lost patience in the warlike atmosphere of the Kids Ski School. This led to a few notable confrontations with both children and their parents. Although it was not necessarily agreed upon, when she was eventually transferred to the Adult Ski School it was a great loss for the kids because this hard side often kept the situation from exploding out of control. The children actually respected her, some parents hated her, and Conrad just felt that a transfer to the Adult Ski School was in everyone's best interest.

As the kids were fond of saying, "Watch out for that lady. She can be mean, just like Mom."

Bobbi's own "Mom" was in the person of the fiery and irrepressible Maria Sanchez, second wife to Robert and a former Ms. Venezuela. From Maria, Bobbi had inherited all the wonderful things that would have looked like money, if money could have ever been personified in the female form: dark eyes—sparkling deep like expensive jewels, the flawless body of an exquisite sports car, hair like the darkest of mink, and a face found only in angels.

When the Old Man died, the estate was pretty much split between the two temperamental women and, while Maria had gone on to remarry yet another successful entrepreneur living in Italy, Bobbi had focused her energies more intently on skiing. It was not a popular decision on Bobbi's part since Ms. Sanchez thought that her daughter was just wasting time on frivolous pursuits. After all, the young woman could be shopping instead.

I used to hear Bobbi claim that, "My Mother and I only get along as long as the bank statements continue to balance."

That didn't seem like a friendly mother/daughter relationship.

I always thought that it must have been difficult for Bobbi to be "Daddy's Little Girl," even though Daddy had passed away. She always seemed torn between the power of his wealth and the unwillingness to give any of it up. She would seem to be embarrassed by her fortune, wanting to be part of the crowd, and then she would do something totally pretentious, like buying herself a new SUV for her own birthday, while others were taking the bus. It certainly was not necessary for the heir of Robert O'Donnell to be living with three or four other people in a cabin, but it seemed a bit much when she purchased one of those high-end condos downtown, and then lived there alone.

While most of the other instructors were struggling weekly to earn enough money to continue their shaky existence, Bobbi donated her "excess funds" to whatever good cause seemed to strike her fancy at the time. To date, she had adopted at least ten kids through some "Save the Children Fund," bought a thousand acres of rainforest, purchased uncountable cases of those awful Girl Scout Cookies, and foolishly sent thousands of dollars to some televangelist in Mobile; a guy with really bad hair.

None of it was intentioned in the true spirit of giving anything to anybody. Bobbi always donated in a loud and apparent way, which was meant to advertise the fact that she was a really great and caring person.

I do not think that Bobbi had any idea of how to lead or how to belong, yet, because of her striking physical appearance, she more often than not found herself to be the center of attention; people gawking, men drooling, women appraising the threat of her charms.

Their gazes, absent in understanding, stared at a flower as though it secretly contained inspiration or answers, never knowing that all the flower contained was beauty, and that in itself should have been enough.

Studying his clipboard as Bobbi slid smoothly next to him, Conrad asked mootly, "How about a three-hour private lesson with a Mr.Grenwald?"

Oh, no thanks Conrad. Very nice of you to ask though. Perhaps some other day. I've just got so much to do right now...

"Yes sir. I would love to," lied Bobbi, while draping Conrad in the sarcasm of her smile.

She then tried to bury her disappointment at having to miss a morning of free skiing with the gang by heaping bad Karma on their heads; *Maybe they'll get screwed later this afternoon; maybe the lift will break down; maybe it will rain.* Immediately her spirits began to perk up by just imagining the negative possibilities that could befall her comrades.

"Level five, and doesn't want to do any moguls," offered Conrad, while continuing to consult his client sheet.

"All right: level five, not bad." *This could be some fun after all. Some nice blue cruisers, learn to carve, and I'll be able to get some good turns in when doing my demos,* thought Bobbi.

"Bobbi, this is Mr. Grenwald," introduced Conrad as the gentleman approached them, "Have fun guys," he added as he hurriedly moved off for another assignment.

"Doctor Grenwald, actually Bobbi. But please call me Roger," smiled her new guest.

Bobbi immediately began sizing up the client. *Tall, not bad looking, nice outfit; must be intelligent seeing he's a doctor and all. Pretty decent equipment. He looks in good shape and those small gold rimmed glasses definitely give him that "Marcus Welby" look. Maybe even a good tipper. Well, this could be fun after all.*

"Of course, Roger," she purred professionally, while flashing her Hollywood smile. *Hey, Daddy spent $20,000 on these great choppers.* "I'm Bobbi O'Donnell, and I'm all yours for the next three hours."

"Jeez," cracked Ivana, who was standing nearby, and to nobody in particular. "What a waste of talent. She could be a great hooker and make lots more money."

"I see that you are a level five skier," Bobbi said.

"That's right," he said fidgeting with his boot buckles.

"Are you a medical doctor?" she asked.

"No," said Roger. "I'm actually a psychologist."

"Great. (*I hope he's not going to analyze me. Hey honey, you should have seen the nut case that I had today as an instructor.*)... You could open up a practice and make a fortune around here," she joked into his blank expression.

Well, that went over like a lead balloon. "So, what would you like to work on today, Roger?" she continued brightly and undeterred.

"Well, I'm starting to parallel ski a little bit," he offered, "but it all seems to fall apart when the terrain gets too steep or too rough."

"That's not uncommon, Roger. We'll work on it," she said professionally. "What do you say we take a ride up the Elk chair? We will get to know each other, do some turns up there on nice intermediate terrain and see what the problem could be. The snow is just perfect for your level," encouraged Bobbi.

"No," he stated flatly.

"No? Do you mean 'no,' as in 'No, not right now'... or 'No, I want to do another lift or...or...what kind of 'no?'" she asked.

"No...as in "No," I don't do lifts," responded Roger.

"Oh, okay (*Now THIS is weird*). Would you mind if I asked why?" quizzed Bobbi.

"I can't ride a chairlift," explained Roger. "It's not that I'm really scared of heights. It's my boots."

"Oh, oh," she commiserated. (*Now here is a problem that I can fix.*) "Are your boots giving you a problem?"

"Yes, they are too damn heavy! I know I'm nuts Bobbi, heck *I'm* the shrink here, but whenever I'm on a chairlift, I'm afraid that they'll pull me out of the chair and I'll fall off."

??????? thought Bobbi, and then she reconsidered and thought again, *??????*.

Well, this is a new one for me. I've dealt with all sorts of phobias, including the lady who refused to open her eyes because she thought she would fall off of the mountain. I've been puked on by cases of mountain sickness and I've had every type of paranoid kid, but this is an intelligent, grown man who is unreasonably afraid of having his boots suck him out of a lift like some giant vacuum cleaner! And all that great snow up there!

She put on her most understanding smile and lied, "Hey, that's okay Doctor, we all have little issues, (*but not like THIS, you moron.*) ... We'll just walk up a ways and start from there." (*Walk up...ha, that will cure him fast....*)

"Great," bubbled Doctor Grenwald. "I'm in really good shape you know."

No kidding. And so he was.

Bobbi and "The Human Mountain Goat," as he was soon dubbed, spent the next two hours repeatedly walking part way up the slope, skis slung over their shoulders, redoing their equipment at the top of their assent and generally sweating like they were on a full out assault of Mt .Everest.

She began to have a new appreciation for the 10th Mountain Division alpine troops of World War II. Bobbi began to wish that perhaps she too could be shot and wounded so that she could finally bid farewell to this battle.

Adding insult to injury, Roger was apparently getting nowhere in improving his technique. He was, as self-diagnosed, "terminally intermediate" and he desperately needed more terrain than the half dozen turns to the bottom that this hill could provide.

Maddeningly however, he seemed to be *enjoying* the exercise. He could have gone to the gym for a mere six bucks and pumped on a Stairmaster for three hours with the same results. Bobbi was getting physically ill from the exertion and Doctor Death was relishing the pain which he was inflicting upon himself.

"Roger, you know, this just isn't going where we want it to." (*You should be dead by now.*) "You are so above and beyond this terrain." (*I'll stroke his male ego.*)

Bobbi was ready to surrender. "We have got to get you onto a lift."

"No. I don't *do* lifts," countered Roger, once more balancing his skies over his shoulder, and in that simple statement he was adamant.

Confused, dehydrated, and contemplating raising the white flag of defeat, the roar of a passing snowmobile shuttling a guest downhill invaded Bobbi's remaining consciousness. *Wait a minute, girl...those things go two ways...down and UP...*

"Paulie!!" screamed Bobbi, "Over here!"

Paulie dropped his downhill load and buzzed over to where the instructor stood with her client.

"Whuz up, pretty lady?" he smiled.

Paulie Genardo had been working lifts and general maintenance off and on at Mount Bellew for over four years now, but this was the first year they allowed him to actually drive one of the big machines. He loved it. He would have paid *them* for the fun. It reminded him of his old Harley—before the crash.

Mount Bellew was very shorthanded this year and Paulie only needed to skip work on the extremely cold days when even his best wool ski hat could not keep the steel plate in his head from freezing up and giving him pain.

Putting on her best seductive smile, Bobbi leaned over the snowmobile and cooed, "Paulie, my handsome Italian stallion, how about being a sweetheart and giving me and the Doctor here a ride up to the top of the run?"

"No can do sweet thing. Rules are rules. You know that. "The Pan" would have my butt fired if he caught me giving taxi rides on the mountain. Besides, what's the matter? Lifts broken? They look okay to me," he said sternly, determined to ignore her charm.

"One, you would never understand," said Bobbi truthfully. "Two, I'll love you forever," she lied. "And three, (*oh god, help me...*) I'll cook you breakfast some morning," she finally promised in desperation.

Carefully contemplating the consequences of being fired by "The Pan"—*Hmmm... no job no car, lots of debt, no food, no rent money—versus having breakfast with Bobbi,* Paulie made the only logical and mature decision that could be expected.

"Okay, get on," he grinned. "But don't make it a habit."

Five thrilling minutes later, Bobbi and Doctor Grenwald were standing at the top of the mountain and grinning at the sun-filled eastern ranges. Roger had made it to the top! His evil boots had not had the chance to suck him to a snow-filled death! He and this wonderful woman had outwitted their diabolical plan! Damn, wait until he tells the other guys about *THIS*!

"Roger, if you don't stop smiling, your teeth will freeze," Bobbi laughed at him.

"You know, I don't care. This is fantastic! I feel like a kid on Christmas morning!" he bubbled excitedly.

Bobbi had a fleeting thought of panic. *Oh no, he's not going to want to go down now.*

Hoping that she was wrong, Bobbi jumped right to her next task. "Roger, now we can really get to work. We're going to ski a trail called "Wanderer" and we're going to ski it all the way to town."

"How far is that?" asked Roger, a bit of apprehension showing in his voice.

"Oh, about three miles I think."

"And just how do we get back?" questioned Roger now suspecting a trick. Perhaps this woman was in evil cahoots with the boot gang.

"I'm not taking a chairlift you know," he was not going to be seduced so easily.

"Yes, I *know* Roger." *Wow...this guy is adamant.*

"Will that guy pick us up again?" he asked hopefully.

"Nope. They have buses which run around down there. We ski to the bottom and the bus will bring us back to the base," said Bobbi, assuringly. *Of course, that is if those goof ball transportation guys showed up today. ...*

"Great! This is absolutely great!" effused Roger, now encouraged. "Let's do it," he said eagerly.

Thirty minutes later, there were hugs of congratulations, laughs, and whoops of accomplishment as both instructor and student finished out their run in a very respectable form of parallel skiing. Ten minutes later, Wally, at the helm of the old ragged school bus, drove up right on time.

Seems he was having an unusually good day.

"Yo, Bobbi! Whata doing down this end of the world? Get lost, or are you just slumming it? You didn't come down here just to see *me* did you?" piped Wally.

"Shut up, Walter. Just drive," she shot back in retaliation.

"As you wish my princess, but don't tell me to take you to your palace. I'm working and I gotta go back to the base. Maybe some other time," he offered trying to let her down easily.

She beamed him her most seductive smile. "In your dreams, sailor."

Is he actually serious?

Conrad was waiting expectantly when she strode back into the afternoon lineup. "Damn, Bobbi, where in the heck did you disappear too?" he asked. "I've been looking everywhere for you."

"Let's see, Conrad, I've been mountain climbing, snow-mobiling, shopping in town, and joy riding with Wally...that's about it." She ticked off.

"You certainly give a full service lesson, girl. Did the good doctor learn anything?"

"A little bit, but we had a lot of fun; and he likes his boots much more now. He also greased me with a $100 tip," bragged Bobbi so that all could hear.

"Holy mackerel! That's a lot of fun! Are you sure you guys went skiing?" Conrad bantered with her.

"Oh, stuff it boss," she grinned back.

Then her smile faded as she remembered that she owed Paulie a breakfast. Maybe he would forget.

Yeah. Right.

YOU ARE WHAT YOU EAT

Most people are scared of those things that don't sit still and pose for our official portrait of reality: which means that they have a lot to be scared about. I suppose that's why they're careful not to look very far in any direction.

Tom Robbins

YOU ARE WHAT YOU EAT

Jack Sprat could eat no fat,
  His wife could eat no lean;

And so betwixt them both,
  They lick'd the platter clean.

Nursery Rhyme

Since no man, including Paulie Genardo, who had any testosterone level whatsoever would forget that he had a breakfast date with the luscious "Bobbi O," she soon found herself cornered like a desperate rat to fulfill her hasty promise.

Now, I'm not prone to bragging, but I am a fairly good cook; in a rather crude army-style sort of way, and so I was pleased to give Bobbi the recipe for my famous *Garbage Omelet*.

Real Food For Real Men. After this, I might write a recipe book. That seems like a good title.

The *Garbage Omelet* has become a culinary fixture around Mount Bellew and persists to this day: much like those *Buffalo Wings* from Buffalo, but it never seemed to really catch on nationally like "the wing thing." I think it has something to do with the name.

Try it: say "Garbage Bellew," or "Mount Omelet," perhaps even "Mount Garbage." Nope, just doesn't seem to have the correct "ring" to it, does it?

Anyway, this simple culinary masterpiece is usually concocted after a long night of drinking. It's after effects can then be attributed to the common hangover. Like the aforementioned "Wings," there is only one true and purist recipe:

The (soon to be famous someday) Mount Bellew Garbage Omelet

1. Open up the reefer (no…that's nautical talk for "refrigerator"). Preferably this is someone else's refrigerator, not yours, so that you can be surprised.

Take out all the meat that you can find. Do NOT ever use tofu. Avoid this at all costs, especially since I personally believe that nobody has ever discovered exactly what that stuff *really* is; and it is spelled weird, too.

Cut up and fry all the meat in a really big pan. Bologna is good. Salami is excellent. Chicken legs should be left on the bone: ribs too.

Drain most of the grease off and give it to the dog. It's good for their coats. Save enough to do the veggies in.

2. While frying up the meat, be cutting up everything else in the reefer: onions, potatoes, celery. Carrots are healthy. Sprouts make it stringy, but that's kind of kinky and maybe should be used only on holidays.

Take all the veggies and fry them up in the leftover grease.

Be looking for cheese during the downtime. All kinds, without exception, are good and will make the ingredients stick together nicely.

3. Beat up as many eggs as possible. One is okay and maybe all that you can find, but it "cheapens" the dish. Twelve are better.

Add some milk, some garlic and a bunch of Tabasco.

Throw the meat and the veggies in together. Let the flavors "marry." That is what Julia Childs says, "Marry"; sounds like they got something good going on in the pan, but it just might turn out to be a mess.

4. Dump in the eggs and don't go touching anything until it starts to harden up. Sometimes you have to stick it under the broiler depending on how deep it all is.

Attempt to fold the omelet.

Do not be disappointed. This is not possible. Try anyway.

5. *Now* look what you've done...okay.

6. Beat it all together with one of those wooden stick things. Add the cheese. *THAT* will make the damned thing stick! Broil it again.

Longer! Until it is nice and brown on the top. Black is bad.

If you need a knife to cut it, that's okay.

7. Serve with the usual condiments of toast, ketchup, and beer.

Bobbi and Paulie's breakfast together was a "great success": success being defined by her as; "He ate it and left." Of course she could have probably served the love struck liftee a steaming plate of cow dung and the fool would have eagerly eaten it just to spend the time around her.

Nevertheless, I think my cookbook is going to be a real hit! You must buy it. I need money. But, speaking of culinary tips... tips for good service... and ski tips in general...

KEEP YOUR TIPS UP!

Wally and I actually heard stories of clients who would tip instructors with such things as four wheel drive vehicles (Aspen) or tickets to concerts (Vail) or trips to swanky resort destinations (Telluride). We read about it in those ski magazines.

There were even stories about these nice little old lady types who would make pies and sweaters and stews for their favorite employees (anywhere in the Midwest).

The only exotic tips I ever saw around Mount Bellew though, was an occasional donation of some farm animal, like a pig or a chicken or maybe a free cat. I think they were meant for dinner (except for the cats), but they all ended up as somebody's pet or mascot.

One clever instructor got pretty inventive and tried giving his friend/student money before the class. This friend/student was then supposed to give it back to him at the end of the session with a great show of tipping in front of the others: kind of motivate them by example you know. The friend/student kept the money and the scheme soon died out. I do not think the friendship lasted much longer after that.

Wally and I never got any tips: I mean like *Ever.* Sometimes we worked damn hard, too. We even tried wearing tee shirts and hats to advertise the fact that we were not proud.

The shirts said, "Tips are appreciated for great service." and the hats proclaimed that, "Tippin' is not a city in China."

We liked them.

"The Pan" made us take them off. He said that we were "begging."

So what?

Now Ivana, there was the true "Queen of the Shakedown." She was a legend around Mount Bellew. She was our heroine and if "The Pan" ever thought about accusing her of "begging" he wisely kept the thought to himself.

After defecting to the good old U.S. of A., it did not take

the girl very long to learn that the inalienable rights of every citizen included life, liberty, and the pursuit of happiness. Pursuing tips made Ivana feel very happy and liberated. God Bless America!

After any lesson she could stand before a client in such a way that they would quickly realize that they were not going to pass "The Wall" without paying some sort of toll. Men threw money at her just to escape, old women offered to make her some nice soup, young children searched the area expectantly seeking their parents and the wallets which they instinctively knew would set them free. Ivana almost always scored something and was damned proud of it.

Once she even got a free tattoo. Her student was appropriately intimidated by her and I imagine that he was afraid not to give her anything. He did not have any extra cash, but he did own a tattoo parlor.

Not a bad job really; right on her butt. She showed it to us. She's very proud of it. Some sort of Czech eagle from the national flag which I imagine will someday look like a road kill turkey, but for right now, it looks real nice.

Kinda big though...

Now you would have reasonably thought that being Transportation Engineers (the only two in this "soon to be world renown resort") that we would have gotten a little more respect for our services. By "respect" I mean the kind shown in money. For many of these skiers we would be the first and last contacts of their day spent at Mount Bellew.

The buses were always quiet in the mornings as the beginners struggled with their anxiety, or the experts tried to get their adrenaline pumped up for the day. We tried to help by occasionally singing, which I feel was never sufficiently appreciated, or by answering a whole myriad of inane questions:

"Are you still open if it's snowing?"

"Yes sir, it's when we do our best business," we would respond.

"How long does it take to come down?"

"Well kid, it depends on exactly how you do it, I guess. Some people can take 10 minutes, some people take the whole day," we would say politely.

"Young man, is the altitude any less here in the summer?"

"Yes madam, but I doubt if you would notice," we would answer courteously.

"When do the deer turn into elk?" "SHUT UP! I'M TRYING TO DRIVE HERE!" we would scream while tearing at our hair.

Still, I reminisce about those days: hurtling up and down the centerline of Route 226, never giving an inch more than necessary to avoid a fiery collision, especially if Wally had the oncoming bus.

He was very competitive, you know.

There I was: I had a busload of blissfully ignorant passengers who knew not whether they were destined for a fine fun-filled day on the sunny slopes or an immediate screaming death; all within dubious control of my hung-over hands.

I felt like a god.

The guys I really felt sorry for were the guys at the ski rental shop. These were the front line troops, the ones who were assigned the task of initially outfitting the neophytes and adapting them to their new equipment. The complexities of ski gear are capable of throwing the new skier, albeit a normally intelligent, rational human being, into a state of complete infancy. It probably would have been like me suiting up for a space shuttle launch and ending up with my helmet on backwards and the air hose in my crotch. So, whether you are a skier, or even an astronaut, there just seems to be so much "stuff" to remember.

I believe that's my point.

Simply fitting the boots could be a complicated matter, since most of the beginners were not even sure what they were supposed to feel like.

"Okay, how does that feel now?" the shop attendant would

ask.

"Lousy," says the customer grimacing in agony. "They're really tight."

"Good, that should be just about perfect then," notes the attendant happily cinching them down yet another notch.

"But I can't feel my feet!" the client moans.

"Excellent."

They sure as hell ain't sneakers, Pal!

No, they were like your first pair of moon boots, but if you could remember to keep the buckles pointed *outwards*, most of your foot discomfort would eventually disappear due to a numbing effect. That was a major step up in the old learning curve.

Then, at least in the thoughts of the student, the sadistic shop technician would apparently *weld* them onto these skis, which for all practical purposes were nothing more than two-by-fours: *designed to twist and break every bone in their lower bodies.*

The final addition to this bizarre outfit was when they are given a pair of sharpened, pointy-ended poles which seemingly had no function, except maybe to kill themselves with when all else failed.

Now, properly attired, they would be sent out of the safety of the warm shop for the experience of sliding uncontrollably across the icy terrain on a pair of waxed, plastic death traps: "designed to twist and break every bone in their lower bodies."

This provides endless entertainment for the entire shop crew; or so this new human missile thinks.

Many beginners go into a state of panic at this point. Some of the very athletic people actually began to mimic other more advanced skiers and, at a great cost to their physical well being, begin to pick up the general idea.

Others, we will call them "the smart ones", check into Ski School.

At the end of the day, it was easy to spot the people who

were really beginning to enjoy the sport. They would ski across the gravel parking lot to the bus and then wait there to load: not a care in the world, not a brain in their heads.

"Sorry, but you'll have to remove those skis to get onto the bus," we would advise.

"Why? I'm just getting used to these things," they would argue.

They had really bonded with their new equipment; either that or they had forgotten how to take it off.

So, all this leads me back to the central theme of this ranting diatribe. Yes, I know, I can not for the life of me remember either; so I re-read it for the both of us.

It is "Tipping!"

Oh sure, the instructor that gets you safe and secure on the mountain and then actually has you skiing down it gets a tip, but what about the other guys? We got you there and got you back. Wasn't that fun, too?

And the ski shop guy, giving you all that great stuff at such a cheap price. How would you like people stepping on your fingers all day or having to play with people's smelly feet and listen to them whine? *That's* not a very good job, is it? Maybe some weirdos like that sort of thing, but not me.

So be generous, bring lots of money, and spread it around. Your donation could be the final little bit that sends a guy, man, woman, or even a person on to medical school where they will cure cancer and save the world.

You never know.

And you would not want to risk it by being cheap.

DECEMBER

Complex systems tend to locate themselves at a place we call "the edge of chaos." It is a zone of conflict and upheaval, where the old and the new are constantly at war. Finding the balance point must be a delicate matter. If the system drifts too close to the edge, it risks falling over into incoherence and dissolution: if the system moves too far away from the edge, it becomes rigid, frozen and totalitarian. Both conditions will lead to extinction. The formation of radical ideas is as important as their abandonment; however it is in their exchange among intelligent men that is of utmost importance. Only at the edge of chaos can complex systems flourish.

Michael Crichton

December

It's okay to kill some people's dreams; because some get the kind of dreams people get by putting marijuana in their brownies.

Journals of Conrad King

She stared forlornly at the image reflecting back to her from the refrigerator door. The doctor had said that she was "fat." She understood what that meant. Without being cynical, it meant another useless round of unsuccessful diets; because she wasn't "fat." She was fluffy. She was horizontally challenged. She had been off and on these diets since she was young and, now that she was approaching middle age, she had pretty much lost any faith in them and just wanted to pig out and be herself. She was tired of being judged. She did not like the doctor anyway and she didn't really care to be lean. Bobbi was lean. She did not find Bobbi attractive. *What's the big deal about being skinny anyway?* She thought.

No, she saw herself as more of an Ivana type; nice and burly. Burly people needed to keep up their strength. Their very burliness depended on constant nourishment. This was evidenced by Ivana; the woman ate like a sumo wrestler. She had watched longingly as the formidable instructor had put two huge sandwiches, fruit, and drinks into the fridge this morning just for lunch. Nobody would dare call Ivana "fat." The woman was like a lunch goddess.

Lunch? Lunch? Damn, now how did that get stuck in her

119

mind?

She had recently finished off a huge breakfast, only a couple of hours ago, and already she was focusing on lunch.

Maybe I do have a problem.

Her soft, dark eyes studied themselves in the reflection. She noted that the gold in her thick hair had achieved a hue which both men and women found irresistible. There was no vanity in her self-appraisal. It was just the way things were.

You know something? You're actually cuter with a little weight on. So, it really wouldn't hurt to just have a quick peek in the old fridge now would it?

Since there was no way that she herself was going to open up the promising treasure chest in front of her, she began to imagine that it would magically spring open of its own accord and afford her access to all the known goodies inside. Then she wouldn't feel guilty. It wouldn't be her fault. It would be some sort of mechanical malfunction. She stared at the humming black box hypnotically, using the force of her will in an attempt to pop open the door. There was bacon in there, and cheese, and lunch meats of all wonderful varieties. *Open...open... open.*

She had comfortably settled in for a long self-pitying contemplation of her fate when Erik startled her from her reverie.

"Okay, Daisy, knock it off. Let's go now. You're making me feel guilty. Get your mind on work," he admonished her.

Erik Nuremburg: the boss, the high commander, the big guy, the alpha-male of her society. Erik made the rules and since he said, "no snacking between meals," then that was the way it would be. Daisy's loyalty to Erik and his command was unquestionable. She had worked for him and his ski patrol for five seasons now. She had lived with him for seven. Where Erik went, she went, and they had teamed up together on the most daring of rescues and the most mundane of ski area tasks.

Together they had bombed precipitous ridges clear of evil overhanging snow lips. The "lips of death" Erik would tell her:

huge protruding ridges of wind-blown snow seemingly packed into rocklike formations that were impervious to the wills of nature, until

nature, which had fashioned them itself, brought them cascading and thundering down into tons of icy boulders. They had evacuated frightened clients from power-starved chairlifts and had occasionally fixed stubborn toilets which had frozen in their jobs.

Erik had brought his considerable skiing talents to Mount Bellew soon after graduating from the Vienna Institute in Austria. The plumbing he had learned on his own.

He was an "alpine ski god." That was what he told Daisy in their moments alone. That was what she believed.

Everybody else thought Erik was a self-important, egotistical ass.

Erik spent a considerable amount of time looking down his long, fine, Austrian nose at American skiing in general and at Mount Bellew in particular. He came from a society which traditionally treated skiing like the national religion and its heroes were treasured celebrities. He had serious difficulty accepting the Americanized version; which was more like a big fun circus, clowns and cowboys included.

The one thing he did not have trouble with was accepting the American money that came with the job.

The big Austrian neither traveled through life nor down a ski hill unnoticed. When Erik would stride into the cafeteria or the little bar at Mahogany Ridge, or speed across a hill with a rescue sled in tow, concentrated conversation would become lost and dim as the eyes of women, and the men too, focused on him.

He loved that feeling.

His athletically tuned body was strong with the sleek muscling of a professional swimmer. He seemed taller than his 6-foot 3-inches would have indicated due to long blond hair which was pulled back into a ponytail. It framed electric green eyes like radars. Those eyes missed nothing. Erik could have been the poster boy for the Aryan nation; a fine example of Hitler's ultimate product. He resembled a Fabio clone in a blond wig—every woman's wet dream; his own much-admired image was a gift to the mirror itself.

He would enter a quieting room, the patrol jacket commanding respect even when not on the slope, his teeth emitting a supernatural light, and he would think, "God, it's wonderful to be me."

It was a good thing that Daisy loved him so dearly, since nobody else seemed to have the tolerance to be around him for very long. It would have been constructive to point this out to him, but he was just too overpowering a personality for confrontation. I wisely never tried.

"Come on. Let's get at it," Erik snapped, interrupting Daisy's happy food dreams, "Time to go."

Daisy resented the fact that she was going to have to head out into the miserable cold with only a half-full belly of food, but Erik was always the boss and so she stretched her square body from the floor and shook out the soft yellow coat which she wore every day.

Although her dedication to Erik himself was unwavering, it was more important to her way of thinking that he might be carrying some interesting snacks in his ever-present backpack. Despite his own command, Erik could only resist her gentle gaze for so long and then he would break down and be willing to share his goodies. She would just have to bide her time. After all, a pretty girl can always get what she wants from a man, eventually.

Daisy followed the lumbering patrolman begrudgingly to the door of the locker room and into the cold, casting a quick backward glance to assure herself that the refrigerator was still there.

Outside, in the fresh crispness of the winter morning, her spirits began to perk up and she momentarily forgot her chronic hunger. As they made their way toward the main lift, she saw that Conrad was there organizing the assignment of private client instructors.

CONRAD! she thought. *I LOVE Conrad!*

With that one and only thought occupying her limited mind, she dropped her butt close to the ground and barreled toward his knees.

Conrad's head snapped in her direction when she first squealed her delight at his presence. He was prepared. He had been involved in this routine before. "Daisy!" he shouted cheerfully, and then squatted low to absorb the inevitable blow from the stout 95-pound labrador body steaming in a full sprint.

Conrad roared in laughter. Daisy whined in love. Soon they were both rolling on the snow while he and the bouncing dog were having a regular contest to see who could slobber on each other more.

"Yeeech," noted one of the young instructors.

"Son, this is the closest thing to sex I've had this month, so why don't you just give us some privacy here," he admonished from under the pile of squirming yellow dog.

Conrad and Daisy were two of the only true natives working at Mount Bellew. While Conrad had grown up on a nearby ranch, Daisy had never known any other place in her life. She traced her lineage back to her mother, Petunia, who had had one last litter before heading off to retirement with Old Pete. She had grown up to be beautiful, sweet, loving, and warm, all the best traits of her admirable breed. She also grew up to be the most educated of her litter and was able to communicate in two languages.

Isn't that odd?

Most everyone else at the resort spoke only English, and generally that was butchered into incomprehensibility, but the rescue dog actually understood two languages that we knew of: Austrian and English.

You could say, "Daisy, come here girl," and she would come right to you. Erik on the other hand would say something like, "Daisy, comen zee here maedchen," and still she would come. Pretty clever, eh? I imagine that she also spoke labradorian, but we did not know any people from Lab Land and so we could not ever test this theory.

Anyway, Daisy had begun avalanche and rescue training as a puppy and had been given over to Erik's care shortly after he arrived at Mount Bellew.

Considering that he personally was such an arrogant jerk, there was no sensible explanation as to why she matured into such a loving and popular girl, except that maybe "god works in strange ways": which, by the way, explains almost nothing.

While Daisy closely mirrored Erik's professionalism toward his job, she nevertheless took a decidedly more hedonistic approach toward her life in general. Food, affection, playing games and sleeping came first; saving people suffocating in the snow came second. This was evident even in her very early days of training.

Puppy education for the rescue of mock "victims" caught in avalanches dictates that volunteers are buried in a sort of hollowed out ice cave under the snow: on purpose mind you. Our little furry heroine pups then run around under the watchful eyes of the patrollers and sniff out their prey. The better you smell, the faster you will get found. Sometimes you will get peed on if they really like you.

Fortunately for Daisy, one of her first volunteers turned out to have the unmistakable stink of a local Burger King still upon him: night job.

She found him almost instantly to the great pride and astonishment of the patrollers. Terms like, "genius" and "gifted" and "awesome" were heaped upon her.

In retrospect, the accolades were a bit premature; one great save does not make a career and she was never able to get that single brief moment of glory out of her mind. In subsequent searches, she would run madly over the "graves" of buried humans in slobbery search of the more important buried hamburger, which often was not ever there.

Understandably, this became a matter of concern, since given the option between finding a real victim or finding their lost lunch, the poor soul would soon perish under a crush of snow while the dog busily pointed to various pieces of scattered sandwiches for the patrollers to dig up.

A pickle. SAVE the pickle! CHIPS? HELP the chips!! That pretty much mirrored Daisy's rescue philosophy.

Most likely, this is why she finally worked at Mount Bellew and not at Aspen. People at Aspen simply do not pack their lunch with them. They "do lunch"; at someplace nice.

Backcountry skiers, who were checking out at the patrol hut, would be given a serious warning to "buy some cheese-burgers and stick 'em in your pockets." This often baffled the uninformed, who would wrongly assume that they were supposed to probably munch on the cold slabs of animal fat while awaiting a delayed rescue. Little did they know that their lives could depend on them *not* devouring the meat and thus magnetizing the ever-starved and sniffing nose of Daisy.

"So, how much longer are you gonna work this old gal," Conrad asked as he got off the snow and wiped his face on his sleeve.

"Probably finish up Friday," Erik answered. "I think the pups will be due in about four weeks or so. Anybody that gets buried in a slide after Friday will just have to wait until spring for a rescue," he joked.

"Doc say how many to expect?" Conrad questioned.

"Four...maybe six. But they have a way of fooling you," Erik answered.

"Yeah, they do at that," Conrad concurred as he knelt back down, rubbed Daisy's welcoming belly, and set off another barrage of whining.

"Now, you take it easy until Friday girl," he cooed, "Then old Conrad is gonna give you a month off from work. Okay?" he asked mootly.

Whatever you are babbling about Conrad...I have no idea...but your face sure tastes good. Musta had sausage this morning...

Erik, festooned in neon-yellow poly line and bright red tape used to mark off the closed trails, led a festive parade as he barked something in Austrian to Daisy and the pair set off to board the chairlift which would carry them to the top of the mountain for their day's work.

Conrad turned back to his private lesson instructors. He caught the eye of Louie Mayfield and let out an involuntary groan.

Bingo! Thought Louie. *Got him again.*

The newly-issued ski school uniform, which had been dry cleaned at the beginning of the season, had finally been relieved of its virginity and fit Louie like a comfortable, worn out bag.

Like a cat preparing for the hunt, Louie had embraced whatever filth he could find in an effort to cleanse it of its domesticated smell. He had spent days chopping wood in it. It had dined with him on numerous occasions and later, finally succumbing to his questionable charms, had gone to bed with him. His reflection that morning had assured him that the sharply pressed lines were now but a memory. Louie took his slovenliness very seriously.

Louie Mayfield's appearance was a bruise won in battle. His sense of taste was a carefully concocted stew of cheap ingredients, a calculated revolution. Conrad had noted that every morning it was Louie, not any of the women, who was in direct competition with Erik for a sufficient amount of mirror time in the locker room. Whatever reflected space was not filled up with the patroller's considerable image would find him carefully tucked into its corners assuring that everything was all carefully disheveled for his day of work.

He would shake his long red hair like a dog shedding water until he was satisfied with the resulting entanglement. The hair was too long and it snaked about his head in mythical Hydra-fashion. Louie fastidiously maintained his day-old beard growth so it always looked like he had absentmindedly forgotten to shave.

An earring dangled tauntingly from his left lobe and, if that was found to be acceptable on that particular day, then he would attach one more in his right. Louie always liked to see just how far he could push the fashion envelope.

Careful to appear to be the epitome of snowboarding chic; Louie considered himself to be the quintessential image for this new and budding counterculture of alternative athletes. He fully expected his reflection to confirm his belief.

Conrad had confronted the young man in the past with his slovenly habits, but was told by Pieter to, "Let the boy pursue his particular brand of beauty."

Pieter thought that this was the image that the snowboard crowd actually wanted to see in their instructors; and, emboldened by the support of his new benefactor, Louie felt secure in challenging Conrad's authority whenever he could.

"Nice," said Louie bouncing on his toes behind Erik in the mirror.

"Why don't you just back off, dude, and wait your turn," grumbled Erik.

"My narcissist friend, if I was required to wait my turn behind your steroidal butt, the only image that I would ever enjoy of myself would be that of an old and wizened man," taunted Louie smiling back at himself.

Erik just grumbled louder. The daily confrontation had become an early morning tradition in the locker room and so far Louie was smart enough never to push it too far. Of course, that was Louie: a master of brinkmanship, able to instigate the smallest of incidents into a confrontation if he cared to.

Conrad did not thoroughly understand the recent craze of snowboarding; except to the extent that it brought in plenty of money to the fledgling ski area and therefore was tolerable. He was no purist. If a cow wanted to slide down the hill in a canoe, then Conrad would have made sure that she was sold a ticket.

Oddly enough, it was that exact cavalier attitude which first attracted the original boarders of the early eighties to Mount Bellew and galvanized their support for the seriously out-of-the-way resort. In 1980 the fledgling sport of snowboarding was tramping the hills of New England in an effort to gain legitimate recognition. Recognition being defined as, "We just want to ride the chairlift, Dude." For a generation that prided itself on marching to the proverbial "different drummer," they had found an alpine home at the little Utah resort.

For the pioneering riders, the powder was always good, the new snow always soft and untouched. Mostly this was because they simply were not allowed on the groomed slopes of any other resort or the use of any other chairlifts; so the walk back up was always grueling. No wonder they sought out Mount Bellew; they were tired.

Snowboarding soon became known as a young people's sport which was immersed in its own alternative ways. This was a perfectly understandable conclusion. The drugs which many were taking were actually needed to help kill the pain. The few heroic "old people" who initially tried the sport soon died off from heart attacks while hiking back up; and the slurred, indecipherable speech which was originally attributed to just "trying to be cool," was soon recognized to be oxygen deprivation at high altitudes.

Since the riders would not just civilly disappear and since they had money with them also, it was erroneously reasoned by large mountain-owning corporations that "Heck, these wonderful children simply need a chairlift to the top and they would soon behave like normal citizens. They will join the

Army. They will get real jobs. They will pay taxes."

Very naïve; but it got the snowboarders on the chairlifts.

The theory that they would become "normal" never quite panned out either and callous little Mount Bellew, well ahead of its time, simply didn't care to fight against the impending tide of popularity. If you had the money for a ticket, you got a ride.

The boarders soon flocked there like the legendary pigeons to Cappachino.

Although Louie had assumed much of the verbiage utilized in the grunged-out clichés of the new snowboarding youth, if you were superficial enough to judge him by his adopted language, you would have guessed him to have attained the education level of a high school dropout. His resume was far more impressive than his language indicated.

Louis Mayfield Jr.

1974 - Bachelor of Arts, College of Economics, Cornell University, graduated Cum Laude.

1978 - Master of Arts, Philosophy, State University of New York, Utica

1979 - Snowboard Instructor, Mount Bellew.

Sometime between 1978 and 1979, after deep introspective thought, physic consultation with the great philosophers of the ages, plus numerous bongs of very good dope, Louie had envisioned the idea of using snowboarding as a way to bring betterment to the world. He also saw a lot of other things in his whacked-out state, but snowboarding as some sort of way to God seemed to stick.

And so he ran away to the fabled Mount Bellew.

Coincidentally, during the same time frame, the elder Mayfield (Louie Sr.) vowed to kill his youngest son. This was not an easy decision, but one which was most whole-heartedly supported by friends at the American Legion Post and many other family members. This excluded Louie's mother, who was leaning toward the idea but wished to abstain, pending more information.

Nobody really blamed the elder Mr. Mayfield or felt compelled to stop him. The man was a moderately successful plumber who had literally gone into about fifty thousand dollars of debt in order to educate his son. When Mayfield senior voiced the opinion of his intentions for young Mayfield junior, it must be said in his defense that he never used the word "kill." His actual words were to the effect that he was going to "beat the crap out of Louie," and at the local Legion bar it was generally agreed that this was a very good idea.

Now some patrons, having known little Louie for most of his aggravating life and also believing that he was totally "full of shit," must have wrongly assumed that this would then logically result in death. So "kill" was mistakenly added to the threat.

See how these things can get distorted?

Anyway, the local judge had kids in school too, and it was thought that he would be more than understanding and lenient at the inevitable trial.

Louie narrowly escaped his fate by slipping out early one morning and heading for some unannounced point west of New York. He felt relatively sure that his father would not have enough money for a number of years in order to buy a plane ticket and track him down. He was probably right. He loved the old man, but he was also scared as hell of him.

Although Louie's steel-trap mind could confront, analyze, and destroy any idea which it had closed upon, he was generally intimidated by the threat of any type of physical confrontation. He relished the feeling that the righteous members of the establishment were all sniffing at his appearance as though he had an offensive odor. The heat of their negative reaction was a gauge of Louie's success.

Like a clever spider, the highly educated boy worked meticulously to set trap upon trap for his unwary victims. His intent: to lead the boldest and most confident headlong into his mental den in search of a seemingly easy meal and then destroy them with his own intellectual poison.

"Violence is the last refugee of the incompetent," he would philosophically taunt and sometimes, being inept at always gauging the steam of his opponents rising frustrations, usually those were the last words out of his mouth before he earned another fat lip.

Conrad had pretty much nailed down the "Louie's" of this world a long time ago and when this one flashed his red curls in his direction, the old bull only moaned and blinked his tired eyes. There would be no enraged charge this day; Louie was much too easy a target for Conrad.

"Mr. Mayfield," Conrad grinned as he studied the clipboard before him, "Since you're looking so extremely handsome today I think I have an assignment which is right up your alley. You do like children, don't you?" he asked rhetorically.

All Louie could do was groan a less then enthusiastic, "yes."

Now, what was officially called the "Employee Party Pot" was more commonly known as "The Goober Jug." This was a fund established at the beginning of the season in order to collect a sizable stash of money for a gigantic final blowout at the end of the year.

Most of the money was collected by a flexible and highly subjective system of fines levied on employees for various "Goobers," or professional screwups, which they were caught committing during the season.

Since the larger the pot, the better the party, the enforcement was rigorous.

These "goobers" covered a wide gamut of infractions ranging from the mere frivolous incident, of perhaps an instructor falling down in front of his or her class while attempting to ski backwards, right on up to the much more serious problem of, say, an accident victim being ejected out of a rescue sled as they were being transported down a mogul run.

It has been known to happen.

Of course this was not funny for *any* of the parties involved, but the fines were substantial and we sadistically looked forward to it.

So, you see, while some infractions were merely *silly* embarrassments, others were downright *dangerous*.

For instance, forgetting to shave before the ski school line-up would cost an instructor five bucks. That was *silly*. Women got off free; nobody wanted to broach the subject. That would have been *dangerous*. Forgetting to occasionally pick up passengers in the bus could cost five bucks too, but only if you were caught: *silly*. Actually running over a passenger: *dangerous*. I don't think there was ever a documented case of that at Mount Bellew, but I bet it would have been an expensive fine.

A good rule of thumb to follow was that anything involving the ski area attorney would be very costly for all parties concerned.

For the lift attendants, the daily occurrence of banging a skier in the head with the chairlift's safety bar or just mashing it down on their fingers was routine enough that they were advised early on to judicially buy the "Platinum Insurance Plan" and then go have fun.

The "Platinum Insurance Plan" was only for the wealthy or the congenitally incompetent employee. The concept of "wealth" is defined in the arena of ski resorts as "being able to live in a house of one bathroom with less than four other people." Simple. The more people sharing the house and the bathroom with you, the poorer you were. It was a direct relationship.

$B/P = M/D$... where "B" is the number of bathrooms you have (usually one) divided by "P" the number of people using it (can be reduced by peeing outside on the lawn) equals "M" which is the money you earn each week (before fines are imposed) divided by "D" the number of dates that you may be expected to get in any month (again, usually one).

Those living in their cars were totally pathetic: zeros across the board.

I like math.

Fairly "wealthy" employees who were versed in the system merely anted up a required preseason price of $100 for "Platinum Goober Insurance." This enabled them to be caught in as many goober incidents as fate allowed throughout the year without paying the requisite fines. Of course, if you had established a reputation for goobers the year before, then your premium could be higher. If an employee tried to buy the insurance midway through the season with a series of goobers already to their credit, well then the cost would again go up.

Sounds a lot like medical insurance doesn't it? If you are healthy and don't need it, then you can get it, and it is relatively cheap. If you are sick, and use it, then you can not get it, or it is exorbitantly expensive. They say insurance is like gambling and they are right; the house always wins. Vegas was built on the losers.

Anyway, people like Bobbi and Erik (i.e. "wealthy people") would opt for the plan. They would pay the $100 bucks up front and then act like some sort of accident police on the rest of the crew for the entire season.

Wally and I did not buy the insurance. We should have. The year cost us at least $200 apiece in five and ten dollar increments. We were heavy contributors.

Fines were levied by Conrad according to his mood at the time. He didn't have to go around collecting the money, like some rodeo Mafia either, because generally the individual always paid up. The peer pressure if you did not was tremendous. Misery truly does love company, as the saying goes, and once one guy was made to pay, then he was damned if he was going to let your weaselly hide slip out of contributing by feigning poverty.

The highest fine I ever heard of was dubiously owned by Louie Mayfield for the time he got lost on the mountain with the three kids. Lost was bad enough, but Louie went and got lost out of bounds. He felt lucky to only have to pay $100 bucks since Conrad had to be restrained from killing him, thus saving Louie's old man the trouble and the plane ticket.

The incident involved a private lesson. Mom and Dad had wanted to go off skiing alone for awhile and so enrolled their children, ages nine, ten, and twelve in the care of the Ski School. After too many boring runs with Mom and Dad, I would imagine that the kids were pretty excited about their three-hour snowboard lesson with a real "hot-dog" instructor and, when they saw how radical looking Louie actually was, they could not wait to get out on the mountain and get some new turns in.

Maybe Pieter was right; Louie had a certain mystique about him.

The way I heard the story was that after about an hour of teaching the little tykes how to do some new "spins and grins," Louie got bored. Spying the yellow rope which was strung along the access trail to the Southside area and, more importantly, seeing that nobody was around to stop him, Louie led the kids under the rope and into the challenging terrain of Mount Bellew's most remote region.

It had not snowed the night before but yesterday that side of the mountain was most excellent for the boards. It was probably still in great shape since the morning sun had time to soften the surface into a corn like texture.

Louie was pretty certain that the only reason for the rope was the fact that the patrollers just hadn't gotten around to skiing the area that morning. He and his band of followers would be the first to explore its intricate tree lines and that would add to the fun he was personally having.

Louie never looked up. He was oblivious to the world around him. Louie only looked after Louie. If he had looked to the west and had noticed the pitch black clouds billowing like evil surf over the highest peaks he might have had second thoughts; then again, maybe not. It was hard to understand the entangled junkyard of Louie's thought process.

The group apparently had only gone a short distance down the access trail when the snow began to fall. It did not come in a gradual and warning wave. It came in a violent and thunder-driven crash which quickly enveloped them in a torrent of wind and blinding white sheets. The kids immediately went into a panic, their fear etched plainly on their reddened faces, while Louie hovered barely out of the reach of its paralyzing grip. He struggled to maintain a little composure. The kids sensed that he was their hope, their rock, and, although he certainly was not inspiring them with the confidence they now needed, he was all they had at this moment.

Louie, not knowing how long the icy mayhem would last, felt that his best option would be a slow descent downward keeping to the trees as best he could. This would at least give him some visibility and depth perception; and right now he had neither. He chose a grade which appeared to be the gentlest slope in an area of radical pitches and tried to keep his board moving through the sticky wetness of the quickly accumulating snow. The kids followed dutifully. Unfortunately for Louie, that particular grade led slowly and inexorably away from the main trails.

Although he did not recognize the area that he was headed for, in Louie's mind if you were going "down" you had to be headed for the bottom of the ski area. He probably still thinks that Canada is uphill from New York and that you can coast in your car all the way to Florida. Louie was a philosophy major. Apparently topography, or even a good stint in the Boy Scouts, never acquainted him with terrain variations; or geography for that matter.

He knew that they were making good time down the hill. The fact that they were hopelessly lost never occurred to him. There comes a time when you are lost that you completely fail to recognize it; that is when you are really in deep trouble.

I've been lost and probably will be again some day. They tell you, "When you are lost, the first rule of survival is: don't panic." That is rule Number One! They say this as though panic is a reasonable and logical decision. Rule Number Two is equally inane. They say something about making a fire, perhaps baking some bread and building yourself a house in your spare time. Oh yeah, maybe a nice two-story ranch with a view.

"They" are nuts. All the advice is just a ploy to keep you busy so you don't go completely bonkers.

Tom Hanks did pretty well following these recommendations in *Castaway*; but let's try to remember that he was not really "lost" (on a two-mile square island?). He just wasn't "found" yet.

I remember PANIC, and I don't remember it as being some petite and effeminate British fellow who taps gently on the front door of your mind and says in his best Oxford accent, "Oh, good day, Sir! I'm Mr. Panic from 'Emotion Express.' Would you mind terribly if I came in to have a seat in your head?"

"Oh really, you mustn't my good man," you say politely. "I was just about to jump out of my skull and have a nice tea with Messieurs Reason and Logic. We might build a nice lodging together, maybe whip up some scones. Perhaps you can come back later in the day? Say, about sevenish...*WHEN IT GETS DARK!!!*"

Hell no! It's MR. PANIC !!!

He is a big, fat, drooling monster dressed up in a pit bull disguise that leaps inside your head and barks "Run! *RUNNN!! RUNNNN!!*"

I imagine that Louie's mind was yelling "Go, GO, *GOOOO!!*" and so it drove him relentlessly into the trees, further and further away from the ski area. The boys' collective mind probably said, "I think this bozo has got us lost," but they were too young to consider mutiny against the authority in the purple jacket and too small to reasonably have a chance in beating him up.

The deluge of snow eventually passed onward, leaving a trace of gray and streaking clouds in its wake. There remained a promise of more white stuff to come and the afternoon sun had faded to a dim, cold glow.

The group stood flat on their boards at the bottom of a frozen creek bed. It was the end of their journey downward and what awaited them now, even on a clear summer day, would be an extremely long and difficult walk toward the south where Louie correctly and instinctively thought the main area lay. How far? He had no idea. Louie unstrapped his board, stepped onto the new surface and immediately sank both his legs, posthole style, into two feet of gooey soft snow.

Back at the area, a mobilization of forces worthy of his days in Vietnam was being orchestrated by Conrad. Louie had not returned with his charges after the three-hour lesson and the parents were quickly going into their own version of adult panic.

The most natural response to danger or stress is an overwhelming desire to flee and hide. Our society, in most cases, has taken that option away from us. We seldom run now. After all, we would look *silly*. Everybody would by running around like rats in business suits each time the Boss lets out a threatening growl. The least little bit of stress would cause us to pull bags over our heads in an effort to disappear; thus adding to the complications of rush hour traffic.

No, now we are civilized; and that can be *dangerous*.

Modern society has conditioned us to deal with stress by condoning our adoption of an aggressive behavior. We need to display to others that WE are in charge and so we raise our voices, we raise our fists, we raise our anxiety levels, and we get ulcers. All because we really want to run and hide.

Civilization is so much better for this, don't you think?

Since they had no where to run, the boys' parents attacked with typical threats of lawsuits, recriminations and the verbal haranguing of anyone associated with the area. They also sweat a lot, questioned their parenting skills, blamed each other, and prayed.

Maybe instead of dealing with all this stress we should just admit that if you are human then screw-ups are inevitable and that we should all be putting money into a "National Goober Jug" for a big party every New Year's Eve where everyone is forgiven.

(just an idea..)

Conrad had placated the parents for an hour after the lesson hoping that Louie would come sliding in with some reasonable excuse; even a half-ass excuse would be acceptable, just as long as he showed up—soon.

Ski school had canceled the afternoon lessons and Conrad had sent every available instructor to search the open terrain. Erik and his patrollers were even now headed into the more remote and roped-off areas, but the searchers were few and the area was vast. After an hour of anxiously listening to the chatter on the radios, Conrad picked up the phone and called in more avalanche dogs and additional help. It would be dark in two more hours and then things would get very bad, very fast, as temperatures began to plummet.

Erik and Daisy had elected to head to the southside, both of them with the fervent hope that one of the young guys might be smuggling a cheeseburger away in some long-forgotten pocket. Since the instructors were all out on the main slopes, Erik glided off the lift and ducked quickly under the yellow rope into the darkening outback.

That obnoxious bastard better not be back here, he thought moving slowly down the winding trail. The anxiety burned in his gut like a knife, but he proceeded with meticulous patience. He needed to let Daisy keep up and to find a scent, if any scent existed. Erik's blood began a slow boil as he noticed her drive her radar-like nose into the ground ahead of him and then begin a familiar circling pattern.

"Search" he ordered. Soon, the concerned dog began to whine and, still keeping her nose tight to the snow, led him slowly into the thickening woods.

Son of a bitch! Was what he thought; but what he said into the radio was, "This is Erik. Send me a backup with a sled to the southside. Bring a snowmobile in as far as you can on Powderhorn; and don't look for me on the main runout. Keep working to the north."

By now, Louie was exhausted and knew that they were in deep trouble. While the lighter weight boys seemed to tread effortlessly on top of the snow, the thin crust formed just below the surface would not support his bulk. He had envisioned himself leading the boys triumphantly into the base area and blowing off all the impending criticism with a snide bravado. Instead, he was now cast in the role of a burdensome whiner and the boys looked on him with a mixture of disgust and pity. He had been sweating like a man in a sauna and had removed his jacket an hour ago, but now the increasingly dim light had brought a new coldness to the creek bed and he knew that the night, and possibly more snow, could not be far away.

Louie had thought of sending the older boy on ahead in

order to get help but wisely shelved that idea for fear of breaking up the group. Now, as he sat upon his board looking up at the fearful young faces, he knew that he was the only reason that they had gotten lost in the first place and that he was the only reason that they had not walked out by now. Louie was the weak link in the chain. Echoes of his father's past lectures, stressing exactly that, pounded repeatedly in his head; and yet he was the one who was still expected to make the right decisions.

He was resting on his board trying to gather all the oxygen he could from the thin air into his burning lungs when he finally admitted the inevitable.

"Guys," the defeated instructor said, "we just might be spending the night here so we better get ready."

The youngest boy began to cry silently. His older brother put a protective arm around him and now shouted defiantly at Louie, "You're an asshole! You know that? You got us into a big mess and now you can't even get us out!"

"I know that, kid," Louie offered in dejection. "Just don't go getting weird on me. Let's be cool here."

"I hope you get fired!" the brother shot back aggressively.

"Somehow, I don't doubt that in the very least," Louie mumbled more to himself. "But before my firing squad arrives, I think that we all better get comfortable." He sparked the boy's curiosity with a mischievous grin and announced, "We're about to play a game called Eskimo."

"What's that?" they all asked suspiciously.

"Simple," Louie offered, "We dig a snow cave, fill it with lots of pine branches and crawl up inside for a nice cozy night on the mountain."

The three boys, unfamiliar and uncertain of their environment, stared at the wild looking young man in front of them as though he had lost his mind. "We're sleeping here?" they cried out.

"Don't worry, we'll be fine," Louie assured them.

"Oh yeah, just as fine as we are now," the older boy said sarcastically, holding back his own tears so his brothers would not see.

"Look, I know I've lost your trust," Louie half pleaded. "And I guess I don't deserve it, but work with me on this one. We'll be okay inside of the cave."

The oldest brother and Louie locked eyes with each other, momentarily judging the soundness of the decision, evaluating each other based only on the past three hours of their lives. The young boy finally backed off and glanced absently toward the forest. He instinctively recognized that they could go no further

"Okay," he said, resigning them to a night on the mountain. "So what are we supposed to do to make this great cave?"

Louie began to issue orders. "You two are the lightest," he indicated to the young ones. "I want you to climb around those trees up there and get as many pine branches or needles as you can. Then your brother and I will dig out the cave using the boards. Keep eating the snow to get some water into you," he said as an afterthought.

He thought hard: what else?

The growl of his stomach was reminding him of how hard he had been working. "Did any of you guys bring anything to eat that we can share? Cliff bars? Candy?" he asked hopefully.

"I still got a baloney sandwich my Mom made me for a snack yesterday," the youngest boy offered. Louie was elated and waited expectantly as the child dug deep into the far recesses of his jacket eventually producing a rather smashed and unappetizing version of baloney and cheese from an inside pocket. His small hands began to slowly unwrap the treasure while the crinkle of the cellophane filled the air.

Approximately one quarter-mile away Daisy's head bolted upright from the snow.

Hey! Is that baloney? I LOVE baloney!

Fifteen minutes later, Erik and Daisy finished navigating their way to the bottom of the creek bed and found the group busily engaged in the construction of a crude igloo. To Daisy's heartfelt disappointment the sandwich was already history, but she was pretty much consoled by finding three children and bounded around them in barking glee.

Erik, on the other hand, could barely look at Louie for fear of losing his temper and Louie judiciously avoided his gaze in embarrassment and fear.

The snowmobiles, which the patroller requested, had been able to push within fifty yards of the party and the boys were soon loaded into sleds and onto machines. Daisy, enjoying her heroine status, was comfortably wedged between two happy young boys. They were all safely down off the mountain as the sun set over the western range and the snow began to again fall lightly from the darkening sky.

Conrad's effort of placating the parents and consoling the

children was infinitely more delicate than Erik's job of rescuing them initially. He bought the family dinner; he bought the relieved parents drinks, and he fussed over the boys like a protective mother bear. He assured that no one was injured in the escapade and cajoled the father into signing a statement to that effect. In the end, he gave them all free passes for the remainder of the season and apologized for the hundredth time for the irresponsible behavior of his instructor. Conrad hoped fervently that they would just walk away with everything being only a bad memory: eventually they did.

Not wanting the obnoxious Louie to be around as a reminder for the upset family, Conrad had ordered him to wait in the locker room for as long as it took; until Conrad came back. Louie did as he was told. There was no need to push the envelope now.

The heavy sound of the slamming metal door felt like an axe cutting through his heart. Louie felt physically ill. Beads of perspiration laced his forehead and betrayed his feigned composure. He half expected an ogre to appear before him, a yellow-eyed beast, which would attack him and tear at his throat with inhuman violence. Instead, it appeared to be only Conrad.

The man stood imposingly at the end of the benches and pointed a pistol-like finger at Louie. "You," he snapped. "Let's go have a talk: my office."

The condemned instructor rose and followed the hangman to the inevitable gallows, fearful, yet accepting of his fate.

They entered a small and windowless cubicle crowded with files. The space was no larger than a oversized storage closet which had been converted for ski school use. The proximity of Conrad, smelling slightly of cow dung, combined with the inability to escape or maneuver, closed around Louie like a tight wool sweater.

A computer sat predominantly upon the small desk. Cold and judgmental, it watched him through a black, dark, uncomprehending eye. His reflection echoed back at him from the blank screen. The long hair hung damp, stringy and matted to his head while his day old beard gave him the haunted look of a recently captured criminal. Wild Manson-like eyes betrayed his fragile composure.

In the office, skis, boots, and other alpine paraphernalia filled the corners of the congested room. More often than not, there was inexplicably only one of anything, as though Conrad ran his own personal lost and found service from these confines.

An opened bag of dog treats sat offensively on the floor and their faint liver odor caused Louie's already acid stomach to heave in protest.

He felt claustrophobic, trapped in a smelly hotbox with no air to keep him cool.

"Shut the door," Conrad ordered abruptly.

Louie wanted to protest, wanted to make some wise remark and preserve an open avenue for his retreat. It did not seem to be a good idea. He swallowed a last gulp of cold air, like a diver going down, and closed the solid door.

"Good. Take a seat," Conrad said as he indicated a small stool by the desk.

As Conrad muscled his way past the nervous young man into the only chair in the room, he brushed lightly against him. Louie stiffened under the physical contact and attempted to put more space between them; a useless maneuver since there was really no place to go.

Conrad leaned closer to Louie, closing the space even further as he settled himself upon his forearms. "Now, young fella," he began reasonably. "Why don't you tell me what the hell happened out there today?"

Conrad's tone was almost conversational and Louie relaxed a bit. He might be cornered now, but that did not mean that it was necessary to concede anything to this uneducated old cowboy.

"Sorry I was late," Louie said nonchalantly. "It took me forever to get here."

"Sorry you're late? " Conrad said incredulously.

"Yeah, I'm way late," the sweating instructor said, dismissing the incident with a wave of his hand.

Conrad felt himself struggling with his own anger. "Son, this ain't no dancing date. You're going to have to do better than 'Sorry, I'm late.' I just busted my ass and ate a whole lot of crap in order to keep this mountain out of a huge lawsuit. I just spent half a day looking for your sorry ass and canceled a thousand bucks worth of lessons. I called in help and favors from halfway across this state," he said with his voice now rising. "And all you can come up with is a wise-ass remark like 'Sorry, I'm late'?"

Louie looked at his boss as though it were impossible for any sane man to understand why somebody could be so upset over such a small incident. After all, didn't everything turn out just fine?

Antagonized by the disdaining look, Conrad's temper flared uncontrollably into his burning face. "Mayfield, you better start coming up with something better than that, *right now* or I'm coming across this desk to beat your skinny butt to a pulp! I don't need this job bad enough to put up with your crap any longer!"

Louie blinked at him over the short distance which separated them and quickly appreciated the fact that Conrad would not even have to take a step in order to get his leathery hands around his throat.

"Try *harder* Mayfield. Try a hell of a lot *harder*," the enraged director glared menacingly at him.

Louie looked at the floor between his legs. He could not face the rising anger in Conrad's flaming eyes and knew that the crusty old rancher was very close to carrying out his threat.

"I...I...screwed up," Louie finally stammered. "Really bad this time," he added in the hope of sounding sincere. "I thought that ducking that rope would be okay, that it would be plenty safe down there. I thought that it would be fun for the kids. I didn't see the storm." *Perhaps some sort of admission would appease the old man*, he thought.

"And that's supposed to be an excuse?" Conrad only sounded angrier now.

"Brother, you don't see the storm anywhere, anytime! You think that all the ropes are put there just for you to challenge? Where's your head man?" He shook his own head in disgust.

"Mayfield, you're so busy trying to buck every authority and rule in your path that you don't even see the one's that are there to benefit you. Do you realize that you and those kids could have died out there tonight? Does that even faze you a little bit? Did you at any point feel *any* sense of responsibility?"

Louie continued to wither under the fire from the heated attack.

"I screwed up," Louie repeated more truthfully now. "I

made a mistake; a big mistake." The emotion of the day's reality now began to settle into his voice. He began to melt in the oppressive warmth of the office. He was tired, he was wet, and he was damned hungry, but all in all he was better off now than if he was out sleeping in the freezing snow.

"Oh shit" he said as he put his head in his hands "I made a lot of mistakes. I shouldn't even be here."

"Well, you made it," Conrad said unsympathetically. "Big deal."

"Not *here*. I don't mean in this office. I mean not here, not in this area, not in these mountains, not in this job," Louie said in way of explanation. "I thought that I was smart. I thought that I was too clever to be caught. I thought, well, I thought that I could play only by my own rules. I never wanted anybody to get hurt. I never wanted to hurt my parents. I just wanted to shake them up. I never wanted to hurt those kids. We were just going to have some fun. I just thought that this could never happen to me."

Conrad stared at the despairing young man for a long moment. "What's your education, son?" he finally asked now leaning back from his attack position at the desk and into the comfort of the chair. "Somebody told me that you were smart."

"I have a college degree," Louie offered.

"From where?" Conrad pressed.

"From Cornell; a Masters degree from Cornell," Louie admitted.

Conrad remained unimpressed. "In what?" he said matter of factly.

"Philosophy."

"Philosophy." Conrad almost spit out the word. "Very nice." he said sarcastically, now squeaking back into the well-worn chair and lighting up another cigarette. He had smoked far too many today, but he was not about to stop now. The hot blue smoke filled the air and chased whatever oxygen was left in the tiny room out under the door.

Louie unzipped his wool fleece in an attempt to breathe.

"Would you mind not smoking?" he asked Conrad with arrogance.

"Yeah, I *would* mind not smoking," Conrad growled back. "You see, this little piece of shit closet is my office, Mayfield, and you *stink*."

Louie recoiled as if he had been slapped.

"You might think that not taking a bath constitutes a statement of some kind. I find it disgusting," he spat on the floor and then challenged a long stream of white smoke into Louie's direction.

"Right now, I'm trying to hide the stench. I spent way too many days not being able to clean the muck and the filth off of me to find your habits to be anywhere near admirable. I lived that way because I had to," Conrad snarled. "You're a pig because you want to be."

He waited a moment and then shifted gears, continuing on in a friendly tone now, "Let's put this on your level for awhile, Mayfield. You ever hear of a guy named, Sartre?"

"Yeah, of course," Louie said suspiciously, ready again to fight a battle on his own turf.

"What do you think of that guy?" Conrad questioned innocently.

"Well…" Louie started.

"He was what you eggheads would call an existentialist, wasn't he?" Conrad interrupted.

"Yeah, he was an existentialist. Most certainly. Why? What would you know about Existentialism?" Louie almost sneered.

"I'm no philosopher Mayfield, so cut the condescending tone," he warned Louie, dragging him back onto his own ground. "I don't care to go into the details of the man's personal life, but don't those guys believe in the theory that you must be responsible for your own actions, that you choose as you go, live with your choice and then suffer the consequences for your actions, both good and bad?"

"I suppose that is part of it; in a rather simplified nutshell," Louie sniffed self-importantly.

147

"Good!" Conrad exploded as he slammed his fist on the desk and sprang to his feet in front of Louie's startled face, "Now, in the same simplified nutshell, because I'm a simple nut, how about *you* telling *me* what exactly happened out there! And don't spare me any details! I got a whole pack of cigarettes here and no place to go, kid!"

The roller coaster style of interrogation being employed by Conrad caught Louie completely off guard. First he was the bad cop, then the good cop, and then he was a philosopher who metamorphosed into a prizefighter. Louie did not know whether to lash out at Conrad with a verbal argument, or run terrified and crying from the office.

He gulped for the diminishing air in the room, a goldfish out of water, and realized that there was going to be no escape. Louie would either have to be forthright with this man, fight his way through him, or die in the confines of the closet while they discussed philosophy.

Of the three choices, it seemed like honesty was the only real and safe alternative.

He wisely began to tell his tale while Conrad collapsed limply back into his chair and acted as though he had all the time in the world for him. The boss only interrupted on occasion in order to ask short and pointed questions, but most of the time, Louie just talked.

He talked of the incident. He talked of his expensive education and of how his dad had sacrificed so much to give him only the best. He talked about how he had left home in the middle of the night, leaving no indication of his final destination. In the end, Louie talked himself into feeling like a spoiled, undisciplined, and ungrateful brat.

After a long time, Louie felt unburdened; the words dried up and he shrugged resignedly to indicate that he had finished.

"So, you screwed up," Conrad said, indicating that only now could that finally be established, only now that he had personally heard the facts. He was smoking languidly in his chair and appeared to be as contented as though he had just heard a fine hunting story.

"You did the right thing by not letting that boy go out for help. You did the right thing by starting the snow cave. That would have saved you. You kept them together, that was good," Conrad analyzed.

Louie was feeling a wave of relief coming over him, riding the praise from the man like a surfboard over the water until it all came crashing down around his head.

"But you got them *lost!*" Conrad again came roaring to his feet. "You got them *scared!*" he pounded on the desk. "*And you did it all while being in a closed off area!*" Conrad shouted loudly now. "Don't start feeling so damned proud of yourself, Mayfield! *You are no hero!*"

Louie winced from the whipping thunder of the voice. It drove solidly into his very soul and he snapped his head away to escape its lash. He feared the fists that he felt were coming and turned his body to protect himself. The reverberations echoed from the metal lockers and he was sure that the entire area had now heard of his condemnation.

The fists never came and the thunder rolled off into the distance. "So, what do we do with Louie Mayfield now?" Conrad questioned wearily. It did not seem to be rhetorical. It seemed, as he sat back down, that he was searching for an answer.

"Fire his ass. Send him home," Louie offered dejectedly. "Send him back to his father where he screwed up, too. Send him back to start over. Don't pass GO, don't collect $200 dollars. Try to make things better…"

He looked trembling and scared at Conrad. *"I don't know!"* he began to cry honestly. "I don't know where I'm supposed to be, or what I'm supposed to do!"

Conrad stared at him for a long time. He saw a young man struggling to rebel against a world he barely understood, a fragile kid engulfed in his own confused tears; his head hanging low and defeated over his crossed arms; arms which offered him meager protection from this emotional storm; a storm, which he now felt the boy had encountered many times before.

"Why don't you just get rid of me?" Louie finally said dejectedly looking at the wall. "That's what it always comes down to anyway."

Conrad sat silently and thought. "No," he finally said. "That would be too easy for you, wouldn't it?"

"What do you mean easy? None of this is easy for me," Louie said defensively.

"Sure it is," Conrad smiled slyly. "I fire you and you walk out of here making up some harebrained story; a story where you would emerge to be the hero and you would take every opportunity to drag down all the good people that made your life right again today. Too easy, kid," he concluded. "You want to run away, Mayfield?" Conrad continued. "I can't hold you here. You'll just keep running the rest of your life. You think that you want a piece of me because I'm screwing up your little rebellion? *That* would be a bad choice too," he warned.

"You want to grow up, Mayfield?" Conrad taunted him now. "Then stay here and face yourself. The *choice* is yours, son," he continued. "I'm not firing you, that would be too easy for the both of us."

He began to nonchalantly straighten the papers upon his desk. "Come or go, I don't give a shit. I've seen cowards before. I don't pay them much mind anymore. You choose, son."

Louie could not believe that this meeting was ending so inconclusively. "Is that it?" he asked incredulously.

"Yeah, that's it," Conrad mumbled.

He then looked hard into Louie's hurt eyes, a challenge in his voice, "You made a bad choice to go under the rope. You can make an even worse one and run away from the consequences. Pack your bags, or, show up tomorrow at lineup, looking decent, smelling better, and we'll work through this. I'm finished," Conrad said with finality, snubbing out his last cigarette.

Louie slowly rose to his feet and looked squarely at Conrad, attempting to judge the temperament of the man and the distance between them. "I am not a coward," he said emphatically.

"So? I told you I didn't give a shit," Conrad said as he also stood, bracing his body for an attack by the boy.

The two eyed each other intently over the expanse of the desk.

"I am not a coward," Louie repeated, and finally thrust out his open hand.

Conrad stared at it for a moment and then took it into the enveloping grip of his own two hands.

"I am sorry that I was late Mr. King," the boy said with resolution, looking squarely into Conrad's eyes. "It took me a long time to get here—not here to this office—but to this moment, to this place in my life and I hope you will understand that it might take a little longer for me to make things all right."

"I understand completely, son," Conrad said pumping his hand. "I'll see you tomorrow at lineup."

"And Louie," he called after the figure now retreating through the maze of lockers, "start by calling your dad. I'm sure that he would want to know where you are."

CHRISTMAS

They will never care how much you know,
Until they know how much you care.

Professional Ski Instructors
of America training manual

CHRISTMAS

A teacher affects eternity; he can never tell where his influence stops.

Henry Adams

L ike a gargantuan tidal wave pounding upon the dike of its meager reserves, Christmas break had descended with a vengeance on tiny Mount Bellew and Conrad was trying to plug the deluge wherever and with whomever he could find. Not a single employee is ever allowed to even think the word "sick" at this time. The words "I can't" do not exist.

"But please, Conrad," you might beg. "I chopped off my left leg last night with a chainsaw. Very unfortunate, really, but it should be healed by next week."

"Don't worry about it," he would say with little sympathy in his voice. "We won't decrease your pay. I'll give you some beginner students. They probably won't even notice the limp. By the way, favor the other leg; and it will probably be best to stay out of the moguls."

Pieter was busy bussing tables at the lodge, Wally and I were frantically speeding buses through town as though we were just let loose for the LeMans Grand Prix, and Erik Nuremburg was running the most efficient evacuation teams ever seen since his Nazi ancestors lost the Battle of the Bulge and had to pull out.

Even Daisy was in danger of losing weight. That wasn't good in her pregnant condition and, much to her immense delight, Erik had been compelled to put her on extra rations.

Students were booking lessons at a record pace and the supply of experienced instructors was dwindling quickly. Caught in a moment of desperation, Conrad searched hopefully down the line of his decimated core of teachers. "Dumbo, you're up!" he hollered to the young man at the end of the line.

Steve Donahue, alias "Dumbo," was a valued and experienced instructor. He had been teaching at Mount Bellew for five years. During that time, he had earned his Level Three instructor certification from the Professional Ski Instructors Association and had become accustomed to dealing with students who were extremely adept at the sport already. More often than not, he would be put out on assignment to ski with those who wished to conquer intimidating fields of tricky moguls or sheets of treacherous ice, not neophyte beginners; but Steve was dedicated and would gladly tackle any job that Conrad would assign to him.

Steve's nickname came from the unfortunate genetic circumstance of sporting a set of ears that protruded from his head in elephantine fashion. He was inclined to wear his wool ski hat on even the most temperate of days, preferring the unwanted warmth to the more unwanted wisecracks.

When he removed his hat, the ears would POP forth like rubber doors and you would be as shocked as if his penis had just as suddenly POPPED from his trousers. To the observer, the ears appeared to extend beyond his narrow shoulders and dwarfed his slight frame. Since the locker room mentality displayed all the human sensitivity of a proctological examination, he was affectionately known as "Dumbo."

"What do you have for me, boss?" Steve inquired as he approached Conrad.

"Your lucky day, my man," Conrad grinned, "Twenty five eager, never-ever students from the First Baptist Church of Somewhere USA. Good luck," he added sardonically as he bustled away.

Now, it is a little known fact that the First Baptist Church of Somewhere USA owns the majority of vans, minibuses, and monster recreational vehicles produced in the United States. I know it. I've seen it. And since I feel that this is a fact, I don't feel compelled to look it up.

Like ducks flocking to the warmer climates of the south with the impending Autumn, the national organization known as the First Baptist Church accumulates all the mobile transportation at their very sizable disposal during the Christmas holiday, fills them with the faithful, and proceeds to send them to every corner of the alpine world.

I could understand this if their function was to actually invade these pits of heathen beliefs and desire in order to convert the sinful to the ways of Jesus, but what is totally perplexing is that they actually come to ski and join in the pagan rituals. Maybe cavorting with the devil is the best way to understand his evil ways. I don't know; but they certainly can raise some hell.

Steve introduced himself to his new students and had them arrange themselves before him in an orderly row. Bear in mind that twenty-five people in a ski class were not normal, but this was Christmas, a desperate time in so many ways; a time for desperate measures.

"This is a ski!" hollered Steve to his new group, holding up the odd instrument for their inspection. "These are your boots!" he pointed, "and please don't get the two mixed up." Dumbo believed strongly in emphasizing the basics.

"The boots should be put on with the *buckles facing out!* Yes sir, that's right, buckles out. You'll need to change them."

"Why?" questioned the man.

"Why what?" (Steve was already confused)

"Why the buckles out?" the fellow insisted.

"Because if you don't, Sir, you'll just ski around in circles and hit trees." *That is a pretty clever answer,* chuckled Steve to himself.

Nobody else laughed. He was all alone in this. People seriously studied their feet to see if they were properly uniformed. Nobody actually *wants* to look like a geek. Sometimes it just happens.

"All right. Pay attention," he continued. "To put the ski on, pick up that foot and make sure that all the snow is off of the boot." Some students, now wobbling precariously on only one leg, inadvertently fall over at this time. It is to be expected.

"Now," Steve hurried on in an effort not to be distracted or to hurl himself onto the snow in hysterics, "put your toe... no, your *toe*. No madam, that is your *heel*. Yes. *That* is your toe. Put your toe under the front binding, look back, and step down hard into the back binding until you hear it click. Step harder. No. Take your fingers out. That will hurt."

Usually at this point another percentage of beginners will go down for no discernable or logical reason. In a group of twenty five this can have the dreaded "domino effect," thus taking out even the more athletic ones. The instructor must be prepared to regroup until all are once more standing and must not give up at this early point.

That will come much later as the frustration level (his and theirs) rises.

Now comes one of the more difficult parts of the first lesson: putting on the *other* ski. This has many odd consequences, since the students will soon be losing the only anchor still remaining for them upon the surface of the earth as they have previously known it: *both* of their feet have now been apparently rendered useless.

Again, an increasingly larger percentage will fall over in place during the process of merely attaching the other ski, and of those who successfully do so, another percentage will begin to inexplicably slide away. Some will go forward, which is not too bad. Others will go backward, which is always much worse. All will panic more or less equally and the heretofore symmetrical lineup will begin to disperse in various compass directions.

The instructor then becomes a hyper-active little sheepdog herding his charges back into a tight group once more.

Over the years, Steve discovered that jabbing them with the pointed end of his ski pole not only stopped them from skiing away, but really elicited no complaint against him. For some odd reason, most people readily accepted that they were paying for a certain amount of physical abuse in a ski lesson, and besides, he also found it to be fun.

Bear in mind that this donning of equipment is all "done in a responsible fashion, on carefully selected and prepared terrain" (PSIA Training Manual) which survey engineers would swear to in a court of law had zero slope.

"The damned thing was flat-assed flat," they would say while defiantly staring down the former student, now encased in medical casts and litigation.

So then, there is no physical or geological explanation for how or why these people begin to ski away on this terrain, save that offered by the earth's rotation around the sun. Apparently it is a Corriolis Force phenomenon which mysteriously begins to suck them in circles.

This deserves more attention from concerned scientists. I feel that a few million dollars of tax payer money would be well spent in the pursuit of this research.

Personally, I just want to know why.

Once the students are regrouped, and the wayward ones are lassoed back into class, the Instructor can begin a series of equipment familiarity lessons.

"Get comfortable with your equipment," Steve encouraged them.

This is easily assumed by any instructor who has just spent 100 days locked into a pair of heavy, stiff, plastic boots which are bolted to seemingly evil-minded 2 x 4's. To the uninitiated, however, it is well… like heavy, stiff, plastic boots bolted onto evil-minded 2x4's which actually have a life and mind of their own and the whole feeling will take some adjustment.

"Lift up one ski," Steve says (three tumble over). "Put it down. Lift up the other ski" (the right-footed people go over). "Put it down. Jump up in the air and bounce." (five more lost.)

He is having *lots* of fun now.

Familiarity does not come easy with this slippery "Monster" and while cursing is not necessarily encouraged, a certain amount from the students must be ignored.

Finally, after fifteen minutes of these high altitude aerobics, Steve notes to the group, "Good, we're all warmed up now." Some of the students have become faint from the altitude while others have already quit in frustration.

Good. I didn't like them anyway, he thinks. *Now, if we can just get rid of the whiners we'll have a pretty decent group.*

"The first thing we must learn to do is to sidestep," Steve continues. "*Side*stepping is walking up the hill *side*ways, while using the *sides* of the skis," he explained in his best Al Gore imitation—meaning, that of a brilliant professor to a bunch of half-wits.

"Why can't we just use the lift?" a woman questions, wondering why in the heck she bought a lift ticket anyway.

"Because we're not ready for that yet," The instructor counters.

"Why not?" she insists

"Because I said so," Steve offers lamely.

Technically speaking, in order to sidestep one must keep the skis perpendicular to the slope and, using the ankles and knees, engage the uphill edges of the alternating skis, (i.e. engage the downhill ski, step with the uphill, engage the uphill ski, step with the downhill ski, etc...etc...etc...) keep them parallel until you reach your destination, which is hopefully not far away.

Practically speaking, the student will now contort every bodily part imaginable *except* his or her ankles, in order to achieve the needed angle. A group of beginners learning to *side*step resembles nothing so much as an unfortunate band of cripples on parade; with Al Gore as the bandmaster.

Oh, eventually the technique will come as they learn to relax, to stand tall, to roll the ankle, but until that time, it is very painful to watch. At least half will achieve about four or five feet of vertical and then go rolling backwards down the slope to the starting point. There is a lot of sweat involved at this time: instructor included.

More students will begin wondering about the validity of "The Chairlift Question" shortly after beginning this exercise and any instructor's explanation of "because I said so" could soon lead to a mutiny: so it's best not to push it too far.

Once the entire group has gained all of about ten feet of vertical, it is time to encourage them to "relax, assume an athletic stance, and experience the thrill and joy of their first downhill glide upon their skis."

That is what the manual says. For a number of them, not having read the manual, it will be a short ride of terror.

Now, unless the instructor emphasizes to them to do this one at a time, this exercise will soon dissolve into a cavalry charge of amusement park bumper cars, each with their own little out-of-control driver. The more inept will run over the better ones and everyone, without exception, will end up in a spaghetti-like pile of arms, legs, and skis. This can be endlessly entertaining, but also very dangerous.

Again, best not to push it too far: but it helps to relieve the tension; the instructor's, not the classes. They, on the other hand, are totally confused and will begin to feel that they have placed themselves into the hands of some Nordic devil.

"Hey, skiing is fun!" This will be the thought of the now remaining fifteen students as they have learned to stand up tall, relaxed and are sliding effortlessly down the small hill. They are sidestepping with total confidence. They are gliding smoothly in the front of their boots. All in all, they are getting too damned cocky!

Time to take them higher up the slope, thinks Dumbo.

Ah ha! Now they begin to try and control this extra speed through a whole new series of contortions. Squatting is a favorite, since the human mind reasons that if you can get low enough, you can not be knocked over. Leaning *waayyy* back is also attempted, despite the fact that Steve has already explained how this will make them go faster. There is also the ever-popular "Windmilling" technique, where one illogically perceives that, by flailing ones arms around in a birdlike fashion, speed must of necessity decrease.

None of these actually work, so once Steve has most of these problems ironed out by systematic cajoling, positive reinforcement, critique and downright yelling, it's time to move onto the braking wedge.

"Why?" a teenager asks.

"Why what?" Steve puzzles.

"Why do we need to stop? I want to go fast," she pouts.

"We're not ready for that yet" he says.

"Don't you go fast?" the kid badgers.

"Yes, but I'm different."

It's good to be King! thinks Steve.

The braking wedge—a significant breakthrough for the beginner skier—a time where we learn that only small children and some anatomically incorrect adults can comfortably achieve this position. A time where some learn to control their downhill speed and others are enlightened to the fact that they have not an inkling of the difference between their toes ("point your toes in, sir") and their heels ("no sir, those are your heels").

Some wedges look like this:

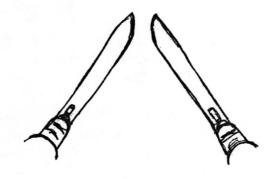

Others look like this:

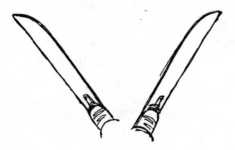

Some are very stubborn and always look like this:

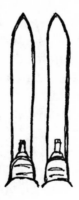

It is the professional ski instructors' job to make sure that none ever look like this:

That is more difficult than it sounds. This is a very hard job and one which does not get much credit.

Observation: Women pick the wedge up much easier than men. Whether this is physiological, because they find it easier to spread their hips apart, or psychological, because they also find it easier to spread their hips apart, again, I don't know.

That is just the way it is and I don't want to discuss it.

By 2 p.m., Steve's original enthusiastic class of twenty-five has dwindled to a very stalwart and determined twelve. Lunch and beer had wiped out the weak ones. They were happily in their condos taking much required naps, glad to be rid of Dumbo and his sadistic ways.

These remaining twelve; these are the ones he wanted: these Dirty Dozen; these stalwart individuals possessed of Navy Seal resilience, unafraid to confront the challenges which lay ahead of them in the afternoon. These alpine commandos are prepared and ready to tackle the first gigantic battle of their lesson. They have no fear, because they have no idea.

They are ready for "The Chairlift." (Ominous music here...)

It is difficult to offer a good visual example for your uninitiated students before their first loading of the chairlift: mostly because the goobers riding up are lousy models and refuse to cooperate by looking competent.

"Okay, now see how that couple is waiting at the red cones," Steve patiently points out. "NO! Wait! Oh, oh..."

"Okay, now see how that chair just slammed into his back. Now we don't want *that* to happen to anybody in our group, do we?" he asks rhetorically. "Noooo, so remember to *wait at the red cones* until the lift attendant calls you out."

Thank you, Al

"So, now they're at the loading point," Dumbo indicates to a new couple. "See how they look to their outside shoulder...their *outside* shoulder!"

"Okay, now did you see how that chair just hit her in the

head?" he winces. "Look to your *outside* shoulder and that won't happen."

"Any questions?" Steve says to the raised hand before him.

"No son, there is no special outside shoulder. It's the one which is away from your partner and depends on whether you are on the right or left of the chair."

"What?" he says baffled about what could be so confusing.

"No, I don't know if you'll be on the right or left. You just pick a side; and don't forget to tell your partner."

"Any *other* questions?" Steve asks, hopeful that there are not.

"What happens at the top?" a small man with oversized goggles now fixed crookedly on his face asks.

"That's the mountain," the instructor says, wearily.

"Before that, how do you get off?" the fidgeting man says with real concern.

Dumbo has forgotten how intimidating this all can be for first-timers. "Lift up the safety bar, stand up tall at the red cones, and just slide down the little incline to a stop," he says, regaining his patience and his empathy.

They all stare blankly in complete and baffled agreement at their instructor, as though what he said was the most logical thing in the world. *Sure, sure,* the group nods their confidence to each other, *Just stand up and glide. Well, what the heck, of course... Easy enough...*

Surprise!

At the top of the lift, particularly during Christmas break, it looks like the scene of a controlled slow motion car crash. There are piles of bodies, usually crashing into other piles of bodies and the attendants are ungraciously sorting them out like amphetamine- fueled wreckers at a Demolition Derby.

Warren Miller, the great ski movie producer, gets some of his finest material from crash sites such as this. His crew will hide surreptitiously in the trees, cameras rolling and at the ready, while Warren delights them with snide and witty remarks concerning the fate of the cannon fodder falling before him. The crew rolls hysterically in the snow. They really enjoy their job. They love working for Warren. It is great stuff and they get a lot of money for it.

The students get no money. They pay to do this. As I said before, they expect a certain amount of physical abuse and could be disappointed if they didn't get it.

The true ski professional comes out in every individual who has dedicated himself/herself to this sport at this point. It is the instructors' job to ride up last with the group. Ostensibly, this is to assure their safety in loading and to provide them with the mental comfort that he/she has indeed not left them behind and dejectedly gone home to drink.

Actually, this will be an opportunity for the students to observe the instructors and their phenomenal skills in action for the first time. They will watch open-mouthed as the professional skier glides effortlessly off of the lift. The students will see their instructor stepping adroitly around, through and between the sprawled bodies at their feet in apparent gravity defying maneuvers.

The professional will never fall. They will never fail. Their razor sharp skis will never touch an innocent body. They are swordsman of unparalleled excellence: Zorros in purple outfits. They will never sweat. They will never become panicked, nor (God forbid) mess up their hair. The students will come to revere them as gods.

This is an illusion which is of most importance to preserve.

The din at the top of a chairlift unloading four skiers from each seat can be overwhelming. Without exaggeration, it is a battle—plain and simple. The chairs are crashing metallic cymbals as they enter the upper station and switch cables. Explosions of sound are rubbing the already raw nerves of the wide-eyed alpine troops. Students are spilling like so many soldiers at Normandy Beach onto the field of snow, while lift attendants unceremoniously drag the fallen bodies from the landing site. Adhering to the supervisor's orders, they are determined to only stop the lift for a major crisis and the invasion cannot be aborted.

Instructors, in imitation of so many battle hardened sergeants before them, are brawling orders above the confusion while students, like young seals, have become attuned only to the voice of their mothers above the cacophony.

"Over here, over here," booms Steve. "On me, gather up everyone...On me. Head count!" A body count is taken: no wounded. Some rookie pride has been hurt, but this group will recover.

Trying to be heard above the wind and the noise of the battle raging before them, Steve explains, "Okay people, good job. Our mission, before we can learn anything more, is to *leave this place*. Nobody passes me, got it? Allan, you're the strongest one; you bring up the rear. Kathy, right behind me. Everybody remember that braking wedge?"

They all nod in confused and numb recollection.

"Okay, everybody in a braking wedge and hold it," Dumbo orders. "Stand tall and relaxed, control your speed and follow me."

He begins a winding and very careful path through the chaos of other classes gone to destruction. Steve needs to move slowly and maintain the student's confidence since he knows that the occasional downed body can present an almost insurmountable obstacle to his green recruits. Still, his jittery squad would be shocked by the sight of small children inexplicably drawn to each other like attracting human magnets. The squealing mass would then continue its uncontrolled downward descent in imitation of copulating midgets.

Additionally, unattached gear would be found everywhere in their path, blown uselessly from the bodies of speeding teenagers.

The sergeant's plan is a sound one. Unfortunately some of his troops have forgotten virtually everything which was taught in their basic training of the morning. The shelling which they took on the chair has mesmerized them. Their heavy lunch has made them sluggish. Most try desperately to follow his path; a few do succeed.

A number of eager heroes have sprinted quickly over small drop-offs in order to engage the enemy mountain and are easily cut down in the unseen land mines of deep snow. A newlywed couple just collapse in desperation and cry where they lay—pathetic.

This is nothing, just wait until they have kids.

Dumbo Donahue is a good sergeant, a seasoned commander. He praises those who were able to follow him to the relative safety of the somewhat flat terrain and cautions them not to move, then he gamely sets out to retrieve the would be Medal of Honor winners who were now neck-deep and struggling in the quicksand of new powder on the side of the trail.

He calms the fears of the desperate, dries the tears of the (soon to be divorced) couple, and, somehow, this group survives.

It is the students first landing off of the chairlift and, like so many other groups who have passed through the fire, like the veterans of many battles before them, each landing will become easier and easier. Soon they will become comfortable on their own and the dim memory of Sergeant Donahue will fade from their minds.

"All Right! You guys are the champs!" Steve grins at his charges in an honest effort to restore their shattered confidence. There is an open slope before him. It is gentle and smooth, with towering pines framing its boundaries. "Now, my little puppies, we're going to *really* learn to ski!"

It is 3:30 p.m. and Dumbo is leading his solid group (now reduced to ten) through the smooth and controlled turns of the Lower Meadow. They look good.

Some are stronger, some a bit weaker, but all are making a flowing movement from one turn to the next. They are learning to dance with gravity. They are floating. The contrived braking wedge has simply disappeared, being replaced by a natural snaking turn as they move gracefully from one foot to the next.

They are birds in flight on a snowy plain, and though the

sun is now setting on the western range, it is perhaps just rising on the smiles of these newfound friends and skiers.

Steve feels good. It had been a long time since he had the opportunity to deal with the intricacies of beginner lessons. There are definitely "mental issues" to overcome, fears which the advanced skier has long ago forgotten—the fear of failure, the fear of being hurt, the fear of looking foolish. The whole alpine world is a new toy for them and with it comes certain dangers and experiences from which they must be protected, or educated.

"We've learned a lot today," Steve says at the bottom of the trail, now wrapping up the day's lesson. "We've come a very long way and I know that you are all tired. I'm proud of you. You people hung in there like real champions. Look up that hill!" Dumbo gestures. "Did you ever believe me this morning when I told you that we would be skiing down that at the end of the day?"

His students are pretty unanimous in their agreement of, "No, Steve, we thought that you were a big liar."

High fives, grins, and laughter are exchanged around the group.

"We learned skills today which will be with us throughout our lives as skiers," Steve continues. "From here at the beginner slopes, to way up there where the experts play," he points to the patrol hut high above them at 11,000 feet above the huge bowl, an awe-inspiring sight, "these skills are the same."

"We learned about our feet and our shoulders and our hands and all the things that make the skis do what we want them to do. *We* are in control," he emphasizes. "But where is the center of skiing?"

"The belly button. The center of mass," someone offers hopefully. (He knows that he heard Steve say that.)

"Put your poles in here, gang," Steve says, as he places the tips upon the snow.

Each student then places his own poles into the center of the ever-growing circle, creating the traditional farewell of camaraderie and fellowship shown to each other after a great day of skiing. Pole upon pole, each touching the other, the circle grows wider.

"Only technically is it found at your center of mass," he addresses the student. Then he intently looks each and every one of them in the eyes. "Actually, it's here," Steve said as he touches his chest.

"It's here—in your *heart*. Unless you have it here," he tapped, "it will always be just a way of getting down a hill and never an expression of freedom. It will never have joy. It will never have life."

He smiles at each and every one of them. "You must ski from your *heart* my friends and all the rest will follow. You will fly down mountains, with wings upon your feet, and your spirits will be lifted to the heavens. And of all the many things that we spoke about today, *that* is your most valuable lesson," Steve concludes.

"Now, go home. Hit the hot tub, have a beer, have fun...and call me when you are ready to continue the adventure," He says. "There is so much more that we have to share."

The grouped poles begin to rattle together, building to a final and clicking crescendo. Steve points to the remaining expanse of terrain before them. "There it is my little birds. It is all yours. You know what to do. Go *fly!*"

With one common shout of conquest, they break from the impromptu huddle like a team seeking victory and, sliding effortlessly across the snowy field, they dance with a mountain.

Steve had a very rewarding day that day—not that anyone tipped Steve—they never do in group lessons. It is not what it is all about anyway. But he did learn a lot. It seems as though you can learn so much as a teacher, if you keep your mind as open as a student.

He reconnected with the basics which makes this sport so exciting and adventurous for the beginners. He saw where there were fears, and found that he could still calm them.

Many of his students had to face doubts which they held

about themselves and, with his guidance they had chased the misgivings away.

He had cajoled athleticism from heretofore undiscovered sources and sun drenched smiles from faces which only hours ago were pale with anticipation.

He had made some new life-long skiers and, well, like any professional instructor, he was just happy to have had the opportunity to help.

STEVE

Don't be dismayed at goodbyes.
A farewell is necessary before you meet again.
And meeting, after moments or lifetime, is certain
For those who are Friends.

Richard Bach

STEVE

And when our time is over here
  And when we've traveled on;

I'll meet you as the pelican that dives upon the shore,
  I'll meet you in the green, green hills

When our lives are nevermore.

Journals of Conrad King

"There is so much more that we have to share," he had told them. But then there wasn't. December 30, 1980: Steve Donahue died today; shortly after the lesson which left him feeling so alive.

Simple as that. Period.

Is today the day, little bird?

Maybe it is the stark simplicity of life and death which has us all screwed up; trying to rationalize, while we avoid what is rational; trying to make some sense of it, while it all makes perfect sense after all. We attempt to disillusion ourselves by buying into stories of afterlife and a system of eternal rewards or punishments. We try to justify a life and wring our hands in despair when we find no soothing answers to comfort us.

Is it because we search for answers which must mirror our material lives here so that we can understand them? Conceptualize them? Do we need heaven to look like the big beach house we always dreamed of—full of family and friends, good weather, good things?

175

Is hell a dirty trailer with a doberman out front keeping us *in*?

When confronted with tragic deaths like this we try to find solace in our religion and logic in our philosophies. Most of it is in an attempt to calm our minds and ease the suffering of our spirit, because we don't understand; and we're scared. Most of the explanations of death, found deep in confusing and unsatisfying language, are all an illusion.

The answers we have been taught from childhood remain shallow. They are meant to satisfy our minds like a parent crooning, "It's all right. It's all right." We are petrified children waking from a nightmare in the dark, inherently knowing that it is not "all right" and that Mommy has nightmares too.

We relish the assurance. We readily accept the comfort because we have no concrete answers and we need to grasp onto something, anything, to keep ourselves from slipping into a depth of despair. The rational part of the human mind wants something logical to grasp onto but we are offered an emotional explanation that says "Have faith. It's all right. It's all right." And we allow it to ring hollow in our hearts, because we have nothing else and the truth is too stark to accept.

Where goes the soul? Certainly I don't know. My mind is not that agile. But after death, I have contemplated an existence of oblivion; at peace with the energy around me.

I have no knowledge, no memory, no recollection, no feeling of ever coming into "Being." I fully expect that I will have a similar experience when my little life-light blinks out and this energy that is me very simply moves onward.

Christians are educated to believe that there is certainty in a life after death, but somehow, inexplicably, they have fashioned that life to look much like this one. I was raised that way. I saw disembodied souls, in a well manicured neighborhood, meeting dead relatives in an ideal setting. It was a vision of an infinite backyard picnic. I saw Grandmom and Aunt Alice sitting in their lawn chairs discussing the gossip of the day. Who died this week? Who will soon be joining the fun? I watched as Grandpop and Uncle Jack shot a never-ending game of horseshoes, while continual "ringers" clanged in the afternoon air.

Dad, looking very god-like, was flipping perfect hamburgers on the grill and Mom laughed ironically at the moist devil's food cake which she was serving. It had never come out so well and the Satan in the kitchen had been defeated. There was never a fear that rain could wipe out our heavenly feast.

Our immortal souls herald all the benefits of life after death, yet we steadfastly refuse to acknowledge that the belief must then logically recognize life before birth. After all, what is the definition of immortal?

Rather than reason it through, we choose to take the easy way out and find a blind and temporary comfort in accepting a story that has us coming into Being from the front door of our birth, passing through the house of our life, and going out the back to join the ethereal picnic of our family upon our death. We close our eyes so as not to see our existence as a circle; preferring a straight-line and linear route: a route of convenience.

It is a pretty cultural tale, but I have trouble with that story now.

Reincarnation consists of a belief in the connection of all living things and the gradual purification of the soul of man until it is returned to a common source and origin of all life. It is a belief that the soul is immortal; at least the religions have that in common. But it does not subscribe to a western, fast-food mentality which demands that it all must happen in the here and now.

When Judeo-Christian religions threw out the doctrine of reincarnation, thus making it more appealing to the developing western mind, they had to replace it with something and an instant quick service judgment earned at the end of a relatively brief mortal life seemed to be a excellent way to keep the masses socially behaving during their short and generally miserable lives on earth.

Perhaps in their wisdom, the religious philosophers of the

day concluded that a "carrot on a string" story was far more successful an approach to keeping the world in harmonious balance then making each man ultimately responsible for his own soul.

I don't completely fault that technique; after all, it was adopted for the uneducated masses that needed structure and discipline in an emerging modern western world, where secular government and the Church were mutually entangled. It was good people management.

After all, lying to the masses for ulterior motives is an age old and honored technique; as effective for 21st century man as it was for his caveman ancestors.

Don't misjudge me. I have enough cynicism to go around for most religions and wouldn't want to confine myself to just picking on any particular one. Personally I like the idea of reincarnation, but can't help and wonder on the value of the lessons lost if there is no recollection of a previous life and the mistakes which it offered.

Where did I go wrong? How can I make it better? Here I was on December 30, 1980, a poor slob driving a ski area bus. Was this because I was once very wealthy and never appreciated the true value of my money? Why then do I wish every day for more wealth? Would it be that now, in my wisdom, I could spend it more humanely?

Hell no, I wanted a new fast sports car! Was I learning nothing? Should I see that wealth is not the judge of a man's value?

I didn't seem to be progressing well with my Karma.

Karma, by definition, is the working out of one's inner burdens; while reincarnation is the physical opportunity to do so. My Karma seemed to be how to work out being poor and liking it, while my reincarnation as a bus driver was offering me great opportunities to do so. I understand it. I just wasn't adapting well to it.

These are two of the oldest beliefs in the history of mankind and more widely accepted than any religious concept on earth. From the Egyptians, to the Greeks, to the

Buddhists and Hindus; the soul is considered to be a pre-existent entity which takes up residence in a succession of bodies, becomes incarnate for a period, then spending time in the astral form as a disembodied entity, it reincarnates itself time and time again.

We are little god-like pieces, tiny lights spat outward from a brilliant star seeking to find our way back home. Millions of people believe in this theory, but the Judeo-Christian upbringing finds it threatening to our material, temporary and worldly standards; and so we create an afterworld that looks much like this one.

It is an arrogant and minority viewpoint.

I'm not knocking Christian teaching on this point; on the contrary, I believe that it has a place. If the theory is comforting to those who subscribe to it, then go for it.

It's all right. It's all right.

I suppose if people can be convinced to be virtuous for a perceived reward it is certainly better than them not being virtuous at all.

It's just that, for me, the Christian concept does not seem to go deep enough in its explanation. Sounds more like animal training and I feel that the Pavlov experiments of action/reward do not just apply to dogs. As humans, we should give ourselves the benefit of following a practice which is a bit more intellectual.

If the central figure of the Christian world, Jesus, is the most visible example of life after death, found in his resurrection, then he is also the most visible example of life before birth; as an eternal god-made man. It is the cornerstone of this belief that "he who believes in me shall have eternal life."

Hey, I believe! I just don't believe that where Jesus was headed is a mirror image of this life. Jesus' tiny light, burning brighter than most, found its way through a world 2000 years ago and while most of our lights are spinning outward and chaotically out of control from the Source because they are looking for an *outside* Source; his, quite happily, was headed home and inward. The awesome thing to contemplate is that

179

I think he knew it.

So my personal belief does not deny God. It glorifies God. It simply denies that the attainment of God is something as easy as that which is being broadcast, "Hey Joe! Be a good person; repent along the way if you screw up; die in relatively few years, and if all went well and the timing is good, go to heaven."

Bing Bango.

"You want fries with that sir?"

By the way, the "timing" thing is of utmost importance. You can be a low life scum who is cheating on the spouse, abusing animals, and trashing the environment with your business; BUT... if you can just get in a little, "Sorry about that, God" before you kick off, then all is forgiven and you are on the express bus to Heaven. Nice. And you don't even have to work out any of the messy details with the crying wife, the damaged dog, or sad old Mother Earth.

So watch the "timing."

Heaven! It's really a GREAT place! Don't miss it!
I can see it on the infomercial now...
For a very small investment of say, 70 years of being good, you can have an *Eternity* of total bliss!
Good deal!

Of course one would have to subtract about 20 years for stupidity and immaturity (early generational faults) at one end and another 10 for being senile, unaware but basically harmless at the other. That's only *40* left for being accountable and a certain amount of that can be blamed on booze, drugs, or other people's fault. Think of it. Less than 40 years investment in exchange for *Eternity*, which I understand is a LOT longer.

That's a sweet investment don't you think?

Or do you think it sounds like the last used car salesman that you ran into?

Complete oblivion. It is really not as bad as it sounds.

Awareness or awakening to the truth does not lessen the fun or the wonder of this life. On the contrary, perhaps I *have* lived other lives in the past and might possibly live other lives in the future. I really don't know, but my belief in that should only serve to intensify my commitment to the present. The time and space that we actually exist in is so overwhelmingly infinite that it serves to make me realize the preciousness of each and every moment on Earth.

Steve had a good life and now he moves on. The cynicism I feel doesn't lessen the pain of his passing. It is something *I* need to deal with; not him. We all seem to see our lives as stories—a tale to be told by a good friend at our wake. If a person survives an ordinary life span of 70 years or more, there is every chance that his life as a story is over and he lays upon his deathbed fearful of the epilogue (it's not so bad, as you will see). Life is not over; only this particular chapter, and the story comes around upon itself.

Carl Jung once wrote, "The dissolution of our time-bound form in eternity brings no loss of meaning."

So why don't we remember our past lives so that we can learn from them? Probably because it is the present lifetime that is ultimately important. Our consciousness blocks out past lives so that we are not continually traumatized by what went before. But that does not mean that we have forgotten its important lessons. They have become what we refer to as part of our nature. We all know the person who is basically mellow, or arrogant, pompous or peaceful. There are those who are wise and those who are boastful. That is their nature and it has developed over long periods of true time and not a mere lifetime.

"A lifetime may be needed to merely gain the virtues which annul the errors of man's preceding life. The Virtues we acquire, which develop slowly within us, are the invisible links that bind each one of our existences to the others—existences which the Spirit alone remembers; for matter has no memory for spiritual things." (Honore DeBalzac)

181

Albert Einstein, that great contemplator of the universe and all its workings, said that there was a greater force at work in the scheme of things that he could not explain. So why should I even try?

If our existence here is logical and rational then it follows in harmony with the rest of the universe which is tremendously logical and rational. And why shouldn't it be? Why should the fate of man be the only thing in the universe which deviates from the rational and harmonic path and attempts to delve into religion for an explanation of its existence?

Religion has brought us ceremony. It has brought us worship of gods. It has brought us mythical rewards and punishments. It has seldom brought us spirituality or an explanation of our existence in logical form. It just doesn't "blend" with what my mind sees and what my heart knows: that I am a part of a Community of Life, no greater than and no less than the honorable creatures with which I share this space.

What is this expanded consciousness? We readily accept the limited dimensions of color, sound, taste, and sight which are experienced every day as being real. Try to think with unlimitedness and recognize the infinity of space and time each day.

And you will see that, "It *is* all right. It *is* all right."

They say that Steve probably caught an edge on his ski and, before he even knew it, before he could respond, he had hooked back uphill into the trees. I believe it. I've seen good skiers do it before.

Lots of people saw this. I heard one lady crying, "It was sickening," she wept into her husband's shoulder. "It was the sound. I heard his head hit the tree. Oh God, it was awful."

Arm in arm they moved slowly back to their car.

He was cruising on an easy intermediate run, a run that he could do in his sleep, a run where an expert like him could be lulled into total relaxation and begin to admire the sky above him, breathing deeply of the clean, cold air which filled his young lungs. I'm sure that it had the strong scent of pine and wood smoke in it.

I hope that was his last memory. It would be a good one.

By the time that Erik and his patrollers had arrived at the scene there was really not much that they could do. They worked on Steve as efficiently as they could. I know that I have said some bad things about Erik but I would have to admit that he is good at what he does.

I remember being at the bottom of the hill and watching the sled come down the mountain behind the snowmobile. I remember thinking, "I'm watching a funeral."

Most of the time the snowmobiles are zipping around like a bunch of busy bees intent on their flowery objectives. Sleds with non-serious injuries often come down with a patroller in the front and another one braking in the back.

This time it was different, sadly different as patrollers and snowmobiles operated in grim teamwork. It was almost eerie as everything seemed to be happening in slow, deliberate and tragic motion.

One snowmobile was leading the sled while two more were spaced out to the sides. They did not zip. They *crawled* down the hill as though they and the people commanding them had accepted the futility of their effort or as though their cargo was too precious to spill a single drop of lifesaving hope for life. They were in no rush to get to the medical center. They did not want to hear the official proclamation of the doctor there.

I felt that I was one of the few at Steve's initial funeral procession and that the service would be redundant. I was seeing all that I needed to see that day. I was watching the passing of a good man.

Behind the lead snowmobile there was the rescue sled. You could not see Steve; he was a bulge in a wad of eerily still orange blankets. I don't think that I wanted to, anyway. There were two patrollers there on the sled with him. One was riding at his head area holding an oxygen mask in place while Erik was pumping methodically on his chest.

I used to think that it would be fun to be Erik, wrapped up in all his male glory: now I don't.

I wanted to cheer him on, "Go Erik! Do your magic!" I would yell.

Instead, I found myself praying to a god that I did not know, praying for the patroller's hands to have the skill to save this man; yelling into a void.

Tiny cat feet snow was falling ever so softly, kneading a blanket of frozen earth. I don't believe that I ever heard an area become as quiet as Mount Bellew while it witnessed the passage of this morbid parade. It's amazing how news can travel so fast in an area of a few thousand acres. Like it has been carried on the wind, people begin to know.

They sense that something has gone very wrong in their world, that this is not just another turned knee or even a heart attack and they become afraid for the man in the sled. They become afraid for themselves. The fact that they are in a dangerous environment suddenly comes home to them. It could have been them this time or their spouse, their child, or their friend. They will all go home early today and supper will be a more subdued affair than the night before. The professions of love made in the dark will be more sincere and desperate.

I waited hopefully for the Life Flight helicopter to come, to whisk Steve away to some big city hospital where serious sounding surgeons would diagnosis, "A very bad head injury.

Will probably have headaches for years, but it seems that he'll be okay."

It never came.

What came instead was the town ambulance. It came about five minutes later and left shortly thereafter. It had no sirens, no lights, no symbols of urgency and no meager symbols of hope.

It was in no rush.

Which do you think is better?

Dying in the glory of your youth with all those muscles and hormones pumping away, your future stretching out before you like a golden highway, then, like a snap of your fingers, lights out. You're dead.

Or wasting away as an old man, pissing in your pants, losing your dignity and being too arthritic to move from your own bed?

At that point, you are probably counting more enemies made than friends and most all of them are dead anyway. You are dying a little bit each day, a burden to your loved ones, and none of you can stop the inevitable progression. You are a cancer eating at your family and they begin to wish that you would just go away so that they can continue to live their own short lives.

I can't determine which is more tragic. Which do you think is better?

The end is the same.

Isn't there anything in between?

I went to the locker room early that day, the day of Steve's death, in order to check out. It was pretty quiet in there. That wasn't unusual at that time of day, but then I saw Conrad, not out on the mountain where he belonged. Conrad never saw me. I didn't want him to.

He was very quiet and a profound sense of peace came from him. He was just sitting there on the floor in front of Daisy and slowly stroking her soft golden fur, speaking to her in unheard whispers, stroking her fur over and over while big tears rained silently and relentlessly down his old cheeks.

He was so silent. No sobs, just a never-ending fountain of tears running unchecked and unashamed from a very deep and pure well. I could hear his heart breaking, without making a sound, so I slipped out the back door and closed it carefully before I was immersed in the pain.

It is too difficult for me to accept that there is a plan for these things, God's Will, God's Plan. What's the difference? To believe that a central force controls the movements of our daily lives in such things makes me think that it must be a diabolical God indeed that we are all working for. Either that or He's gone away on vacation, or maybe washed his hands of the whole mess we have made of ourselves and went on to create a better life from somewhere else. Hey, we all make mistakes.

And if you don't believe that He is controlling our lives then you must think that after creating man, He said, "Well, by gosh, I think that's about the very best that I can ever do. Maybe I'll just have a little rest and let my little man/god run things for me. He certainly looks quite competent."

Ha Ha. Good joke, God.

Isn't there anything in between?

No, I don't think that God is capable of abandoning us, just as we are not capable of abandoning Him. We are all in this thing together.

I don't know what I am saying here; I babble because I'm not tough enough, or cynical enough, to tell you that I handled it "like a man." Like a man with the wisdom to know all of the deep answers. No, I bawled like a child at Steve's service, at the graveside, and by myself.

We say that we cry to morn the departed. I think that we cry for ourselves. I think that we have this sudden void and emptiness in our lives, our souls, our hearts, and we simply don't know how to fill it except with tears.

I went to the viewing to look at him again. That was not my friend. It did not even look like him, some stranger in a box. He never combed his hair that way. It must be the wrong guy, someone that was not included in my life and so had always been dead to me.

His ears: they should have covered his ears. Dumbo never would have let his ears hang out like that! They looked even bigger in the small, narrow box. Why didn't they put his ski hat on him? Should I do it for him? Would that be crude? Would they all hate me for it?

The day after the viewing, the church was overflowing with people. They stood in the aisles and spilled out onto the icy walkways. Unable to get a seat, some were peering into the windows hoping to get a glimpse of the magnificent ceremony. All of them had come to wish farewell to Steve, to hear the fiery words that would eulogize him forever into their memories. Angels floated above the rafters, touching the shoulders of the most bereaved, assuring them of the righteousness found in his early death, drying their tears with an ethereal touch.

I had no need to arrive early. My place was assured. I heard my name called and strode down the center aisle, confident and self-possessed. The Church fell into a muted hush as all heads turned in my direction.

I made my way to the stage with purpose, stopping dramatically along the way to comfort a weeping soul, to lift a sagging shoulder here, to hold a trembling hand there, to whisper encouragement to the inconsolable. All smiled at me like tiny suns breaking out of their own clouds as my compassion and love lifted some of the burden from their hearts.

I grasped my place behind the great wooden podium while the crowd wrestled with expectation. My voice was clear. My voice was strong. It was full of words which reverberated from the cold stone walls, across the high mountains and into the very heavens above. I was thunder, crashing defiance at this evil death. I was lightening, sparking flashes of fire and light into every open mind. I was the tide rising unstoppable to its crest, bringing new life and hope to this barren shore. Parched souls reached to me with vacant eyes and I brought them the rain of pure insight and love.

I was a god, in God's own house and there, on His very

doorstep, I challenged his righteousness. I weepingly beseeched His compassion and, appropriately humbled, I showered His Eternal Truth upon the questioning faces before me.

I made it all seem right and fair. I made it all seem sane and acceptable. I chased dark death from the doors of their hearts and brought new hope to all mankind.

I brought them nothing.

I sat.

I sat in the rear of the small, cold chapel and looked at the backs of the heads of the fifty or so people spaced sporadically about and I wondered. Who was the priest? Were he and Steve very close? Why did he speak so vaguely of him? Why didn't more people show up? Didn't Steve have many friends?

We are afraid to look on death. Uncomprehending and confused by the fairy tale explanations which we have been given since childhood, we are paralyzed into doing nothing. We are afraid to ask the questions gnawing at our hearts— afraid that we will be seen as sacrilegious non-believers not satisfied with the story.

Ultimately, we are afraid to set ourselves free by just seeing the Truth and so we run back to the fragile cage of our beliefs, knowing full well that the myths and the bars give us no protection.

After all, we will still have another wish; to get out of the cage. And maybe tomorrow we will.

Is today the day little bird?

Should I go to the gravesite, or would I be out of place? Maybe the family wants it to be private. This priest, he gave me no answers.

I feel nothing, only confusion.

I waited in line with everyone else in order to shake the hands of the family standing in the vestibule, to offer my condolences. I dug into the pockets of my old ski coat to give what I could.

His mother was red-eyed, vacant, and thanked me for coming. She had no idea who I might be but was grateful that

I wanted to be there at all. His father was silent, stalwart and gray. I took his hand. It was difficult to look into his eyes. This was a moment where I wanted so much more from myself. I was a disappointment. I handed him the old knit cap from the recesses of my coat and told him that I thought that Steve would have wanted this. At first he looked uncomprehendingly at my gift. I didn't know what else to do so I mumbled something, incomprehensible tears in my throat making me foolish and inelegant at that very moment.

I left.

I stepped carefully down the ice-covered steps and looked back at the small group behind me. The old man caught my eye and he slowly waved the tattered red wool hat in my direction. A weak and understanding smile crossed his face.

I think that he will be okay now, never the same, but okay and wherever Steve goes from here, well...at least he will have his hat on.

And it *will* be all right.

Mount Bellew

A Feeling is Something Your
Mind Can't Express

Take up your pen and write out your heart.
Tell us the feelings that lie deep inside.
Tell us the loves that make you feel warm.
Tell us the times that made you cry.

Words.

Now look at your work and see what you've done
For it's now on paper for all men to see,
But men that they are, they'll see through the work.
It's really not what it was meant to be.

Just Words.

These words seem so useless, so gray, so dead:
They never express what a man can feel.
They never serve to bring you his heart,
And emotions of his can never be real.

Yes, you'll read all his works and say that you know
That which is going around in his mind;
Yet, he will cry for a way to express only himself;
But inadequate words are all he may find.

Journals of Conrad King, 1980

I will miss you my young friend.

JANUARY

Love is a trap. When it appears, we see only its light, not its shadows.

Paul Coelho

JANUARY

You'll hear people say that birth is a miracle and death is a tragedy, but a sportsman eventually comes to see that everything that happens every day is just plain ordinary. Life is just life, and even brook trout get the blues. The trick is not to get too bent out of shape about it.

John Gierach

His corncob pipe is clasped tightly between a set of grouper-like jaws, which, like the prow of a ship, cleaves its way toward us. The first thing you notice are the forearms: abnormally large and simian, they explode from beneath a tightly fitted tee shirt and dwarf the banty rooster body to which they are attached. The almost indecipherable chortled of his voice bubbles over the pipe as he grumbles, "I yam what I yam, and that's all that I yam."

"Go, Popeye," Wally encouraged halfheartedly as he continued to set up our ritualistic game of backgammon. "Kick some ass."

"Yeah, you just wait, man," I warned him as though he was totally unaware of what was going to happen next. "The dude is going to actually suck down an entire can of spinach through his pipe in this one. That stuff is like hot-wired to his testosterone producing testicles and then all hell is going to break loose for old Brutus."

Wally stared at me blankly for a brief moment. "You're really into this aren't you?" he asked.

"No, not really," I countered. "It's just that I find him more interesting than you."

"I yam what I yam and that's all that I yam," I began to softly chant.

"You do know that he's not real," Wally continued to eye me with some concern.

I refused to answer.

Popeye's fatalistic chortle often wanders in my mind, especially when I'm involved in something wayyyyy over my head, like electrical wiring for instance. Of course, Conrad had a more pragmatic approach to the issue when he said to me, "Listen son, you know what you know, and after that you don't know crap. Just admit it and go drive your bus."

I think this was after I gave him some unsolicited advice on how to run his Ski School more efficiently.

Anyway, either one of those approaches could be pretty philosophic dependent on how much substance abuse you were into, but I still think that Popeye was more poetic.

Now the sailor boy was no yam, nor even a "potatoe," as Mr. Quayle would say. *Now there's a guy who should have hung his hat on a Popeye philosophy rather than throwing it into the political ring.* But, I digress. Popeye was just another merchant sailor on leave, with a strange attraction to an incredibly ugly chick.

It happens and so, perhaps, he is real after all.

Popeye apparently did not expect much of himself after the fact of just being himself, but oddly a severe chemical dependency which he had developed for something found in spinach caused him to assume unnatural heroic proportions in times of stress. He could no more run away from his beloved old hag of a girlfriend, Olive Oil, than we could have run away from our own Mount Bellew.

Maybe our own similar heroism was found in the clear mountain water.

Anyway, I know what I "yam" and I know what Wally "yam" and what we "yam" is we "yam" no doctors and what we know has nothing to do with medicine or anatomy.

This was evidenced by our sad dating records: which is to say that if we *were* physicians or understood *anything* about the human body (especially the female one) we might have been more popular.

Oh sure, Wally and I had been to a few medical training courses in order to prepare for our lives which were supposed to be spent at sea, but in the grand scheme of things they turned out to be fairly useless (the courses; not necessarily the lives). If I were a seaman watching *me* approach *him* with a knife in order to remove his appendix or something, I would have enthusiastically jumped from my bed, wrestled myself to the ground and plunged the dull and rusty instrument Harakiri style directly into my own heart.

Disregarding actual surgery, however, I must admit that we were fairly adept at dispensing the ship's supply of drugs.

"Here, eat a few of these blue things," we would say to an unsuspecting seaman, "and see how you feel in the morning. Call me if the vomiting doesn't stop by say, oh, noon tomorrow."

We had even gone to a school up in Maine where we got to practice sewing chickens and things. The birds never complained (they were dead) and it always led to a pretty good barbecue that evening even if you failed the course.

Our vaguely realized medical ineptitude became a source of real concern one evening when Daisy wandered into the locker room looking rather anxious and nervous. She would not approach us at all, even though we were some of her favorite people. We had that nice earthy smell of past dinners and dirt upon us, which she loved.

"What's the matter, girl? Are you feeling unsociable tonight? Where's your Nazi leader? Donde esta el fuehrer?" I kidded her, trying a new language. "Where's Erik?" I encouraged in better English.

I knew where Erik was, I was just testing her language skills. He was at the monthly management meeting in the administration building doing important management stuff. We were not invited, but being dedicated employees (on overtime) we waited in the locker room for one last run into town with the bosses and occupied our time with the eternal backgammon game. As was his usual habit at these times, Erik allowed Daisy to roam the now empty parking lots and buildings in her continual quest for discarded lunches and late night companionship.

I think that is how she got pregnant in the first place.

Kids nowadays: what are we going to do with them?

"You know, Walter," I said. "Old Daisy there doesn't look so hot."

"What's it to you? You gonna ask her for a date or something?"

"Don't be sarcastic butthead; I can do better than that. I don't mean "hot" like sexy "hot," I mean "hot" like not looking so well," I attempted to explain. "It just looks like she's all stressed out—like she's going to be sick."

"You're sick," he added "and I'm not worried about you. Besides, it's your turn."

"I yam what I yam and that's all that I yam," I intoned mindlessly.

"Oh shut up," he muttered.

We returned to our game while Daisy continued her wandering survey of the room, complete with much sniffing and scratching under our watchful eyes. Like an obese woman after an enormous meal, she could not get comfortable and thus waddled from corner to corner in her seemingly aimless search. She finally selected the large pile of ski school jackets which were due to be sent out the next morning for a cleaning and settled into them with a loud and contented groan.

Good, I thought. I presumed that she had finally gone to sleep.

Somewhere during the third game of getting my butt thoroughly kicked, I looked toward the corner and saw a distressing sight.

"Dude..." I said in a singsong voice.

"What?"

"I think we should call 911 or something, Dude..." I con-

196

tinued singing.

"Why? It's not that bad," he said. "I think that you can still catch up."

"Wally!" I now barked seriously, snapping him out of his concentration "I think Daisy is having her puppies, man. I mean I think she is having them like *right now*," I emphasized.

"Holy shit," he whispered in order to show that he was now paying attention.

"Holy shit," I echoed louder in order to show that we were now prepared to deal with this immediate problem.

"What do we do now?" he asked. "You're from the country."

Wally always referred to me as "being from the country" as though it somehow qualified me to deal with large animals or repair farm equipment.

"Should we get help; call the vet or something?" he offered searching for a solution.

"One," I began calmly, "I don't think we're supposed to do anything. They know how to do it themselves." This was a very Zen-like approach on my part; where doing nothing was an actual option as opposed to doing something. Doing nothing had resolved many immediate problems for me in the past.

"And two," I began to yell, "Jesus H. Christ! Get Erik or Conrad in here like now!"

Wally bolted for the door, a true man of action, not sure of whether I wanted him to find Conrad, Erik, or Jesus. He just wanted more help than I could offer.

I, on the other hand, being the Great Thinker of our Dynamic Duo, bolted for the back of my mind in order to better understand the scene unfolding before me. And so I thought: in the process of baby birth, the weak biological human must spend about nine months reading numerous books and manuals on what this process entails. It is a very good thing that someone wrote it all down so we don't forget what to do.

Somehow people got the laying of the keel all right just by

following their natural instincts, but when it comes to the launching of this little vessel, well, you would imagine with all our anxiety and preparation that it was the first space shuttle going up and not about the 100 billionth person in the world.

We are supposed to practice for hours, sometimes with the spouse, sometimes not, on how to *breathe* for God's sake. I got that part down and have been doing it for many years. I hope to continue (even without the manual).

Then we are supposed to practice on how to *relaxxxxx*; but no beer, or music, or dancing is allowed in the room. So how are we supposed to do that?

Okay, say that none of this New Age stuff is quite working out the way we had planned during the birth. Things are not exactly looking like the movie they showed us. The woman is tearing the hair out of her head in pain and is screaming obscenities at some medical student. Her makeup has become a clown's mask of mottled streaks as the sweat pours unrelentingly down her contorted face. It looks like a scene from *The Exorcist* in there. Perhaps, in a moment of self-preservation, the hubby has unwisely gone off to the cafeteria for a hamburger. It does not look good for anybody involved. Well, we still have the medical miracle of powerful drugs at our disposal, don't we?

Oh yeah, just have the new mom pop a few of those little pills, lay back into LaLa Land and be assured that the high priced doctor, now squatting between her thighs like Johnny Bench, actually went through medical school on a scholarship as a catcher on the university baseball team.

Rest assured! His steady hands will just grab that squirmy little humanoid when it pops out then whack 'em, wrap 'em, band 'em, stack 'em, feed 'em and throw the runner out at second. All while "Mommy" catatonically counts the bumps on the ceiling. Easy.

Of course, I'm just saying this from a male point of view: a guy whose major concern at the time of birth would be, "I wonder how I'm going to pay for college?"

Don't get me wrong, I am not callous. I appreciate the fact

that the more emotionally involved member of the team is presently sweating bullets on a gurney in total concentration for an attempt to pass a watermelon sideways out her loins.

During the brief respites between labor pains, she is not thinking lovingly of her future family given to her by the devoted husband standing next to her. Oh no, she is thinking, "you SON-OF-A-BITCH...unhhhh...If you EVER touch me with that thing again...unhhhh...unhhhhh...I'LL RIP IT RIGHT OFF YOUR BODY ! Ow...ow...ow..."

They tell me that this childbirth thing is even more painful than a serious groin pull; therefore I would want nothing to do with it.

So, while waiting for Wally to return, this led me to think: "Damn, I'm not sure *what* we're supposed to do. Either dogs have it a lot easier in these things or else we've all gone soft due to the pampering of modern medicine".

I can only speak for myself when I say that if I was the woman, or even the dog, I'd want to be *knocked out completely*! And I want the good drugs, not just the local stuff. I want to go to sleep at the first sign of discomfort and wake up fully relaxed and refreshed as though I had gone to the Bahamas for a month.

I'd awake after a fine nap and the sun would be twinkling through my window. The sea breeze would be gently ruffling the clean white curtains of my private room. My eyes would flutter open to find my new and perfect child lying contentedly in the arms of her fat Jamaican nurse, named NaNa. My beautiful daughter (looking much like myself) would resemble a perfect little angel. She would be very quiet.

She would stay that way.

My extremely handsome husband (looking much like myself) would be smiling paternally upon me with the keys to a shiny new Jaguar tinkling in his hand. He would have bought it for me; and not stolen it this time.

"For you, my love, for all you've been through," he would purr devotedly.

He would look "hot." I would want him to take me, right

there, right now, but for the sake of the baby (and the Jamaican nurse) we would have to wait.

"I am truly sorry if I have caused you any inconvenience, dear," I would say subserviently, "but I will be on my feet very soon after lunch and will then skip home to make you a fine dinner and prepare our perfect daughter for college."

I just don't understand what all the big fuss is about anymore.

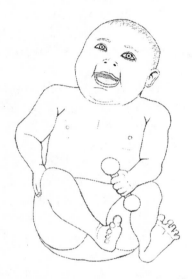

While I was engaged in these escapist thoughts of how my future life would be, Erik, Conrad and Hermann came hurrying through the door. Apparently Jesus was not available. Even though Erik had seen his own share of medical emergencies, he was as concerned and as nervous as an expectant dad was supposed to be. He had even delivered a real human once, but somehow things become quite different when they get personal.

The fretful father-to-be attempted to approach Daisy and was greeted with a deep and unaccustomed growl which made him back off immediately. None of the human mothers had ever done that before: maybe some of his dates, but never the mothers.

"Stay away from her, Erik," Conrad cautioned. "She's

doing just fine."

"But, shouldn't we help or something?" Erik asked.

The patroller's experience with humans had led him to believe that he had to do *something*. Erik was very un-Zen.

"Maybe later," Conrad continued. "Right now, she's doing all that needs to be done. They know how to do it themselves."

I grinned at Wally, vindicated in my medical analysis of the situation.

"Shut up," he muttered. "Why don't you go boil some water or something?"

"What? I didn't say anything," I said innocently. "Besides, boiling water has nothing to do with babies. Did you know that, dufus?"

"You're right there, son," Conrad broke in, "but if we plan on watching this show tonight, we're going to need some coffee and I don't plan on drinking it cold. So why don't you do like your buddy says and boil us some water."

"Guys," Hermann piped up, "We can do better than instant coffee. Go to the cafeteria and brew up some real Java," he ordered while fumbling unsuccessfully in his pants for the key, "and while you're in there pull out some sandwiches and fruit, too."

"That's okay, Hermann," Conrad offered. "Save the effort. They don't need a key. They can break in just like they usually do. Right, boys?"

Conrad caught our astonished eyes at the same time and we quickly looked embarrassingly down at the floor. He had known of our little forays into the cafeteria in search of food for some time now, but had discreetly overlooked our little "hunting" trips. We only took what we needed and only when we were hungry and broke. I guess he thought that was acceptable enough, but any future dining experiences were now going to come at the price of honesty.

"That's right, Mr. Olsen," Wally confessed. "We don't need the key. We can find our way in."

Hermann winked slyly at Conrad. "Yeah, I know," he said.

"You guys are doing a good job here. Thanks for the help."

We both brightened at the small compliment and silently vowed never to eat more than we ever needed again.

"Hey Conrad, that's not us all the time you know," I said defensively, happy now for our new assignment. "You want some soup, too?" I added hopefully. "They have great soup."

"You're pushing it, boy," Conrad growled. "Now git!"

And we git: while the gitting was still good.

"Hey, you're no longer on overtime anymore," he yelled after us. "This is now a family matter.

The night passed by slowly as the pups took their time

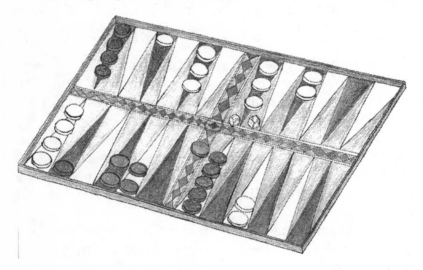

entering their new and purple world. Daisy went about her mothering business in a rather matter-of-fact and professional way, delivering puppies with no more fanfare or enthusiasm than a UPS man dropping off a load of brown, in descript packages. We kept our distance from her as Conrad had ordered, but each little squirming yellow or black package was greeted with excited buzzing like another Christmas present brought by our own hairy Santa Claws.

An echo in the dark spread word of the event from the locker room. It quickly reverberated around the mountain and eventually faded into the town. Soon other employees, who had not gone home yet, entered the building in whispers like concerned relatives in a hospital waiting room. Those hearing the news down in the village drove up to be with the family.

We drank coffee; far too much of it. We played interminable rounds of a never ending backgammon game, but nobody kept score. We ate sandwiches and Wally showed Hermann how to make his soon-to-be-famous "Leftover Soup."

We talked about the things that we had done and all the things that we still wanted to do. Some talked about their "glory days," while others admitted that they never had any. Some of the former later confessed that they had lied.

Ivana cried because she had never gone to a prom and so we severely criticized every institution we could think of including the CIA, Immigration Service, and the damned Prom Committee for denying her this life-changing opportunity.

Bobbie showed us her newest frivolous purchase: the FUD. That's short for Female Urinary Device. It looks like a catcher's cup with a hose sticking out of it and a valve on the end.

Apparently the girls can wear it secured under their clothes and when the need arises to pee, they just hang the hose out of their ski pants like any blue-blooded male would do. This lets them pee in the trees with the guys without taking off all of those clothes, which must be a real pain in the butt—especially in winter.

I imagine they'll soon be trying to write their names in the snow; equal opportunity and all that. Anyway, Bobbi bought some stock in the company and figures that it will make her even richer; but I wouldn't advise investing in it right now.

You'll just piss your money away.

Conrad even opened up a bit about Vietnam, telling the lighter stories about his adventures while on leave and away from the fighting. He knew that we were already stressed enough and so we didn't need to hear any gory stories of real life in the jungle.

We grew close. We bonded with each other's lives and I felt as though I was with my own relatives waiting for my sister to give birth. Our flaws seemed to slip away, at least for a while, into the mesmerizing hum of our own voices. Nature was having a most magnificent moment. The night was soothing; the lights were dimmed; and by the dawn it was all over.

I suppose I always thought of miracles as an instantaneous event. Jesus cures the cripple and "bingo" in a wink and a flash this guy runs away and joins the Hebrew Soccer Club. The blind man not only can see again, but he has 20/20 vision! The leper suddenly looks a lot like Tom Cruise, etc. etc.

I know now that it simply does not happen that way. Miracles are a transformation over time and emotion. And while time seems to be a concept recognizable by only one of God's creatures—man—emotion seems inherent to all sentient beings.

Men apparently are the only ones that attempt to count their existence in the gauge able fashion of "time" and so we seem to prefer our miracles in some equally measurable fashion.

I see the slinky caterpillar, not marking time but only feeling the seasons, spinning a nest and retreating into it full of self-doubt and low self-esteem. She emerges as a reflection of rainbows and light.

Surprised at what she became; or fully expecting it? Is that a miracle?

The ugly duckling hooks up with the wrong crowd only to discover one magical day that she is truly a queen in disguise. But you know, I thought that the ducks were kind of nice too.

A young girl runs Bambi-like down a beach, a disconnected loose-jointed mass of wire and springs. You turn away so as not to laugh and when you turn back she is a flowing woman of power and grace. She will break your heart, and that is a miracle too.

All in their time. All in their nature. All as they were intended to be.

That night we watched, transfixed as a miracle evolved into six small, precious, and delicate creatures. Six little fur balls emerged from Daisy's womb, kicking and struggling like baby birds emerging from their warm shell. She treated each one as though they were the first; chewing through the umbilical cord, bathing them thoroughly, and then warming them against her teats as they immediately began to nurse on her.

They were born blind, like all puppies are, and it was a good thing, because if they had crawled out full-sighted onto the bright, ugly, grape parka world awaiting them, they would have thought, "WOW! What is THIS!" And gone right back in.

The Mount Bellew signature purple jackets had been significantly and heroically stained beyond the normal ability of any dry cleaner to rectify.

"Hermann, they're a mess," Erik offered at one point. "I am very sorry."

"About what? I like 'em better that way," Hermann snickered, "Hell, guess The Pan will just have to get himself some more; doubt if there is a big backorder on purple."

We all laughed at his use of Pieter's nickname. We had thought that it was a secret. Guess there aren't many secrets at Mount Bellew. The echoes carry far.

When it seemed that the birthing had come to a close and that Daisy was resting securely with her new pups, Conrad gingerly approached the tired girl with a bowl of cold water. Sometimes the mother may snap, you never know. But with an old friend like Daisy, he felt that she would give him sufficient warning of any sour disposition.

"How about some water, gal?" he asked as he gingerly moved the bowl under her muzzle. The quick wag of her tail told him all he wanted to know.

"We're going to be fine here," he announced to the throng of new uncles and aunts.

"You're going to be just fine," he whispered encouragingly to Daisy as he grinned and stroked her head.

Conrad was wrong. It was only "fine" for a while and weeks passed.

The desecrated uniforms were replaced by a bed of soft blankets and the area around it was sealed off with boxes. The makeshift pen was ostensibly constructed to keep the now active puppies *in*, but more pragmatically to keep the marshmallow hearts and heavy hands of the employees out. It was "fine" as the pen filled with small stuffed toys competing for space with the pups. It was even "fine" as the number of employees taking their lunch in the before empty locker room seemed to increase daily and "The Name Game" kept them continually occupied.

"Caesar. I would call mine Caesar," Ivana would offer.

"Too hard and demanding" was the consensus. "Look how sweet they are."

"How about Rose?" someone would inject.

"They're yellow and black, you moron," was the cry. "What's that got to do with Rose?"

"My mother's name is Rose," they would try defensively.

"So what? My Mom's name is Yadwegah; and that seems wrong, too."

"I like Nugget," would be an offer, "like in a golden nugget."

"Not bad," they would concede, "but not for a girl dog."

"You guys ever hear of the joke about the guy who called his dog 'Sex,'" I jumped in. "Well, when the dog would run away he would have to go around the neighborhood looking for 'Sex' and..."

"We heard it! It's not funny! Shut up!" I would be attacked.

The game never had a conclusion, or a winner, and, as in most games like that, (*Monopoly* or *Famous People* come immediately to mind), they are found to be interminably fascinating by the intellectually challenged.

And so this went on for weeks.

One afternoon Conrad had taken to softly examining each little ball of fur as they lay against their mother's warm stomach. Daisy trusted Conrad exclusively and had no reservations about letting him near her new brood.

"So, what in the world are we going to do with six pups?" Bobbi asked gleefully to the crowded lunch room.

"Well, I guess we'll sell them to some good homes around here," Erik said. "Labs will go pretty fast. I don't expect to keep the money or anything," he added rather magnanimously for him. "We'll just put it into the 'Employee Party Pot' or donate it or something."

"Erik, you should have one, if you want it," said Hermann, "and I'll buy one for the ski area," he continued. "It can be our new Avie dog someday. Take Daisy's place just as she took Petunia's. I like it. It's kind of a legacy."

It was generally agreed that this was a good idea.

"No," grumbled Conrad from his corner with the dogs.

"No? No what, Conrad?" Hermann asked, incredulously. "You telling me that I can't have one of my own dogs?" he growled back.

"No, Hermann, I'm telling you that you can have one dog, Erik can have one dog and you'll sell three dogs," said Conrad as he turned to the owner.

"So, what happens to the sixth dog?" cracked Louie. "He gonna go to Hollywood and be on TV like Rin Tin Tin or something?"

"No, son: *she* is going with me." Conrad fixed the snowboarder with a glare that made it readily apparent that this was no time to screw with him, and Louie wisely shut his mouth around the top of his soda bottle.

Conrad slowly creaked to his feet with an extremely small and quiet black puppy in his large hands. His voice was like a father's whose duty it was to inform the children that their long anticipated summer vacation was about to be canceled due to circumstances beyond his control.

"People," he began, "this puppy is going to die. She's bad off."

We all stared at him, uncomprehending his concern or his manner. "You see her hind legs," he continued while gently pulling on the little paws. "This one was born crippled. I thought so on that very first day, but it was too early to be sure. Now I know."

"She doesn't walk like the others, doesn't walk hardly at all," he said. "Mostly she just lies there, and Daisy is rejecting her. The others won't let her eat. They know she's not right."

"But, Conrad, we can fix that," Bobbi said with authority. "Can't we?" she added, not so sure now.

"That's not how the breed survives, girl," Conrad instructed. "The weak one must go. It's nature's way and we have no say about it. She's going to be crippled and eventually will need to be destroyed. It's better to do it now," he said with finality.

"Oh no, Conrad," cried Bobbi above the rising murmurs. "Don't do that. Don't hurt her! I'll pay for a vet to get her better," she offered hopefully.

"It doesn't work that way, Bobbi," he said gently. "It's something all your money can't fix." With that, Conrad, cradling the pup in his arms, moved quickly out the door. Bobbi followed him hurriedly and watched as he placed the puppy in his truck. She tried to grasp his arm, but he effortlessly shrugged her off.

"You cruel heartless BASTARD!" she screamed in his face. "Don't do this, Conrad. Don't do this! Don't hurt her!" She pleaded again now, while tears of frustration streaked down her cheeks.

Conrad firmly moved her an arm's length away and stared into her eyes with the pain of the moment etched deeply into his sun-cracked face. "I'm sorry, Bobbi," is all he could say, "It's nature's way."

Then he started the truck and drove silently away.

When Bobbi returned to the locker room, she found that it had suddenly become empty, as though an evil sorcerer had instantly made twenty people vanish into the thin mountain air. The warm magic which had been building since the day of the puppies' birth had evaporated out the frost-covered windows and all that was left was the void of her own soft sobs echoing off the metallic locker walls. Her shaking shoulders were suddenly held steady in the firm grip of Hermann's warm hands. He had slipped up quietly behind her, not wanting to leave the building with the others, not wanting to leave any of his kids to face this alone.

"Conrad is only doing what he thinks is right, honey," Hermann whispered.

"I know, Hermann. I know." She held his hands on her shoulders, seeking their understanding. "But why does he have to be such a hard ass *all* the time?" she lashed out.

"Bobbi, I've known that man for awhile now and I'm not sure of that answer," Hermann said. "I believe that under that crusty, impenetrable shell is a heart so soft, that he's afraid for it. He's afraid that if he ever lets his heart go, the world will break it."

"I don't mean to defend him, Bobbi," he continued, "but I believe that it's not easy being Conrad. Try and remember that before you condemn him completely."

With that, Hermann slowly loosened his protective hug, and now, suddenly feeling tired, old and defeated, he moved out the door.

DOWNHILL BOOGIE SOUP

UMmm, UMmm, Good.
UMmm, UMmm, Good.
That's what Campbell's soup is
UMmm, UMmm, Good!

Campbell's Soup jingle

DOWNHILL BOOGIE SOUP

My greatest happiness has almost always been connected with nature; occasionally people, but very seldom with my work. I've gone many places alone; physical places; mental places. I am not afraid. I need to be alone. I need my time and space to reflect.

Journals of Conrad King

In the many weeks before and after the birth of the puppies, Erik had become accustomed to skiing the mountain by himself. He did not necessarily like it. He missed the constant companionship of his loyal canine friend during work, but Daisy needed to rest. She was not yet ready for the rigors of the mountain and had her mothering duties which came first. Uncharacteristically, Erik would find himself thinking absently of her on his solitary ride up the chairlift. He would find himself getting excited about seeing the pups at the end of the day. He loved the way they would crawl over him, how their soft fur felt in his hands. He relished the smell of their sweet milk-laden breath and the sharp bite of their pin-like teeth. Erik had never known that you could miss being away from somebody, or something, so much.

I suppose that he was becoming a pretty good father after all. Nobody actually knows how to do it. It just takes a lot of love.

It had been snowing for hours and you could sense the soft electricity in the air, fresh, clean, and exciting. There would soon be a powdered sugar blanket laid upon the earth that would swallow you to your knees and then offer you the opportunity to float down the mountain in a fluffy cloud-like experience which was worshiped by fanatical powder skiers around the world.

Deep powder skiing: there are not that many who have done it, not many that can do it, and fewer who can do it well. Once you have accomplished the soft extension and retraction of powerful legs seeking an unattainable bottom, you become like a cocaine addict seeking to obtain more and more of the elusive white powder.

No stash is too remote or forbidding to access. You will hike for an hour in lung burning altitudes for a mere five minute rush of untracked virgin snow. You will drop unconcerned through a forest of brain damaging trees and rocks for fresh tracks that reach seductively up to your hips.

It is a sickness, and you don't desire a cure.

I had come into work early just to be sure that I could make it up the winding, icy road to the mountain. I was sitting in the locker room, bored and alone, and had taken to examining the rescue gear there. There were all sorts of contraptions: plastic bottles of clear liquids, nylon bags full of strange tools and complicated splints, things which would have baffled Houdini in his plans to escape them. The patrollers either carried this stuff on their backs or they had access to it at a moment's notice by calling for it on their radios. I'm sure that if you were the injured skier it would seem like an eternity before help ever arrived, before somebody came to keep you warm, but I've seen these guys and gals in action. They are as good and as fast as their hostile environment will allow.

Consider the huge territory that the patrollers have to cover and the myriad of unusual problems they must face. They might have 2,000 acres of forest, often much more in the larger resorts, and it has been recently invaded by 15,000 maniacs who generally have no appreciation for the environment that they have just entered.

There are the experts seeking ultimate thrills and just as

many who are afraid of their own skis. Each day the patroller must deal with the possibility of climbing an ice covered metal lift tower in order to evacuate unwieldy and often unwilling passengers from a broken down chairlift. This will almost never occur when the weather is nice. It will always be in a blizzard with 40-knot winds. Why? Because *that* is when things break.

Early in the morning, the patrollers ski around at high speeds with a load of dynamite on their backs through areas which are determined to be unsafe for skiing. Why? Because the terrain has avalanche problems! What do they do? They ski *into* it and blow it up (of course), all the while hoping that they do not exacerbate the problem by burying themselves, or all the cars in the parking lot, under tons of snow and rock in the process.

Later on, they might find themselves trying to get a lost, half frozen and totally scared child back to its parents, or maybe having the golden opportunity to guide a speeding hundred-pound sled occupied by a two-hundred-pound passenger with a bone sticking out of his leg down a run designated for experts only.

Appreciate the skill level here for a moment, people!

The more mundane days can be spent with a small shovel in their hands, digging out protective pads around chairlift towers, repositioning snow fences, or closing off un-skiable trails. How do they know they're un-skiable you ask? Well, simply, they ski them first (of course).

As the evening gloom begins to darken and solidify the mountain into a forbidding and inhospitable mass of ice, the weather beaten patrollers remain on its trails, "sweeping" each run in order to assure that none of the fifteen thousand clients have been left behind and all have made it home to the comfort of their hot tubs.

During this entire process, these heroic men and women have the unique opportunity to trash all of their own equipment, often fixing or replacing it at their own expense, so that they can warn the paying public that certain trails are "un-skiable." This is often the same public that then cops an attitude when tracked down for skiing under the closed rope, or for skiing out of bounds, or for skiing too fast or too recklessly in a Slow Skiing zone. Most of this "public" deserves a good slap to the head.

That is what I would do, but the patroller has been trained to have patience with snotty guests.

Despite their best efforts, some people die in these mountains and that is tough for everybody to accept. It happens, but you cannot take that attitude. It is difficult to be that cavalier. The patrollers go home at those times and wonder, "What if I had been able to get there sooner? What if I had been able to stabilize him quicker? Are my skills up to par? Would he have lived if I was better?"

Sometimes they do not sleep well at nights.

I could never have been on the Patrol. It is a fine job, though. Many are volunteers, the rest work for something just above minimum wage. They have a huge personal commitment to duty and service.

I needed the money, so I chose to drive a bus instead.

I watched as Erik entered the locker room. He was stomping his feet to relieve them of the snow on his boots and sweeping at the mess of flakes which had accumulated on his jacket with a tattered baseball cap. He saw me at the back of the long room sitting amongst the patrol gear.

"Get out of my shit," he growled as he approached his locker. "And stay out of that stuff from now on. You hear me?"

"Okay Erik. No problem," I stammered. "I didn't touch anything," I offered in the way of an apology. "I was just looking at it."

"Well, look someplace else," he said.

When it came to patrolmen I believe that Erik, despite his personality faults, was as good as you could ever have. He just needed to lighten up.

I figured that I would try to mollify him a bit by striking up a nice early morning conversation—something that he could ramble on about. So I said, "Hey Erik, do you think that in

Rome they would call IV's something like, '4's?'"

"What?" he said, looking confused.

"The IV's. You know, those bags of stuff," I said to clarify the issue. "Would some doctor in Rome say, like in his most professional doctor voice, 'Start this guy on a 4; stat.'"

He continued to stare at me blankly. "You're weird. And stay out of my shit," he repeated.

So much for pleasant morning conversation.

Ten minutes later, Erik had disappeared out the back door and I was left alone again, still contemplating this new medical conundrum and wondering if I could jiggle the soda machine to get a free coke.

All right!! Now THIS was a mistake, Erik thought. *First, you should not even be back here and second, you should not be alone. You dumb shit. Hey, at least when I screw up nobody will be around to diss me. Of course, nobody will be around to rescue me either. I could be the Edmund Hillery of the Rockies: "Man found frozen after 50 years. Cliff bars still edible." Good headline.*

Erik had slipped over to the south side of the mountain; colloquially known as "The Darkside" (as in "come to the Darkside...hahahaha"), for the chance at the new and continually falling snow, which he knew would be there.

He was dressed for storm skiing: good warm suit, top of the line goggles, glove liners in, and the prerequisite survival food of two Cliff Bars squirreled somewhere away in his many pockets. He was cozy and warm in a little portable tent.

Not many people out today. Not exactly the place to be when the snow, plummeting down, is driven by thirty-knot winds. Not real popular on the double diamonds he had been searching for all morning, but then again, the "carvers" wanted groomed corduroy and tended to avoid this stuff.

Weenies, he concluded derisively. *Probably all at an early lunch by now.*

What the Patrol Chief had not counted on were the increasing winds and now there were gusts popping up to almost 40 knots. He had ridden the chair up, one of only a few brave souls, and was almost sure that nobody had followed him on the traverse to this side of the mountain.

He was feeling a bit alone (*Should be at least some other demented skier over here: be rather nice to see another patroller about now*), but felt comforted by the occasional chatter being passed between other patrollers on the VHF radio which was tucked securely near his chest.

Although he could not see it, or hear it, he was almost sure that the lift would soon be closed down behind him until these gusts subsided. It wasn't safe to operate the equipment in the unpredictable conditions and the head of the lift department wanted to treat his aging chairs with as much TLC has he could muster.

The wind pounded in Erik's ears like the rumble of distant thunder. He was a solitary explorer on a very mean mountain; it was kind of the way he had wanted it, but really... not so dramatic.

There had been intermittent whiteouts throughout the day, but visibility was now totally obscured. It would be hard to believe that conditions could be worse, but then again he felt a perverse security in knowing that at least they were *consistently* bad. The snow was blowing a horizontal sheet from seemingly every direction. He could see his skis. He could see his hands and, well, that was about it. He thought of holding up in some trees for protection, but was not exactly sure of where they were just now. *Probably just fall down a tree well anyway. And then what?*

Like a ship in a dense fog, his sense of direction was totally gone. Well, not totally: right was right and left was left, but where do they lead? Up was when the skis stopped. Down was when they got rolling. That was pretty basic stuff, but not enough to avoid the numerous obstacles which he knew from experience lay somewhere below him. While Erik adjusted his goggles and tightened up on his pack straps, he composed himself. *Okay, let's not panic. Let's just figure this all out. Hiding in the trees is "bad" because I have no idea where they are. I'd never be found there anyway. Waiting is "bad" because this crap is just going to get worse. Going down actually sucks because there are lots of immovable objects in the way, like unseen rocks and submerged trees, and going up is no option at all. Shit man, you are going to DIE up here!*

This logical conclusion actually began to motivate him, since going "down" was the best of the worst alternatives. He had skied this mountain almost one hundred days every year for the past eight years and the accomplished outdoorsman knew her intimately. There was not a bump or a crevice or a glade that he had not explored, and most times found to be pleasurable. He had been on this exact run dozens of times. She was his mountain and he was good. Heck, he *knew* he was good!

He had lots of other mountains before he came to love this one and settled down with her. He had tried those kinky rope tows in New England and had ridden the finest high-speed gondolas in Europe. Erik prided himself in being a true expert skier. He doubted that there was much a mountain could throw at him that he could not handle or had not tried at least once. But what was THIS? He was totally blind! He checked his goggles again, concerned that they were malfunctioning. No fog.

Yep, he was just plain snow-blind and totally disoriented.

(Come on, sugar…let me wear the disguise this time,) the mountain whispered to him.

No. Take it off. Let me see you, his mind answered back.

(*Why, baby?*)

Because you're scaring me. That's why.

(*That's okay, Sweet thing. Pretend I'm another woman. Pretend you've never met me before. See if you can do me and not know me. It's okay, I want it this way.*)

Pleassse take it off? He begged.

(*No!*)

Well, this conversation is going nowhere, he concluded as he began a slow shuffle forward. He knew that somewhere just before him was a series of drop-offs which would lead into the body of the bowl.

Due to the prevailing winds, the snow would build up on the usually small, but now hidden cliffs, transforming them into intimidating obstacles at this time of year, and so he moved hesitantly, almost mechanically, for the lips he knew to be there. When he sensed a space under his right foot, he knew that he had reached a moment of decision and must either start his decent or hike back to the patrol shack a quarter mile above him. The mountain was waiting his next move.

Relax, relax, relax, Erik told himself. *You've done this all before. Think of something else and just go with the feelings. Don't tense up or you'll lose it. You need to perform here.*

(*Hey Baby, why don't you put on some nice music in that pretty head of yours?*)

What? You again? Go away!...Like what? He thought with curiosity.

(*Got any Barry White, sweetie?*)

Not a big collector of his albums. Let's try some Eagles. He hummed.

(*That'll do just fine, Baby.*)

Then, with the lyrics of "Take it Easy" playing inside his head, he gently brushed over the waiting lips.

"Take it easy....Take it easy....Don't let the sound of your own wheels...drive you crazy..."

Erik stretched his powerful legs to meet the expected softness of the mountain, but, as he landed, he was thrown back unexpectedly, skidding sideways on the hard surface beneath him.

What the hell is this? Ice? You finicky bitch. Where the heck do you get off throwing ice at me on a day like this? he demand-ed. *I'll just give her a little bite.* And he rolled his edges into the unexpected sheet to feel them carve the slope into sub-mission.

Okay, this should be a piece of cake now, he smiled. *Three turns. Four turns.* He was getting her under control.

(*Where you going so fast, Baby?*) She reprimanded him. (*You better just slow down, Hotshot, because you and me got a long way to go now. I ain't seen none of your stuff. Nothing I ain't ever seen before. You just think it's all over because you got one little purrrr out of me? What you got in that little sack of tricks, Baby? Come on, show Mama!*)

I wonder if this is what it was like for Ray Charles to make love? he laughed. *Can he have a different woman every night if he just pretends about it? And do looks make much difference to him? Heck, old Ray just wakes up every morning and says, "Whoa! Hold the phone! I'm bad. I'm a stud. I wonder who THIS is?"*

Okay, okay: hands. Keep them where you can see them, Erik reminded himself. *Damn, that is all that I can see. Powder here and maybe some bumps below. Avoid the bumps. Go left. "Get moving" the Lady says. So...get moving boy.*

He dropped into the fluid and soft motion of an accom-plished powder lover, strong legs extending and retracting under him like reliable old pistons, his whole body a long and supple spring, his hips absorbing the undulations below.

Sweet, sweet stuff, he smiled. *Heck, I could do this all day. Good rhythm, good slope.*

He had just settled into a confident second verse of "Take it Easy" when he suddenly found himself to be airborne!

Hold on! he panicked. *I am not going to fly through this stuff! Land the plane, Dude! I thought that I had missed the bumps.*

(*Come on, Baby. We always do it that-a-way. You just pump-*

ing along and me just singing a song. Put some action into it boy! Don't make me be rough with you now. I got some issues here that I'm expecting you to be taking care of and you just being your same old selfish self!)

Erik slammed on the brakes to catch his breath. *Okay, game's over Ms. Mountain,* he thought peevishly. *I need to see these bumps: time to take off the disguise; drop the wind, drop the snow, and let me out of here!*

(Don't see no future in that, Sugar. Bumps is the best part. Never the same line. You're a good bumper, Baby. You just got to feel 'em more. Stop using your head. You know they're there. Come on now, be sensitive, be gentle to Mama's old Darkside.)

Yada, Yada, Yada. ...Been there before...Breathe deep and go. Don't turn the shoulders, keep up the rhythm, absorb in the hips...hands, hands, hands. Feel each bump as you weight and unweight. Be sensitive now. Feel the mountain, he instructed himself. *You know, if she put a tree out there ahead of me, I'll kill her!*

(No trees, Baby. Not this time, maybe next. Maybe after the boy gets use to this fun game the Lady will throw a little brush in his way to shake 'em up. Work the bushes. Lots of fun. But just keep going now, Sugar. Those bumps you are doing are feeling real nice.)

She was leveling out now, feeling soft and gentle. Erik was pretty sure that he had made it to the flat traverse at the bottom, but this was where the real work began. The excitement of gravity pulling you down the hill was gone for now and all that remained was the slow and steady skating in the traverse. The snow here was soft and deep through the forest. He could usually get through this part in about three or four minutes, but today she was not going to give an inch.

(Come on, Baby! You gonna have to pump harder than that if you want to get out of here. Move them legs! Move them hands! That's right, sweet thing. Now you is sweating! And you thought you was gonna freeze? Brother, you is hot! You is soooo hot! I think you gonna catch afire!)

One more drop, one more big drop. I know it's steep. Saw it

222

before, he panted. *Don't need to see it now. It's usually clear. Hell, I don't care if a lift tower is in the way! I'll go through it! I'm taking it full out downhill boogie!* His mind now screamed at him full of confidence.

(Oh, that is IT, Baby! Full tilt confident boogie! You are the badest dude on the Mountain today, my man! You are the best! The Beast of the West! Nobody else could have done that run like you. You are the blind master of the Mountain, Baby! Stevie Wonder in a Kung-fu robe. Hooah!!)

The gusts had started to back off some by now and the lift was running once more. The exhausted patroller approached the empty lifeline, tired and hot, yet exhilarated with his last run.

The adrenaline was still pumping furiously as he thought, *Damn, that was GREAT! My legs are shot. I don't think the shaking is a good sign.*

He looked at the empty chairs parading before him. He looked up at the waiting mountain wondering what more she had to offer. Five years of the same old gal and still he could not get enough of her. Everyday, every run was different. The mountain always called the shots. He just responded.

A smile cracked through the ice of his frozen beard as he slid up to the solitary attendant at the lift who was stomping his feet to stay warm.

"You headed up again?" the liftee noted in disbelief.

"Hell, it's early, Charlie," laughed Erik. "Maybe just one more run."

"Well, be careful up there, Chief," the attendant said with real concern. "That mountain is pretty temperamental today."

"Oh yeah: so it seems, so it seems," he answered. "But, you know Charlie; a ski patroller's work is never done. We just have to keep working in this lousy stuff," he silently laughed.

Then Erik's mind filled with a thrill of private joy as he eyed his new challenge. *Get ready for The Man!* he thought defiantly as he loaded the empty lift; but he instinctively knew that his confidence was a flimsy shield against the dangerous mysteries of the mountain.

(*Bring it on, Bad Boy!*) He heard her answer.

Erik could not wait to get home and tell Daisy and the "kids" about this day.

WALLY'S (soon-to-be famous) LEFTOVER SOUP

I knew that you were just *dying* to ask about this unique dish but did not want to interrupt Erik in an intimate moment. Wally's soup is sort of like an Italian Puttanesca (i.e."whore's stew") but for Anglo-Saxons (i.e. "white guys").

1. Start by calling as many friends as you know, but try sticking with people that actually cook "things" during the week. This should help to limit the party, and besides, all those other guys just bring leftover pizza crusts which do not go into the soup—unless you are desperate. Have your guests empty out their refrigerators and bring all the stuff that is "leftover" in there to your house (hence the name). It is even better if you can use a friend's house, since this can get messy.

2. Get a pot—a BIG pot—since this stuff seems to have a way of growing to larger proportions than you would expect.

3. Separate the food into manageable piles using the Basic Food Groups System, which is a lot like the Dewy Decimal System. For instance: meat goes over there (NO TOFU!), veggies and green things there; pasta, rice, and potatoes somewhere else; spices, beer, and wine close by for easy handling.

4. Check the meat closely for any signs of mold or green hairy things growing on it. Blue is also not a good color and all those pieces should be thrown out. Smell the remaining pile. Anything vaguely resembling the odor given off by well-used sweat socks should be highly suspect and perhaps dumped into the garbage also. If you are unsure, then vote on it. That way you can't be blamed. If any of the remaining meat is raw, it should be cooked at this time. Do that. If it has already been cooked in some fashion then set it aside until later.

5. Gather up all the veggies and chop them into nice big pieces. When the "new" meat looks done, add the "old" meat and then throw everything into the pot.

6. Now the real secret to good soup. Number one: never use water. Use that vegetable broth that you can buy in the store and dump in a lot of cans of that. It's cheap, so splurge. Number two: add as much wine as you can get away with, usually until someone yells, "Hey, you moron, I brought that stuff for dinner." That should be your clue to stop, or else fights break out and ruin the party.

7. You'll need some spices now, but not necessarily *all* of them: garlic powder, salt, dill, basil leaves, and Tabasco sauce are basic, but don't hesitate if something else really piques your fancy.

8. Let it all come to a boil, turn down the heat, and let it "marry." Very important.
Just at the end, you can dump in the *cooked* pasta, *cooked* rice and *cooked* potatoes. I stress that they must have been *cooked*, otherwise the result will be a big hard lump.

9. Ladle the soup into bowls. If you weren't paying close attention to the recipe (particularly #8... *cooked*), you might need a knife to chop it up, so have one of those handy.

10. Serve with the usual condiments: toast, ketchup, and beer.

HOME TO THE HILLS

Here he lies where he long'd to be;
Home is the sailor, home from the sea,
And the hunter Home from the hill.

Robert Louis Stevenson
Requiem

HOME TO THE HILLS

If we could see ourselves and other objects as they really are,
we should see ourselves in a world of spiritual natures,
our community with which neither began at our birth nor
will end with the death of the body.

Immanuel Kant

er wet nose hovered no more than two inches above the ground, like a fat black bug in search of its home. *I know that it was here*, she thought. *And it wasn't that long ago either—maybe a few days. That's all. I'm sure it's still good.*

The highly developed olfactory radar, tipping the end of her snout, probed intensely for the target as she scanned the spaces before her. Daisy's tail stood ridged upon her rump and wagged a stiff, formal salute at the stars gleaming above her. *Seems like cheese, and some sort of meat, and mustard. I like mustard.* The scents came to her in wonderful new waves now, stronger than the original and ethereal whiffs which had greeted her when she first trotted out of the locker room door. *It is definitely cheese, but some sort of new and foreign variety. It's close now.*

The ever-hungry girl began to salivate at the thought of the lost and abandoned lunch, and secretly hoped that one of those horrible snowplows hadn't buried it vindictively under a few feet of gray, dirty snow. Then she would have to dig for her treat and she was tired. Erik had worked her hard that

229

day. This was supposed to be her playtime, and so she continued her ever-narrowing and circular route in the hopes of eventually zeroing in on her valued prize.

Now that her mothering duties had drawn to a close, Daisy was once more put to work with the Patrol—a task she actually loved. Three of her pups had been sold off to good homes in the area and Conrad had personally assured himself of the new owner's impeccable credentials.

A beautiful and pudgy yellow female had gone to Hermann. He called her Marigold; "Goldie" for short, and while she spent most her present day either sleeping in his office or chewing up his furniture, she would eventually be given the same training as her mom and someday take over Daisy's duties.

Erik had opted for a feisty black ball of muscle and had named him Miska. That is Polish for "little boy," and by the loving and proud way which the gruff patroller treated the pup you would have thought that they were blood relatives.

Erik had let Daisy roam the parking lots after hours since she was small. It was her custom during the weekly meetings. He knew that she hunted down the leftovers, but saw no harm in it. The area had gone dark and cold with the end of the day and there was seldom any activity in the lots except for the few managers left behind to finish up the paperwork. Everyone kept a communal eye on their favorite dog. She never wandered far, keeping mostly to the banks directly outside of the windows where Erik could see her. She never liked to let him too far out of her sight. Erik never knew whether this was out of loyalty, or just the fact that she was insecure about everything if he was not there to protect her. She never really recovered much in the way of food and, true to her breed, she was capable of digesting almost anything. It could be a hot dog or a dead frog. It seemed to make no difference to her nuclear powered digestive system. The evening game of "hide and seek" seemed to offer her a relaxing end to the stressful day.

Most people envied Daisy's easy simplicity.

The UPS man was named Gary. He had been delivering packages in this area for almost ten years now and knew every dirt road and ranch in the county. The long distances between some of the farms gave him an expansive territory to cover. He never seemed to mind. He actually enjoyed the driving, but today the weather had been extremely temperamental: a constant sheet of blowing snow. He was on his last run of the day and was looking forward to dropping off the final packages. Gary wanted to head home for a well-deserved cold beer and a warm dinner with his family.

If he hurried, he could make it back before the kids were sent off to bed and hear what they had done in school that day. He gunned the heavy brown truck up the hill as fast as he dared under the conditions and hoped that the local constable was happily enjoying his own warm meal. They seldom gave him trouble anyway, instinctively knowing that the timely and intact delivery of their own packages somehow lay in the temperamental hands of the man in the dark brown uniform.

Daisy shook the cold accumulation of flakes from her long yellow coat, flinging them in a mini-blizzard around her stout body. Cold weather never bothered her. It made her feel like a puppy again. *This is the best,* she thought. Her tail betrayed her enthusiasm for the hunt. *This smells good. It won't run away if I scare it. I know I'm close; maybe over by that snow bank... I think that's where it went.* She ran head down, intent upon her suspected treasure. There was never any traffic this time of night, nobody ever came here. All her senses were focused into total concentration upon her prize, led by the quivering nerves of her highly sensitive nose.

One more package and I'm out of here, Gary thought as he turned onto the road leading to Mount Bellew. *Maybe I'll be home before this snow gets any more serious for the night.*

A sudden flash of yellow, coming like a comet from the sky, caught the driver's peripheral vision as he swung into the parking lot. *Shit!* It was coming from the left and crossing in front of the quickly moving truck: *Brakes!* His mind screamed at him. *Too fast, asshole!* He slammed the brakes and the heavy truck began to skid sideways on the frozen road. He swung the wheel into the skid to avoid whipping the vehicle into a 360-degree turn. It began to straighten out. The truck was safe.

The oblivious yellow mass continued to bolt across the road as though the huge brown vehicle never existed. Gary's shaking hands laid on the horn. *Scare it! Scare it away!*

The golden mass halted its pursuit and stopped to stare uncomprehendingly at the blaring, skidding monster before it. Daisy's soft brown eyes could not comprehend where this thing had come from. Why did it make such a noise? Was it there to harm her? Should she run away? The lights hurt her eyes, but she remained frozen in their grip, unable to react.

She had always been scared of anything bigger than her. She was frightened to death of the occasional hot air balloon which traversed the valley and would run home with her tail tucked protectively between her legs. She was intimidated by the mountain elk and thought of them as hormonally imbalanced dogs which had invaded her territory. They would hurt her. She was sure of that. Daisy hated the massiveness of cars, and trucks, and large people who would dominate her by their very size.

She loved small children and would shrink into a whining ball at their feet, happy to have found a human scaled to her world, reveling in their innocent and soft touch, excited by the sound of their joyful voices. She had an acute sense of how relatively insignificant she was in a very scary world. Her non-existent ego had never led her to believe otherwise. She did not understand the tiny dogs that would yap at her; little noisy things that she could destroy in one strong bite. They were annoying and she preferred to send them scurrying away with a deep warning growl. She was scared of the cat, because it killed the defenseless mice. She was scared of the mice, because they allowed themselves to get dead. She was scared of the crows, because they screamed piercingly for their tidbits of food. Daisy was pure. Daisy was simple. She had more sense than most of the humans around her and that made her scared of many things.

The soft thud which the immobilized dog made with the huge metal bumper felt gentle and forgiving inside of the truck, as though she meant the mass no harm and was only there to rub up against the stranger in a friendly greeting. She never had a chance to be really scared of the screaming monster bearing down upon her. She only had a momentary thought of, *I wonder what this thing is?*

Daisy felt very little—a solid uncomprehending blow and her brief fear was quickly eliminated with the unstoppable impact of the 2,000-pound truck.

Her body was flung into the far ditch. It landed, ironically enough, near her sought-after sandwich so that she could smell it in all its glory. *Oh, there it is...* she thought; and quietly passed away. Her deep brown eyes glazed over with a gaze into an uncomplicated world which many men never had the wisdom to seek.

The truck had squealed in protest as the loose gravel under its wheels pelted dirt and rock under its metal frame. Daisy had yelped in fear and shock as the monster threw her effortlessly aside. Inside the administration building, the sudden noise had brought them all quickly to their feet, knowing almost instantly, instinctively, what had transpired. They ran as one from the building hoping not to find that which they were already sure of.

With all their power, with all their training, with all of their expertise, when death came to call, they could only watch in helplessness and there was nothing that any of them could do.

It happens.

At times like this, you want to assign blame. You want to grab someone and yell: "You...you...you!" There is a need to find someone responsible, someone besides yourself, someone to stand up and say, "Yes, Judge, I did it. I'm the guy who brought this man's life crashing down upon him. I am at fault."

Trust me; that will never happen.

There is never a 100 percent fault. There is never a 100 percent man. Excuses, happenstance, fate, ignorance, and lies, all will cloud the issue and serve to hide the facts. Legalities will take precedence over the simple rights and simple wrongs which are perceived by the heart. And morality becomes relative.

Soon you will begin to doubt your righteousness. Apathy precludes us from taking a proactive stance when we are not personally involved. Bitterness follows us when we are. This is life, and, sadly, despite many deaths, little will change.

I sometimes think that we are all in a war in which everyone, everything, will be killed, and no one, nothing, will be remembered. Whole generations will spring up and die without leaving a trace. And you, with all of your accomplishments, will be a victim like the billions who have gone before you. Everyone is slowly forgotten.

Is there hope? Of course.

Ask yourself: is there someone that you love? Then go home to them, call them, be with them, tell them. And who will remember them? No one. That's just the point. Don't wait to write your love for them upon their tombstones.

You must take care of all of that now.

Gary bubbled, cried, and justified, "I never saw her. I don't think that I was going too fast or anything. I just made the turn and there she was, right in front of me. I'm sorry. It wasn't my fault. I didn't mean to hit her."

The more he talked, the more he would have talked himself out of it. Pretty soon he wouldn't have even been there at all.

Erik was like a volcano about to blow. He had become extremely quiet, a very bad sign for Erik, a sign which Conrad recognized from his years of experience with him. Erik knew that his nightly game of giving Daisy her freedom to roam the vacant parking lots of the mountain had been risky. He never thought that it would come to this. He had made a gamble and now he lost. Gary eyed him with leery caution, not sure of how the man was going to react.

Conrad quickly stepped between them and gently steered the driver toward his truck. "Look, son," he said as he took his arm. "I know it wasn't your fault, but I think that I want you out of here *right now*," he emphasized. "I don't think that you want to be around. Get on back into your truck and drive on home to your family."

Conrad guided him back to the waiting beast. It grinned maliciously at them through its grillwork and continued to purr like a large cat satisfied with its kill.

"Give me the package and then get on out of here. We know this stuff happens. Drive on home. Drive safe, Gary," he said as he took the large box. "I'll call you in the morning, but you get going now," he said as he helped the shaken young man into his truck.

"Oh shit, Mr. King," he said one more time, the truth finally sinking into him; "I never saw her. I am so sorry. I'll buy him another dog."

"We'll talk about it later, son," he said. "Things happen. We'll take care of it now. Go home to your family and rest."

Gary shifted the truck into reverse and backed slowly down the road, unable to shift his own eyes from the scene which he and fate had inadvertently created.

Erik sat by the side of the road and stroked the still warm and golden fur. Daisy did not look hurt. She looked like she was sleeping.

"Do you think that we should get her to the vet?" Erik asked hopefully as Conrad approached.

"No, son. I believe that we're too late for that," he said as he laid a hand on the young man's shoulder.

"Really?" Erik asked, with tears beginning to form uncontrollably in his eyes.

"Really," Conrad confirmed, squeezing the young man's neck in understanding.

In the space of the cold night, which now wrapped its frozen fingers around them, Erik thought that maybe, just maybe, the old man was wrong, but in his heart he knew.

"Oh damn," he finally said, beginning to weep silently as reality came crashing in. "She was such a good dog."

"She was the best," Conrad said assuredly. "She was the best dog we have ever had. I don't think she felt a thing, Erik. I think that it happened so fast."

"What do we do now?" Erik looked at him with hopeful eyes, as though Conrad could control the situation, make everything better again.

"Well, we better get her out of here," He said. "Why don't you grab her back feet..."

"No!" Erik yelled at the thought of the indignity. "Daisy is *not* going like that! She's not one of your cattle! She's my *friend*," he pleaded almost apologetically.

"Okay then," Conrad eyed him cautiously. "What do we do?"

"I don't know," Erik struggled to reason. "But you get a blanket, a big blanket, a soft blanket, that one she likes in the locker room and bring it back here," he ordered, now taking charge again.

"Okay," Conrad said, as though he was assessing a mental patient. But he hustled to the locker room.

Soon, a large gray blanket arrived on the scene and was quickly handed to Erik who had not ceased stroking the dog's quiet head.

"You know," he explained as he spread it upon the snow. "She had a lot of fur, but she never really liked to be cold." He put his arms under Daisy's body and gently lifted her off the hard snow.

"Sometimes she would lie in front of the fire until I thought that she would start to spontaneously combust," he said whimsically. "I'd have to move her then, too. Like this..."

Erik brushed at Daisy's coat to wipe off the attacking flakes and began ever so carefully to wrap her warm body carefully into the folds of the gray shroud.

"It's almost dinner time, girl," he crooned softly, only to her. "Maybe we'll go home and get a special treat."

He raised her from the frozen ground and began to move slowly under the load to his jeep. "I'll let you ride in the front tonight," he said to her, "as long as you don't go shedding all over everything. You'll like that."

He placed Daisy's limp body gently onto the front seat and turned, with tears etching his face, to Hermann who had been holding the door for him.

"I'm taking her to the meadow tonight, Boss. I'm burying her up there," he said emphatically.

"I can't let you do that Erik," Hermann said, apologetically. "The lifts are all shut down. It's dark up there," he continued on helplessly. He knew that he was not making much of a case at all. "You just can't go burying animals on the mountain in the middle of the night!" Hermann stated more emphatically. "Besides, this entire mountain is frozen!" he tried to rationalize.

Erik stared at him defiantly and repeated, "I'm taking her up to the meadow and it's going to be *tonight*—just Daisy and me. I'll build her a cairn of rocks until the spring but I don't want her lying around in some old box until the thaw. That just would not be right for her. So, I'm burying her up there, in the meadow, *tonight*," he concluded.

Erik held Hermann's eyes defiantly in the gaze of his own and, after a long moment, moved into the jeep and drove slowly out of the parking lot.

Hermann shrugged after the retreating tail lights, "I guess you gotta do what you gotta do, son. Do what you gotta do..."

FEBRUARY

As individuals, as families, as neighbors, as members of one community, people of all races and political views are usually decent, kind, and compassionate. But in large corporations or governments, when great power accumulates in their hands, some become monsters, even with good intentions.

Dean Koontz

FEBRUARY

*When you do not appreciate someone's corporate, material,
or political strivings they will begin to resent you since you
do not have similar needs or ambitions. This resentment
will soon lead to a quiet and progressive isolation. You
will be marginalized; you will be ostracized; notably
because you dare to view the world differently.*

Journals of Conrad King

Frank Hayes rumbled his stout bulldozer body into
Mount Bellew's small administration building as though
it should be presumed that he already owned it and was
ready to begin the demolition.

"Frank Hayes to see Hermann Olsen," he growled to the
receptionist as he brushed the top of his crew cut into imaginary place.

It was not an announcement. It was not a request. As in all
things surrounding Frank, it was a simple and unquestionable
command, but before the properly intimidated young woman
at the desk could ring into Hermann's office, Pieter, who had
been excitedly awaiting his arrival, breathlessly appeared to
greet the present-day hero of the ski industry and slather him
with subservience.

During the last ten years, Frank, and his Black Granite Ski
Corporation, had been busily purchasing and developing
small ski areas throughout the West. It was a niche which fell
between the publicly traded giants like Vail and Intrawest and

the "Mom and Pop" operations of small town hills. In that niche Frank had been hugely successful.

The theory was simple, really. Since Frank was not an original thinker, he had stolen the concept from watching how the private golf clubs worked around the states, then, to his personal credit, he applied the same principles to other outdoor sports.

Among other things, Frank had built clubs which specialized in equestrian activities. Then there were those which reserved huge tracts of land for private hunting and fishing preserves. Some developments had cross-country ski trails wandering through them. One resort was dedicated exclusively to snowmobiling.

He purchased land which would be unaffordable to an individual, but well within the means of a group, and divided it into comfortable parcels where high end, top quality but smaller houses could be built. The amount of deeded land around any given house was insignificant since the majority of the tract was left as common property dedicated to a mutual interest and then maintained by the group.

Recently, Frank Hayes had turned his pit-bull demeanor to alpine skiing and was hungrily eyeing the juicy steak bone called Mount Bellew.

After he had been ushered into the close confines of Hermann's office, Frank arrogantly positioned himself at the head of the conference table; like an adversary in full command of the situation the space itself seemed to shrink around him. He was a Bradley tank in a very bad suit entrenched in an unassailable position. He had become accustomed to crushing things in his path and the pint-sized ski area would be just another small obstacle for which he held little respect and from which he expected little resistance. Frank often won these battles through sheer intimidation and, although he had nothing to lose by listening to Frank's proposal, it was immediately clear to Hermann that he just might have a considerable amount to gain by hearing him out.

Hermann Olsen was also very intimidated by the "tank" now squeezed into his chair.

As they exchanged polite pleasantries, Pieter was bustling about being as condescending as possible. He brought juice, he brought coffee, he assured that the Danish was just right, although untouched; and he smiled constantly at Frank. It was not everyday that you had the opportunity to be in the presence of a true capitalist hero. Pieter knew that Frank Hayes could be his ticket out of Mount Bellew and he nervously wanted to make the best impression possible.

Frank thought that Pieter was a sniveling underling.

Frank was very insightful.

"Olsen," Frank said, abruptly cutting off the small talk in mid-conversation. "I am sure that you know that I've been watching Mount Bellew for some time now and I believe that it would make a fine addition to the portfolio of Black Granite. Of course, we would have to get some exact financials from you," he added as though Hermann had requested this meeting. "But generally, an area like this will market for five to seven million." He gave Hermann a playful poke on the shoulder and an insincere chuckle as he winked. "But don't hold me to that figure."

That was the extent of Frank's cold attempt to show what a regular guy he really was, a regular backslapping kind of buddy, and since Hermann was now mentally picking himself up from the floor, he missed the entire tender scene and fake camaraderie of the moment.

Don't hold you to it? his mind screamed at him. *I was thinking that this place was good for a couple of million...but not this!*

Hermann sat in stunned silence, struck mute by the fact that his small area was worth such an exorbitant amount and that he could be a very wealthy man. Frank took Hermann's silence as a signal to barge onward and so barely noticed Pieter's hands trembling on his own coffee cup.

"This place has a lot of promise as we see it," Frank growled. "Most of this land around here," he indicated with a wave of his massive hand at the unseen mountains, "Well,

Olsen, you're not really using it to its full potential."

While he allowed Hermann to absorb the admonishment and feel as though the owner had been scolded for missing school, or not doing as well as he could have on his math test, Frank slurped noisily at his black coffee from the small cup. His fat fingers struggled with the delicate handle. He did not do well with tiny things. Frank was a mug kind of guy and detested the dainty china now being offered to him. With rising frustration he continued to count off Hermann's failings in methodical fashion.

"One, Black Granite has the financial resources to put this place on the map and you don't," he taunted. "We've got room for two or three different style condo projects, a small village at the bottom and some pretty high-end private homes. Two:" he ticked, "those lifts are getting old. Haven't you ever heard of high speed detachable quads, Olsen? Those antiques need to be replaced," he ordered.

Sorry, thought Hermann. *I didn't know that they were giving them away to deserving ski areas.*

"And Three: there's room for another three or four good trails that you haven't even opened up yet," Frank pointed out in exasperation. "Hell, there's an entire meadow up there that hasn't been touched! The key to this market is *expansion*, Olsen. What have you been doing up here all this time?"

Hermann followed the sausage-like finger now scolding him and seeming to ask, "What's *wrong* with you Olsen?"

Should I apologize? he thought. *Should I tell him that I'd take a lot less for doing such a poor job?*

Frank seemed to feel that he had made his point and stared expectantly at Hermann, awaiting a reply. Hermann stared at Frank. Hermann did not seem to grasp the conversational concept that it was now his turn to speak.

He had just hit the jackpot on the world's largest slot machine and he now blinked uncomprehendingly at the burly machine, staring at the tray as though he expected more tokens to come tumbling his way.

But the machine was silent.

He was being admonished for *not* doing a good job and so this guy was offering him a huge sum of money to do what...just walk away?

This just doesn't make sense, Hermann thought, now genuinely confused.

Pieter, sensing the awful awkwardness of the moment in his churning stomach, felt that the interminable silence must be broken or else this entire offer would die like a newborn and neglected baby. His first thought was to pop up and down like a mechanical toy while singing a Broadway rendition of *We're in the Money.*

He shelved that, figuring that he would lose a considerable amount of respect in the eyes of his newfound god.

His next reaction was to kiss Mr. Hayes full on the lips and offer himself in unholy union. That seemed like a poor idea, too, given the fact that they had just been introduced.

What Pieter did do was slowly remove his shaking hands from the table and hide their obvious enthusiasm in his lap. Then, like a remote controlled mannequin operated by the clairvoyant Hermann, he softly spoke.

"Mr. Hayes, this prospective offer is indeed generous and very exciting for all of us at Mount Bellew," he said, nodding his curly blond locks in Hermann's direction in an attempt to indicate that the boss was still alive. "However, I'm sure that you appreciate that it is rather sudden and that we will need to discuss it among our partners."

Frank's ape-like grunt in reply was meant to show how appreciative and sensitive a guy he really was. *Maybe I'm talking to the wrong man here*, he thought. *Maybe this effeminate little prig is the real money and brains behind Mount Bellew.* Maybe Frank should go home and fire half of his staff for giving him false information.

"We would be happy to gather the necessary financials together in order that we might work toward a more concrete figure," Pieter continued on quickly. "But that will take us a couple of weeks. Can we arrange to meet again around that time?" he asked.

Oh god, oh god, oh god, oh god...PLEASE say "yes"...

"Yeah. Sure," Frank responded, still staring at the mute Hermann.

Hayes was generally perplexed how this guy could do that. Hermann would stare. Pieter would talk. Weird. Maybe some ESP thing. Maybe he was smarter than he was giving him credit for. You never even saw his lips move.

"I'll have my administrative assistant give you a call to set up some dates," Frank said to Pieter. "Perhaps you and he can do one of those 'lunch' things that you people do."

Is he mocking me? Pieter thought. *I don't care.*

Frank had perfected the motion of dismissing people around him with an apathetic wave of his immense hand. No general in battle could have executed the gesture with more aplomb. In this case, he brushed the air around him, as if shooing off a pesky fly, and abruptly stood up, leaving no doubt that this unsatisfactory business was concluded for the day. He felt a need to regroup. He had expected a more animated reply. Frank Hayes had the distinct feeling that he had been yelling down a well and the only answers that he had heard had been the sound of his own voice.

"A pleasure to meet you, Olsen," he smiled cynically as he pried his considerable mass from the embrace of the conference chair. "And you, Petroski," he continued, "You could have a bright future at Black Granite. Hopefully we can talk about your involvement with our organization later on."

Pieter almost fainted as Hayes engulfed his small hand. In contrast, Hermann stared at the handshake as though he was watching a movie unfold in his office.

And then the tank rolled resolutely out of the building.

"Holy shit," said Hermann.

"Holy shit," echoed the mannequin.

Email, snail mail, no mail ever works faster and more inaccurately, than good old rumor mail. You do not keep secrets at a place like Mount Bellew and you would be foolish to even try.

The morning after Frank Hayes's visit, the word had spread upon the mountain like a new fallen snow. Some of it was right: "Frank Hayes of Black Granite—" Some of it was wrong; "Going to give Hermann thirty million for the whole place." The rest of it was just convoluted: "They're going to build an entire village down here with a Marriott Hotel, a movie theater and an ice rink."

Hermann's reputation as a particularly astute businessman suddenly soared. "Sly as a fox," people would whisper. "Laid-back and low-key, but not someone you want to mess with," others would offer. "Definitely has his fingers on the pulse of this business," more would say with self-importance.

Only Conrad understood that his old friend had just been blindsided by a speeding train and probably had no idea what to do about any of it.

King was just finishing his second Jim Beam and noisily crunching on the ice when Hermann pulled up a seat at the corner table. They ordered another round for the both of them and Hermann's bleary eyes left no doubt that he had already gotten a good start on the bottle which was squirreled away in his desk somewhere.

"So what's this guy's thing, Hermann?" Conrad questioned while waiting for their drinks to arrive. "What is Frank Hayes doing sniffing around an area like this?"

Hermann took a long pull on his bourbon and stared at Conrad. Hell, if he could not confide in his old friend, he might as well just pack up and go home, he thought.

"Hayes is the majority partner in Black Granite, Conrad," he started. "Basically it's his company, with some other financial backing, of course. These guys are always looking for small mountains like ours."

"Why? They like losing money?" asked Conrad sarcastically.

"Nope. Do you have to chew ice like that?" Hermann said with the irritation of the past days showing in his voice.

"Yep," Conrad crunched louder. "So, go on."

"Nooooo, they like making money, lots of money," Hermann giggled. "The primary reason that we caught their attention is because all of the forestland up there is private. It's 'clean' Conrad. No forest leases of any kind. It makes us verrry special," he offered coyly.

Conrad was truly interested now and slid his chair closer to the table. "Why is that, old Buddy?" he questioned.

"Well, almost all the big areas are on Federal Forest Service leases," Hermann began. "You can develop the mountain facilities, you can even develop some of the real estate around it, but you can't privatize the mountain itself. It's illegal," he lectured.

"Okay, I get that part," Conrad nodded, "but why in the hell would you want to 'privatize a mountain' as you say? How in the world are you going to make any money if only a few special snobs can ski on it?"

Hermann signaled for another round, convinced that old Jim Beam would clarify his thinking, and he waited for the waitress to move respectfully away.

"Let me back up," he said after a long swallow. "First, what Black Granite does is buy the whole kit and caboodle. Then they put in a pretty high-end village at the base with all the nice little amenities which, you might have noted, we don't

have. Things like a couple of theme restaurants, some boo-
tiques, that kind of stuff," he burped.

"Big deal; you can do that anywhere," Conrad broke in.
"That doesn't sound like much of a way to make a few million
bucks. What if the ski business dries up, like it *always* does?"
he cautioned. "What if he doesn't sell any tickets? What happens then? Those few pretty shops of his aren't going to pay
the electric bills for his mountain, that's for damned sure," he
said assuredly.

"That's his trick, amigo," Hermann snapped his fingers.
"It's not *his* mountain, and he doesn't sell tickets. Mr. 'Big-
hearted' Hayes generously donates the entire ski area to a
homeowners association which he has formed for a whopping
$1.00."

Like a star mechanic listening to a pinging engine, Conrad
studied his friend to gauge the extent of the problem and pretty much found that Hermann was still functioning well
enough to continue.

"Oh, okay, he buys a mountain for a few million bucks;
then he drops a few more million into it; then he *gives* it away,"
he said cynically, "and we're supposed to consider this guy to
be brilliant, right? Sounds more like a lunatic to me," Conrad
concluded cynically.

"Doesn't *give* it away," Hermann clarified as though
Conrad was not listening "*donates* it for a buck."

Conrad was incredulous. "A buck... and that's not giving
it away?" he questioned.

"A buck makes a difference in the eyes of the law,
Conrad," Hermann offered slyly. "A buck *and a contract*
which gives him the exclusive development rights around the
area. Black Granite then goes about the process of subdivid-
ing all the land into house lots and condo complexes."

"Sounds like he already had that opportunity when he first
bought the place," observed Conrad.

"He did; but now he doesn't have the direct financial
responsibility for running the mountain operation. That
responsibility lies with a homeowners association which he

formed at the outset. That's the entity that he donated the land to," he clarified.

"Oh sure, he shoulders the burden for awhile, but it is self-limiting. Every sale reduces his responsibility a little bit less. As time progresses more and more of the burden shifts onto the ever-growing association."

"You mean he creates his own buyers right from the beginning?" Conrad asked, now crunching a little louder.

"Yep," Hermann said through a mouthful of peanuts. "Pretty soon Black Granite is left solely in the real estate development area and Hayes makes money on each and every house or condo that is sold. The last 25 percent of everything he builds, the really high end stuff, which he saved until the last, becomes pure profit."

Conrad's mouth worked furiously on the ice at the thought.

"Figure this, my man, and stop straining your little brain," Hermann laughed. "Out of every ticket we sell, 35 percent goes toward insurance of some kind. It's not cheap in this business. Another 35 percent goes toward the operation: salaries, upgrades, benefits, that sort of stuff. Another 20 percent goes to debt reduction because me and the banks are still very close friends. Now, if you didn't completely fail your math class, that leaves me with a 10 percent profit on each $35 ticket we sell. I make a lousy $3 dollars and 50 cents and half of that goes back to my partners." Hermann paused to take a long slug of his bourbon.

"We totaled somewhere around 150,000 skiers last year. You do the math, Conrad, and tell me if I'm getting rich here."

"Still sounds pretty good to me," Conrad retorted. "But then again, I'm a simple man."

"Conrad," Hermann stressed. "Black Granite will make my annual profit on the very first one or two homes which they sell after the association assumes full control: about five years. And I presume that Hayes will keep at least a dozen of the best lots in his back pocket for himself,"

Hermann concluded.

"What about the restaurant?" Conrad asked still trying to drive up his boss's profit. "You must make something there."

"The restaurant is successful if it pays for itself," Hermann instructed. "It's an amenity which we need to offer, basically a break-even operation."

"And if it's a bad snow year?" Conrad asked a bit bewildered, still trying to crash the plan, "Like *always* happens?"

"No difference to Black Granite, Conrad. Everybody who buys real estate from them must also join Hayes's little homeowner association and then pay annual social membership dues on top of that. Each of these equity memberships is then returned at 80 percent value when the property changes hands and 20 percent goes back to the association for upgrading facilities and more expansion. That, then in turn, increases everyone's value. Everybody wants to be in on the bottom floor of a Black Granite project because the first thing to skyrocket is the membership fee and then, as the club becomes more and more exclusive, the facilities become better and the real estate values shoot up, too. Etcetera, etcetera, etcetera," he beat a count with his empty glass on the table.

"Let me give you an example," Hermann said as he waved for another round. "Some hunting club, up in Wyoming I think, started with a membership fee of ten thousand bucks. Within five years, that fee doubled to a cool twenty thousand. The first guys in made a very respectable six grand: 12 percent annual return on their money. And they had some great fun to boot. That's better than most stocks in the market today, Conrad," he instructed.

"And that's just the membership fee," he continued. "They probably made much more than that with their own properties. Once Hayes announces that he is even contemplating a new development, the sales will start and will probably be sold out within the year."

Conrad stared at Hermann thoughtfully. "So, Hayes owns the village but leases it out long term to the association."

"Right," said Hermann.

"Then he sells the real estate as Black Granite, but the membership fees as the association and uses the member's own money to upgrade the facilities."

"Right again!" Hermann boomed in his best game show voice.

"And finally, correct me if I'm wrong here," Conrad eyeballed him, "Hayes controls the association until at least 51 percent of the real estate is sold, thereby directing the rise of the fees, the extent of the upgrades and ultimately the property values."

"Bingo!" Hermann popped a peanut.

"And, I gather, he's the broker, too, with a little exclusive office in the village, right? And that is why he holds the very best lots for last, the lots that he owns, and bought at the initial price."

"You're a sharp guy for a ski bum," Hermann smiled at him like a pet student.

"So, why can't we do this?" Conrad questioned

"Because I'm poor and you're old," he answered sardonically.

"Is any of this illegal?" Conrad asked hopefully.

"Not one bit of it, amigo," Hermann sighed.

"Okay, last hurdle in this rusty mind, then I think I'm going to go talk to my cows instead of *you*," Conrad crunched onward. "Why in the holy hell would someone want to lay out that sort of cash when they can just go ski at Park City or someplace?"

"Been to Park City lately, Conrad? Or Vail? Or Killington?" he laughed. "You should get out more often, my friend. It's kinda like a weekend in Disneyland. It's a bunch of sardines all packed up tight and fighting for some space." He took a long draw on his drink.

"Exclusivity, Conrad, *Exclusivity*," he emphasized, and

poked the cowboy with his finger. "People with the big bucks, the real bucks do not want to be rubbing flesh with the common folk. People like you," he kidded. "They pay and pay big for the opportunity to find service and solitude and keep away from you. Think about it: all the big exclusive country clubs are members only. And why are there so many of these mega-yachts around when those people could just book a first class cruise? The real money doesn't want to be around all those people and there is plenty of real money out there, too," he added.

"So why not the same for the ski business?" Hermann continued. "Why not the same for any outdoor business? It's a niche that we had not filled; until Black Granite found it."

"The skiing crowd seems to be a pretty small niche, though," Conrad said.

"Hayes isn't just about skiing, Conrad. He has taken this concept and used it to develop equestrian centers where you can ride thousands of acres alone and have the privilege of leaving your horse in a private stable at the end of the day; or use indoor riding rinks that you could never afford to own yourself.

He has developed hunting and fishing clubs where the only other people out there are the other wealthy homeowners and you have no fear of getting shot or hooked by some wild-eyed asshole. They stock and control their own game. Everyday is a trophy day, no matter what you're into, and everything Hayes develops is top notch. His reputation precedes him and people are waiting in line, money in hand, for his next specialized project."

"The land is disappearing before our eyes, Conrad," Hermann continued on bleakly. "They're talking seriously now of restricting access to the National Forests. They're literally being loved to death. Most of us can't afford thousands of acres to indulge our passions, but many of us can afford to share those thousands of acres with a limited number of people who also share our passions. It's quickly becoming evident that we can't have a quality experience on a public basis anymore, but we can still do it on a private basis."

"So, the great outdoors will eventually become the domain of the wealthy? Is that where this all leads?" Conrad asked.

"In many cases, yeah," Hermann concluded. "If you don't want to be trampled by the masses or hike through their trash. If you don't want to get run over by the RV's or subjected to the sight of begging bears, yeah."

"That sucks, Hermann," Conrad said resignedly.

"I know it sucks, Conrad. It is sad. But we have too many people trying to use a finite resource and the experience they are seeking just gets progressively cheapened every day."

"How to preserve the experience?" Hermann noted in contemplation. "That's the question that Frank Hayes must have had to ask himself and, to his arrogant credit, he found the answer. At least from the skiing side, Hayes saw that all the big mountains are on National Park Service land. It's public and he can't make it private. But if he finds private land, on a private ski area, then he can turn his little trick. I admit, there are few cases like us, but the mere fact of that helps to get Hayes's little ball of exclusivity rolling."

"All the small areas that the big guys had put out of business years ago are sitting there vacant," Hermann concluded, "and depending on what Hayes has to pay for the property determines just how exclusive it becomes. Hell those areas aren't dead, they're just taking a break and Frank Hayes is their new savior. He knows that he doesn't have the gnarly terrain of the big mountains, but he sacrifices that and replaces it with impeccable service, smooth as silk runs, and high-tech snowmaking. Conrad, these people have big money. They are quite naturally older. They have no desire to flash a double diamond bump run like a hotshot, but they sure as hell want a lobster for lunch, someone to know their name, and a cute kid to carry their skis or run them home on a snowmobile: a place for the family and grandkids to come and be treated to a first class experience."

Conrad drank his last drink in one long gulp. "And they don't sell any lift tickets?"

Hermann laughed at his old friend still trying to catch up to the strange concept.

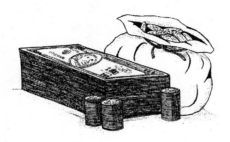

MARCH

Nothing that exists in the world of senses is everlasting: people die, marble crumbles, feelings fade, and everyday is fragile. We can therefore never have a true knowledge of anything that is in a constant state of flux. We can only have opinions based upon the time of the moment about inexact things that belong to the world of senses. These are tangible things. We can only have true knowledge of things that can be understood with our reason.

Jostein Gaarder

MARCH

*Men do change, and the change comes like the wind that
 ruffles the curtains at dawn, and it comes like the stealthy
 perfume of wildflowers hidden in the grass.*

John Steinbeck

Despite all of his assurances to Conrad that there was an
eager waiting line of wealthy investors simply salivat-
ing for the opportunity to throw money at Mount
Bellew, Hermann did not have any of those well moneyed
homeowners to support *him*. They were still in Black
Granite's future, not his. All Hermann had now was a group of
growing and angry locals screaming for his head on a platter.
There were wide-eyed environmentalists meeting with steely-
eyed traditionalists at the Town Hall. Liberals, conservatives,
and Green Party members were having pancake breakfasts
together and raising money for a campaign against him.
Grunged-out snowboarders were holding hands with even
grungier ranchers in candlelight vigils. People who had long
ago adopted Mount Bellew as their own personal place
adamantly did not want it to change at all.

Nothing brings people together like a common enemy,
and they were united in their outrage against Hermann Olsen
and his rumored plans. They applauded Mount Bellew and its
stagnation as being quirkily progressive. People who could
barely tolerate an occasional change in the menu were now
being asked to accept a major innovation in their midst. Worse

259

than that, the mountain was to become a private club from which they would be financially excluded. Hermann doubted that many even understood how that was going to happen. All they cared to understand was that they would lose their hill, a place they had come to believe they owned, and they were outraged at the insult.

This was a place where many had donned their very first pair of skis and where they now spent weekends with their grandkids. This was a place where Dad could share the joys of a downhill run with old friends without buying all the modern gear or stylish clothes. This was a place where Grandpa could still show them "how a really good skier does it" and, when you could not afford the restaurant lunch, you barbequed in the parking lot and shared a six-pack of beer on the tailgate of the truck. This was a place steeped in blue-collar tradition and one which was not planning on surrendering easily.

Mount Bellew was the comfortable old recliner, festooned with tears and stains, which the decorator always insists must be thrown out. The tenants however were having a problem with that.

It was inevitable that the "Save Mount Bellew" movement began and just as inevitable that Hermann Olsen (alias "The Traitor") was cast in the leading role of villain. Soon there were posters on the highways, signs on the cars, stickers on the chairlifts, and graffiti on the buildings—all of them hating Hermann and his plans.

Even the bathroom by his own office had been invaded with a "Fuck you, Hermann" scrawl on the wall which, try as he might, he could not wipe off. He secretly suspected his sweet secretary and recognized her handwriting, which gave him cause for concern at the depth of the rebellion. Hermann was not being seen as a victim here. He was being seen as a collaborator with the evil Black Granite people; their puppet, their dupe. And he became the lightening rod for all of the local frustrations and anger.

He sat in his office and thought, *I like these people. I've spent 10 great years with these people. I loved this mountain. This isn't my fault! Hell, I was just having coffee when this guy Hayes tried to buy me out. I haven't said "yes." This is all Hayes fault! The people should hate Hayes!*

Hermann was startled at the blare of the phone, as though a bomb had suddenly been lobbed into his office by a crazed eco-terrorist.

"Olsen, Frank Hayes here," the booming voice began abruptly. "So how are you handling the brouhaha down there? Got everything under control for us?"

Oh, nice personal touch, thought Hermann. *No "How's the family?" No "Nice weather we're having." No "Hope you're enjoying that case of wine I sent you." Us? Shit, when the hell did I join his gang? This guy should be putting out the fires which he started, not me. What a jerk.*

"Everything's fine down here, Frank," he said condescendingly. "Good to hear from you again," he lied. "Things are pretty calm, really, (*having the building "egged" certainly doesn't count*) A few signs here and there. (*Maybe they'll fire bomb my car next*), but I think the folks are kinda catching onto the benefits of the idea (*like working as waiters for rich assholes*). I'm sure that they'll appreciate all the new jobs which the project will bring in," he finished. (*They all like working for minimum wage.*)

"That's great, Olsen!" Hayes thundered over the phone. "Tell you what, let's get together in about two weeks and we'll start dealing with some final numbers. That sound okay with you?" he asked rhetorically.

There was a lengthy silence hissing at him through the line like a long distance snake.

"You still there, Olsen?" Frank thought that with Olsen you could never be sure.

"Sure, Frank," he responded. "I'm still here; just thinking."

"About what, Olsen? We got a problem?" Hayes asked aggressively.

"No problem, Frank." *This would be a good time to discuss things,* Hermann thought. Instead he said, "I'll make sure that

Pieter has everything in order and we'll set up a time." *Like I have a choice.*

"Good. We'll be in touch," Frank said with a sense of finality. "Take care of us down there Olsen and we'll see you later."

The echo of the abrupt cutoff rang in his head. *More of that "Us" and "We" crap. I bet the bastard doesn't even know my first name,* Hermann thought angrily. He hung up the phone and realized that he really did not like this guy Hayes all that much, just his money.

Hell, he thought, *I'm nothing more than a prostitute for Frank 'fucking' Hayes. He acts like all of this is a done deal and I'll just jump at the smell of his money. What pisses me off most is that he's probably right. Everybody I know is mad at me and I haven't even done anything yet. They hate me just because of the rumors. What happens when I actually sell the place?*

Hermann morosely settled into a long and catatonic contemplation of self-pity. He was trying to work himself into a better mood, more decisive action, by daydreaming about just how he could spend all that money, when the speaker on his desk jolted him from the deck of his new yacht and back into the cold water of reality at Mount Bellew.

"Hermann," his secretary squawked from the box, "Bobbi O'Donnell is here and wants to know if she can see you for a few minutes."

"Sure," said Hermann, "send her on in." *And stay out of my bathroom…*

Looking at Bobbi would definitely cheer him up and as she floated into his office like a warm breeze on a pleasant day, Hermann found himself bounding to his feet and smiling in greeting.

"Bobbi, you don't know how good it is to see you today, or any day for that matter. Take a seat," he offered. "What brings you up here to consult with the god of Mount Olympus?" he teased.

Hermann loved to banter with his employees, but Bobbi was a definite favorite, never giving an inch in their exchanges.

"Oh Hermann, you know, every once in awhile I have a craving for a handsome, rugged individualist; a real man, not one of those little boys down there on earth." She could flirt shamelessly and Hermann ate up every minute of it.

"Sorry girl, I'm not your type," he acted as though he was letting her down easy. "I'm way too powerful, and besides, I'm already involved with at least a dozen other women. You'll just have to wait your turn; perhaps if you take a number on your way out."

"Don't want a number, sweetie, but I will take a cup of that coffee," she said indicating the pot with a nod of her head.

"I'm sorry, Bobbi," Hermann bolted quickly back to his feet, "I'm forgetting my manners."

"Now the truth, sweetheart; what's on your pretty little mind?" he said as he fixed their cups.

"Hermann," she began a bit hesitantly, "rumors are flying everywhere out there and some of them aren't very nice. You're my boss, but you're my friend, too. Hermann, what the *hell* is happening around here?"

One thing about Bobbi, she was a woman that could get to the point. Hermann respected that and so, as they drank their coffee together, he laid the whole thing out for her, just as he had done with Conrad.

The truth can't be half as bad as the rumors being passed around, he thought.

Bobbi listened patiently, asked a few pointed questions here and there, but generally just let her boss talk it all out. When he had finished, they quietly stared at each other for awhile, neither knowing quite where to go next.

"My father belonged to clubs like that," she finally said. "It's kind of what I thought was going on. Could you tell me what Black Granite offered you for this place?" she inquired.

"That's supposed to be confidential Bobbi, besides, there is no final offer yet," he hedged.

"About how much Hermann?" she pressed him.

"About as much as I've ever dreamed of in my life," he joked. "Want to go on a cruise? I'd get a lot more respect with a beautiful young woman on my arm."

"Not just now, Hermann," Bobbi sighed seriously.

Hermann sensed that his frivolous banter had become tedious to her and it brought all of his old depression crashing back into him again. "Bobbi, this is business," he said rather sadly in way of explanation. "I just can't tell you that."

"And, Hermann, this is business," she said seriously. "This is business too."

"What kind of business?" he questioned with curiosity.

"Ski business, Hermann," she said flatly. "I'm prepared to make an offer, but you need to be honest with me."

Hermann was floored and stared at her in stunned silence.

"An offer? I think that you better go on," was all he managed to squeak out as he closed the door.

"Mr. Olsen," she began formally. "As you know, I have some family money. Not enough, I'm sure, but I also have other financial connections. My father left me pretty well off.

Unfortunately he also left me with nothing to do," she said much more softly now.

"He died when I was 21. He gave me all the good things that money could buy in life but he didn't leave me the things that were most important. He didn't leave me all the things inside of himself that made him so wonderful. He was feisty. He was independent. In some ways, you remind me of him," she teased. "Daddy persevered in a business that everyone else thought was foolish. He always told me of how he pulled himself up from his own bootstraps, and yet when he died, all he left me was a pile of money. He didn't leave me any bootstraps for myself, or the instructions that go with them."

Bobbi's eyes now glistened over at the thoughts of her father, but she continued resolutely onward. "Hermann, it's like he left me with a big pile of bricks, and no mortar to put them together. I know I've been pretty flaky over the last few years, trying to throw enough money around in order to feel useful, but most of it was just bullshit," she stated honestly. "This is the first time that I think that I can really do some good. I think I've learned a lot about Bobbi O'Donnell here at

Mount Bellew. I think that I'm ready to fly on my own. I believe that I want to buy this mountain. I just didn't know that it was for sale."

Hermann swallowed hard, old memories gnawing at the corners of his mind, "Neither did I, Bobbi," he said. "Neither did I."

"You know, honey," he continued. "I think your daddy's still alive and well inside of you. Don't shortchange yourself. I see all sorts of bootstraps. Now, let's be business people and you tell me what's on your mind," he said as he refilled their cups.

Then they grinned at each other like co-conspirators about to outfox the fox.

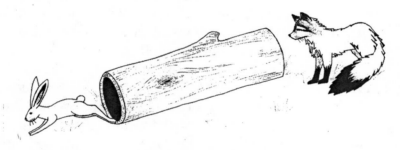

"This is a poker game that we have going on here," Hermann explained. "Hayes says the area will be worth between five and seven million. He's full of shit. He just wants to wet my whistle," Hermann added cynically. "Let's say I fold at the low end of five, and resign myself to a smaller yacht," he laughed.

"That is still a lot," Bobbi countered slyly. "More than it is worth."

"Oh?" he said vaguely.

"Obviously you know what he plans to do with it," she continued. "He plans to turn it into an exclusive country club for fellow high rollers."

"Yep," he shrugged. "I guess if it's his, he can do with it what he wants."

"Does that bother you, Hermann?" Bobbi asked.

"Yep," he said again, "but not enough to pass up five million bucks. I'll move out, pay off the banks, the locals will hate me, but I'll be gone fishing." Hermann was taking the hard line now.

"You're full of it yourself, Hermann, and you know it!" she countered sharply. "These people are your friends. Hell, they are *more* than that; they are your only family. You don't have anyone else you care for, or anyone else who cares for you as much as the people of this town," she lectured. "You run out of here under these conditions and you will be a miserable and lonely old coot for the rest of your rich life. No one can possibly be happy if they act against their better judgment. Do you believe that you can live a happy life if you do things that you know deep down are wrong?" she questioned the now thoughtful Hermann. "A person who knows what is right will do right, because why would anybody choose to be unhappy?"

"Hermann," she went on, "we both know people who lie and cheat and speak maliciously of others behind their backs, but are they aware that these things are not right or fair? If they don't, then they are ignorant, they are sad cases of humanity. And if they do, then they are unforgivably evil. You are neither, Hermann Olsen," she concluded, wagging her finger at him. "You already know what is right here. Do you choose to be unhappy?"

Like a slap in the face awakening him to something that he had already known, Hermann looked at her, shocked that she had reached into him so deeply.

"Damn! I'm rich, too," she continued, "but I've never been as rich until I met Mount Bellew; a place that *you* created, a place where you belong. It's like you're willing to throw your own child to the wolves!" she said in disgust.

Her endless black eyes stared into him as though seeking his very soul. "Is that you in there, Hermann, or only a shadow? I'm having trouble seeing you now."

Hermann stared back for a long moment, his heart and his conscience fighting for space in his mind, then he sadly chuckled, "Okay, tough girl. Where's your counter offer, then? And be nice, I feel very fragile right now."

The afternoon was fading into alpenglow, the evening sun setting behind the clouds when Bobbi, relaxed into her chair, no longer afraid of her proposal, and said, "I think I can get five and maybe, with some innovation, even the seven," she finally offered.

"Aw, hell," Hermann winced. "This boat just keeps getting smaller and smaller, and now it's a *maybe*. Pretty soon I'll have one of those goofy sit-on-top kayaks with nobody to row the damned thing."

"No. Listen!" she chirped, warming to the subject at hand now.

"I, and some of the family friends, would form a Limited Liability Corporation. Bear in mind now, Hermann, that anybody I'm talking about here are financially comfortable trust babies like myself or some powerful compadres that still owe my daddy old favors," she continued. "We don't need an immediate return on our money to live on. We're here for the long term. Even a small return keeps everyone happy and the bragging rights that they own part of a ski area makes them feel important at cocktail parties. To them that's even more important than the money," Bobbi smiled sardonically.

"What's your profit margin here, Hermann," she pressed on, now warming to her subject, "ten maybe fifteen percent?"

"Somewhere around there," offered Hermann coyly.

"And I would presume that half of that is going back to your partners?" she concluded.

Hermann nodded in dejection, "Unfortunately, yes."

"Okay then," she grabbed at the yellow legal tablet on his desk. "Since it seems that you're going to have me make all the presumptions here, let me presume this..."

Bobbi began to scrawl furiously on the pad, listing numbers as her mind ran on: "150,000 skiers at $35 bucks a ticket; that's no secret. The restaurants don't pay. I know that Hermann, so don't try to con me," she warned. "Gross revenue of about $5,250,000: 35 percent of that goes to insurance and another 35 percent goes back into the operation: 20 percent goes into debt reduction: 5 percent goes to Hermann's partner and 5 percent goes to Hermann. Hermann takes home about $260,000 for all of his work and risk," she noted sadly, looking at the truth on the tablet before her.

"So, how am I doing so far?" she eyed the owner.

"Pretty good. Sounds like you've either done your homework, have been snooping in my desk, or are sleeping with my accountant," he teased. "Keep going."

"Can't," Bobbi said. "Can't until you give me a number that only you would know."

"And what would that be?" he said secretively.

"What do you owe the banks, the principle on the debt reduction?" she said directly.

"Pencil in two million," he said throwing up his hands like a man giving up the keys to the safe.

"Okay then, Mr. Olsen," she leaned back in her chair, now satisfied. "My partners and I come in with two million in cash in order to get the banks off of your back. We then pay you as our senior consultant an annual salary of $300,000 for the next ten years. That's more than you make now for a hell of a lot less aggravation," She added. "You tell me that your partner has indicated that he will bolt out of here for a cool million for his share. Will you do the same?" she asked.

"Yes, I would," said Hermann directly.

"Then, there is four million bucks that I just spent upfront," she calculated, "and another three million spaced over the next ten years. That's about the high end of the offer that you said you would accept from Hayes, and it buys me some time. Without the 20 percent bank debt, my group will have enough profit to pay each of the investors a decent return. Like I said, we're here for the long term and that's what I'm counting on."

"It all sounds good, Bobbi," Hermann said, "but the final three million is risky; more risky for you than it is for me," he advised. "I don't want to see you get into trouble over this. I'd rather see Hayes fall on his fat old butt than you on your pretty young one."

"Hermann, anytime within the ten years, if we go under, I'll guarantee the balance due to you out of my own trust fund, and, if anyone 'falls on her butt' as you say, then I'll be happy knowing that I gave it a shot," she said sincerely. "I need my own time in the sun, Hermann. And I believe that this is it."

Hermann studied the young woman's open face. She was not scared. She returned his gaze unwaveringly. Her eyes shone with the confidence and idealism of youth. *Maybe this is what Mount Bellew needs,* he thought. *A new fire to bring the snows back to life again. Maybe I've been here too long. Maybe it's time to move on. I wonder if my eyes ever glowed with that enthusiasm. I wonder where or when I lost it.*

A soft tapping began on the windowpanes and filled the silence of the space which had come between them.

"Rain," said Hermann flatly.

"Yes," said Bobbi.

"I suppose that means that this season will be coming to a close soon," he added.

"It also means that spring is on the way," she said optimistically.

"So it is," agreed Hermann.

"Listen, Bobbi," he said as softly as the gentle rain. "When I came here in 1972, I wasn't looking for money, or an investment, or an opportunity. I was looking for a place to hide from my parents and from my responsibilities. This was a good place," he remembered with contentment. "The rest just evolved around me. Suddenly, I'm some sort of big shot and I never planned it that way. It just rolled over me."

He stared into a past which was pasted on the ceiling only for him to see.

"Anyway, when I bought the place, there was an old dog named Petunia, who was satisfied to lay under the table, get fat, love everyone. She seemed happy to let the world revolve and change around her. I loved that dog," he said. "She was kind of like a spiritual anchor for me—what I wanted to be, simple and content; a canine guru in an ever-changing world. She never judged, she never aspired to any greatness, she just

269

flowed through her life and accepted whatever was thrown her way."

Bobbi sat quietly and listened to Hermann's voice blend musically with the rain.

"The day Petunia died I carried her up to the meadow and buried her there among all the flowers and pines and animals that she loved so well. It took me a long time to leave that meadow that day. I wanted to stay with her. I wanted nothing to change, but had to face the fact that all things do. Death comes to all of us and change, in so many subtle forms, is always present."

"So," Hermann said clearing his throat from the tears forming there, "she left a pup here. That was Daisy, you know. Erik kind of adopted Daisy and the two made the most out-standing pair. Erik all puffed out and efficient and important," Hermann mimicked. "He tried to control every aspect of every day; yet steadfastly beside him ambled old Daisy just doing her thing in her laid back way, never wanting much except affection and food, lots of food," he now laughed.

"She became an avalanche dog because we *wanted* her to be an avalanche dog. Then Erik learned, just as I learned. We learned more from the example of a pair of avie dogs than they ever learned from us, damn it." Hermann cursed and paused to control the rising emotion in his voice.

"Erik learned from Daisy, just as I learned from Petunia," he continued, "learned that all of this really doesn't matter." He indicated nothing with a wave of his hand. "We saw that by being simple, accepting the life that we've been given, accept-ing the people that we deal with, accepting it all, and then dealing with it in good faith, is the most important lesson. And the changes—both good and bad—will happen as they will, in their own time."

"There is your life, Bobbi, and it means nothing to any-body except yourself. Like you said before, did you choose to be happy? I also believe that you can, you know." Hermann leaned toward her now. "Every day there are decisions. And every decision has some sort of consequence; some more monumental than others, but consequences nevertheless. Everything our senses reveal to us flows in continual changes. Hell, we *can not* control things," he emphasized. "We don't *need* to control everything. Only a fool believes that he can. We can only deal with them in good faith and choose to be happy."

"The dogs seem to know it," he continued, "so why can't we, with all of our intellect, know the same. Our graveyards are full of dead men and women, none of whom were able to control their fate or their inevitable demise. Many of them probably went to their deaths wondering 'Why me? How could this have happened to me? I was special. I was important. I was in control of things.'"

"Bullshit," Hermann now murmured to himself. "Steve Donahue didn't want to die that day. It just happens. It happens to the young, to the old, to the best of them, and to the wicked. Anyway, Daisy died, too. So what? It happens everywhere. What was more important was that Erik came back and, against my orders, fired up a chairlift and rode her back up to the meadow: knowing instinctively that she belonged there. It was an act of defiance, totally out of character for Erik," he pointed out for the now engrossed Bobbi.

"That one moment of rebellion did more to make him a man than all the 'yessirs' and 'nosirs' in the years before. Maybe something in her passing spirit inspired him to do the right thing in spite of the consequences."

Hermann's eyes streamed with tears now as he quietly said, "I am so glad that he did. I have the feeling that he will have a chance to become a good man; because of a good dog that never gave up on him."

"And now, Bobbi, I have the same decision," Hermann said looking intently into her eyes. "Do I follow my heart or do I follow my mind? Do I make good business by taking Black Granite's assured offer; or do I do what is right and risk your rather shaky one? Do I depend on others to tell me how happy I must be for being so smart and so rich, or do I hear people say, 'he had it all... and then made a bad deal'?"

"What do *you* think?" he questioned. "Do I do what is simple and right, or do I complicate my life with greed? Do I choose to be happy? What would the dog do, Bobbi?" he added with a slight wry smile.

The quiet filled the room while the ticking of Hermann's old railroad clock on the wall pounded the air with sound.

"Well, Hermann, what do you do?" whispered Bobbi back to him. "Now, I don't care anymore because I understand that your decision is out of my control."

"But I care, Bobbi," Hermann emphasized. "I care because a long time ago a man offered me a chance to follow my own dream, a chance to fly out of the cage; even when I didn't know what the dream meant or where it would lead me.

"I liked that man," he thought aloud. "He had a wisdom which we don't see much of anymore. I always thought that I would want to be like that man someday. He didn't charge me much to live in my dream, just the cost of admission, just what the dream was worth and it wasn't worth much, I'll tell you that! The ticket was cheap, Honey," he rasped conspiratorially. "I didn't pay much for this place going in, and I believe that it would be wrong to charge much going out. My reward has been all the fun and joy I had in building it. I probably owe that old man more than any other man I have ever dealt with," he continued, "but I never knew how to repay him, because I never knew where he went. Disappeared like a genie back into his bottle."

Hermann stared into the open space above her head. "Maybe, just now, I finally know what the real price would be: something called integrity."

"I once told that man that, when the time came, I wanted to see if I could do the right thing," he said with excitement, as though seeing a revelation. "I thought that I was talking about facing my failures. It seems now that I was talking about defining my success."

All of this was complicated and foreign in Bobbi's mind, but she instinctively knew that Hermann was arguing himself toward a decision, and she let him rattle on.

"Sweetheart," Hermann finally bubbled, "I don't think I want to depend on other people for their definition of my own god damn happiness. I'll tell you what we do:" Hermann was on a roll now, "you get your package together and I tell Frank 'fucking' Hayes to kiss my old ass. Then you sign a contract that says you'll never develop anything in my Daisy meadow, or anywhere near it."

"It would scare my dogs, you know," he added. "I won't back off on that, girl," he warned. "I'll have it in the contract."

"Can you live with *that*, Bobbi?" Hermann inquired as he held out his hands, "because it's all that I honestly have."

"Not only can I live with it Mr. Olsen," Bobbi beamed at him, "I respect it. I'd have it no other way. The Daisy meadow will be our tribute to the simplicity and beauty of an ever changing life. Write it up. Ironclad. I'll sign it!" she ordered. "Matter-of-fact, make it a contingency for any future owners. The meadow stays," Bobbi smiled, "as a symbol of Mount Bellew and a tribute to you."

"No Bobbi, as a tribute to all of us," Hermann corrected her. "This is about all of us."

"What the hell!" He finally boomed. "I never figured I'd get seven million for this place anyway! I guess I could learn to paddle the kayak myself if it all falls through. The exercise would do me good!"

He began to ramble on, now excited with the new prospect. "I would despise the idea of everyone hating me. Besides," he whispered conspiratorially now, "I really abhor that self-important ass, Hayes. And you gotta promise that I get free drinks whenever I come up here to ski or visit you guys," he laughed, now on a roll. "And I'm not paying for a lift ticket either!"

How can people be smiling so broadly and have tears streaming down their faces at the same time? Somehow it seems a contradiction. How can life be such an enigma?

Just when you think that you have it all worked out, just when you start enjoying it all, just when you have it all under control, it makes you cry.

"Screw the money!" Hermann yelled. "Maybe I'll just get a fishing boat for me and Conrad."

"Oh, Hermann, thank you, thank you, thank you," Bobbi bubbled. "You are a sweet, sweet man and I love you."

"No, Bobbi, thank *you*. I think you just saved me from myself. This will work. We all win."

"And now Mr. Olsen, thanks to you, I have got about a zillion things to do," said Bobbi as she leaned across the old desk to kiss Hermann on the cheek.

"I think my father would have been proud to call you his friend," she whispered as she pulled away from the embrace.

Hermann pretended not to hear.

"Will you be telling Frank Hayes soon?" she added.

"Bobbi, I'm going to thoroughly enjoy telling that pompous asshole that I sold my area to a pretty woman just for the sake of love," Hermann kidded. "He'll think that I am absolutely nuts, which is just fine by me. I've got a reputation to keep up you know. Hermann Olsen…'Senile Old Coot'… and loving it! Want to try my chair?" he asked playfully.

"Not just yet, Hermann," she tried to calm him down. "You know, you're a hell of a guy," she beamed at him.

A slush began to fall from the darkening sky, coming down harder now, a mixture of snow, sleet, and rain. It was as though the weather was having trouble making up its mind as to which season it wished to turn. Hermann had moved to the window and was contemplating the coming storm on the darkening mountain.

"Take care that you run around the big drops, Bobbi, so you don't get too wet," he said, apparently to himself, not really about the weather. "It's going to get serious out there now."

"And you know what that means," she said moving behind him.

"Spring?" Hermann answered like a bright student.

"Yes," Bobbi smiled at him, "new beginnings."

"Yes." Hermann agreed. "Wonderful new beginnings."

"Goodbye, Bobbi," Hermann said as he opened the door for her. "And you know," he called after the departing woman down the hall, "I believe that you got a lot of your Old Man in you. Wish I had met him. I think he would have been a hell of a friend to have. Bet you're a lot prettier, though."

With that, Bobbi O'Donnell waved and walked out of the office knowing, only to herself, that she was going to be the next COO of a small fading ski area, with questionable clientele, unreliable personnel, and a meadow dedicated to some old dogs.

Isn't life great! she thought to herself and turned her face up to the dripping sky.

APRIL

"The time has come," the Walrus said, "to talk of many things:
    of shoes—and ships—and ceiling wax,
    of cabbages and Kings-
    And why the sea is boiling hot—
    And whether pigs have wings.

Lewis Caroll
The Walrus and the Carpenter

APRIL

I'm off to see someplace Magic; and so, I really don't want to stay of course...

Harry Potter

The flyers had been posted around the locker room, throughout the town, and in the restaurants for almost a month now.

they announced.

they shouted.

279

they importantly heralded.

Various brightly colored banners, all advertising the same impending orgy.

The annual event of debauchery was the social highlight of the season for a group of individuals well known for their ability to socially debauch. The Prom had survived brawls, protests, the Vietnam War and two or three small fires. It was held near the end of the ski season, when spring filled the air and mud season was imminent. Most of the serious skiing customers had since turned their thoughts to the golf courses and tennis courts of the lowlands and had departed the sloppy ridges of Mount Bellew.

Those clients who still visited would not recognize a good ski lesson from a police interrogation and everyone without exception realistically expected that lousy ski conditions and poor service would be the penalty endured for the deeply discounted lift tickets. That seemed to be a pretty good justification to slack off and so most of the remaining employees felt quite comfortable in pursuing the gargantuan hangovers promised by the Prom. The pounding headaches, sour stomachs, and gruff attitudes would persist for a week thus adding to the ambiance of spring skiing.

The Prom had actually originated many years ago, in the

very early days of the original Mount Bellew. It was adopted as a means of defense for the skiing cowboys who grew tired of their females whining a constant wail of, "We never get to dress up and go out anywhere," or, "We always do the same old stupid stuff."

The men concluded that a formal dance where they could really get blasted with their friends struck just the right note of compromise. The girls would have the opportunity to dress up for each other, shave their legs for a reason, and the guys got to do the same "stupid stuff" (i.e. get drunk). Both agreed that it was certainly a welcome break from the never-ending barbecues.

And so the "Mount Bellew Cotillion and Ball" was launched, and like a defective rocket to space, spinning in lunatic circles, it never came down.

"The Cotillion" was not like one of those stuffy Wall Street black tie affairs where rich people never sweat. Oh no. It was not like one of those phony office parties thrown at the end of the year either, where everybody pretended to like each other. People got beat up at this party.

And it certainly was not a sedate and intellectual sort of art gallery opening where people stroll around and give intelligent and well informed opinions. As a matter of fact, a bit of local art often got destroyed in the process; and intelligent opinions were generally not well received.

What "The Prom" was, what it prided itself on, was a Mad Magazine parody of all those other parties. Season-long grudges were often settled by large men uncomfortably stuffed into rented tuxedos. Undying friendships (very often declared by the same now disheveled and bleeding men) were drowned in strong glasses of liquor. One night stands and sexual fantasies were finally secured. Spontaneous table dancing, featuring both male and female performers, were a standard ritual, and the occasional food fight tolerated.

Hearts were broken, teeth were broken, glasses were broken, tables buckled under the weight, and all ended up shattered in the debris of the new morning. Many of the tuxes had to be bought from the store due to "irreparable damage."

Pretty much of a damn good party.

"Gentlemen," Pieter was laboring on at the end of the weekly meeting, "I don't think that this Prom is such a good idea. Let us look at the liability we are incurring here if something goes wrong. Every year we stick our necks out a little bit further for this crazy thing and I don't think it is necessary."

"Oh come on, Pieter," Conrad argued, "These kids have worked hard for us all year long and now they deserve to blow off a little steam. I believe that we're covered for most of the shit that they could break."

"Oh yeah, Conrad," Pieter taunted, "what about if they break themselves? You of all people know that most of these kids have the maturity level of high school ruffians. Nothing good is going to come out of this thing," he warned with finality.

"The good that will come out if it, the good that comes out of it every year, is that it is damn good for the morale around here!" Conrad growled. "*Especially* this year," he emphasized. "These kids have put together a tribute to Steve which they want to present. They need to get this out of their system. They need to have closure. This should be a time in their lives that they'll always remember with relish, not with dread."

"And if we go ahead with this thing, if it looks like we are the ones sponsoring it, then I'm telling you, we are the ones that are going to regret it the most when it all goes bad. How about the cost, Conrad? What is this all going to cost us?" Pieter pressed on, hoping to shift the argument into an arena which he could dominate.

"Okay guys, enough," broke in Hermann wearily. He had grown tired of the same arguments being hashed over every day. "It's getting late, and my mind is already made up. First, I don't care about the cost. It can't be that much. The kids have their Goober Jug money which they are always eager to throw in and then I'll cover the rest. Second, this Cotillion is a tradition which I rather like and, until I have a real reason to shut it down," he emphasized, "I don't plan to. Hell, I'd feel like Santa Claus canceling Christmas."

"Okay," Pieter shrugged in defeat, "but what about security? What do we do to keep all the little monkeys in line? This thing could turn into a complete brawl," he added in dire warning, still hoping to convince Hermann.

"You have a point there, Pieter," Hermann conceded "and what I'm going to do is to hire two or three of the local grenadier to make a presence and then pay a couple of those big liftees out there to work as bouncers."

"Conrad, you want a party," he winked, "then your job is to keep them all in line. No runaway monkeys. Don't give me the reason that Pieter is looking for here to shut this down."

"Does that satisfy your concerns?" Hermann addressed Pieter. "Conrad gets his little barn burner, and now he is responsible. Something goes wrong and we get to chew on his butt. And nobody will chew on it harder than me," he said looking sternly at Conrad.

"We'll be downright angelic, Boss," Conrad smiled from his chair. "I promise you," he added seriously noting Hermann's scowl.

"Pieter?" Hermann questioned.

"I guess so," Pieter whined like a child not having his way, "but put me down as being against this thing from the start."

"Yes, Pieter," Hermann said sarcastically as he rose to his feet. "We'll remember that you were against it...again. Now if that is all, I guess this meeting is over and I can go home and feed the dog."

"That's all I have," Pieter said crisply while tiding up the papers before him.

He liked to pretend that it was his meeting and got to close it whenever he wished.

"Good. See you both tomorrow," Hermann concluded as he strode out of Pieter's office. "And pray for snow. It's getting pretty thin out there."

Conrad quietly shut the door behind the departing Hermann and said, "Pieter, do you mind if you and I have a word together?"

"Well, since it doesn't look like I have much of a choice, sure. Have any seat," Pieter indicated to the couple of empty chairs.

"I need to know something," Conrad began while pulling up a chair close to the desk. "I need to know why you are so against these things. Not just *this* thing, this party, but all of these things: a keg of beer at the end of a hard week, the kid's Goober Jug, the safety meetings which always turn into sledding contests...all that stuff? Why do you and I have to wrestle over every employee issue?" he asked

Pieter quietly watched him through pale blue eyes devoid of any expression.

"It seems that you're just mad at us all the time," Conrad confronted him. "Why is that, Pieter?"

"I thought that this was going to be about something on the mountain," Pieter started defensively. "Some sort of business, Conrad, not about me or whether you think I have a problem or not."

"It *is* business, Pieter," Conrad emphasized. "It's my business to make this operation run smoothly out there and you're always a speed bump in my way. What *is* your problem, man?" he stressed.

Antagonized now, Pieter stared cold and blankly at the man before him. "My 'problem' as you put it, my friend..." he began.

"First!" Conrad's voice cut him off in mid-sentence and cracked like a bullwhip commanding attention, "cut your crap! Do not ever refer to me as your 'Friend'! Save that condescending tone for your employees. My friends are few and far between. If we ever became friends, and that seems very doubtful, then I'll let you know."

Pieter, flushed into silence as though his words had been strangled by the strong hands before him, stared angrily at the old rancher, hating him, hating what he stood for, but not daring to cross him.

"Now, let's try again," Conrad said softly, encouragingly,

as though he was trying to regain his patience. "I'm a simple man, Pieter. Try to humor me and keep it simple so that an ill-educated old fool can understand it. That *is* what you think of me, isn't it?" He asked slyly, already knowing the answer.

"Pretty much so, you bastard," Pieter replied coolly. He knew that in any argument he could give it out as well as take it; as long as it did not turn to violence. Pieter never wanted to push a physical man like this too far.

"If you *need* simple, then we will be simple," he sneered.

"Those 'things' that you're always talking about," he continued, "all the little nice social events and party games that you want to play with your employees," his shaking hands lit his cigarette in the pause of the moment, "I *hate* them," he hissed out with the smoke, like a dragon rousing from his sleep. "I hate them because they are a distraction to the business around here. I hate them mostly because I don't belong at them. I hate them because they're silly, and I hate them because…because…" he paused not knowing whether to continue in this way.

Pieter nervously took another deep drag on his cigarette to steady himself, "Because I'm always standing alone. Standing alone and hearing people talking about me, but nobody is ever talking to me. I don't belong at them and I don't belong to them," he said with his voice rising with emotion.

"To who, Pieter?" Conrad now said questioningly.

"To *all* of you!" Pieter shouted now. "I haven't been a part of this whole group since I arrived here! I'm always the Big Bad Wolf who has to blow the whistle on all the bad boys around here so it doesn't all get out of control," he said more calmly now.

"God knows you're not going to do it," he sneered contemptuously.

"So, who gave you that job?" Conrad said mildly amused, not rising to the bait.

"Nobody *gave* me the job, Conrad," Pieter countered importantly, as though instructing a small child. "It came with the position."

"The position is what you make of it, man. I've known plenty of men with far greater 'positions' than yours that were at least able to act with a sense of humanness."

"Humanness?" Pieter spat out. "What about some humanness or respect for my feelings?" he said incredulously. "Now Conrad, *you* cut the crap!" he snapped and Conrad fell into silence.

"Look at me, Conrad," Pieter commanded, leaning over the desk toward him. "You know what I am? I'm a damn freak around here," he continued. "I'm presuming that I don't need to tell you that I'm gay, and if that is the first time you've heard that so-called 'rumor,' then I'll be more shocked than you. Everybody knows it and everybody makes fun of it."

"I've heard it," Conrad conceded, "and I guess I'm as guilty as anybody else."

"Good, then we can save time," Pieter angrily snubbed out the cigarette. "I'm a little fag in a whole herd of macho cowboys who couldn't verbalize the difference between a flan and a buffalo steak. I dress neatly because I like to dress neatly. I speak properly because it is correct and it pleases me. I actually bathe twice a day instead of once a god damn week, because I don't find stinking to be attractive. I have a boyfriend in Chicago who I see on occasion, and who is more attractive than most of the bimbos around here. And for all of that, Conrad…they hate me!" he concluded.

"I have power here," Pieter continued in defiance to his slowly blinking antagonist, "and if the bastards want to make me miserable because of whom I am, then I'll make them equally miserable because of whom I am."

"I don't belong here," he now said quietly, "but I'll be damned if I'm going to be forced out by a crowd like this; not yet at least."

Silence filled the air and the only sound was the sound of their mutual breathing.

"Well, at least we got *that* out on the table," Conrad said leaning away from the desk.

"Yeah," Pieter now indicated an imaginary gift on his desk, "there it is, and now what are we going to do about it?"

"Most likely nothing." Conrad concluded. He did not know where to go with this conversation anymore. He was grasping at straws. "Pieter, have you ever gotten out of this office and opened your eyes to what is around us out there?" he questioned while waving at the mountains outside the window. "Have you ever really seen what kind of show we are running here?"

"Besides a three ring circus, I would have no idea what you mean," Pieter said guardedly.

"Yeah. A circus! That's *exactly* what it is," Conrad noticeably brightened to the idea.

"Look at them. Look at me. Look at the people we have here," he started. "We're all some sort of freaks! Everybody I know at this mountain seems to be running away from somebody or something. Running away to the circus; like Toby Tyler did in the movie! Do you think that we've chosen to live at Mount Bellew because we even remotely belong to that other world out there?" Conrad asked. "No sir! We're in The Land of Misfit Toys, and I'm just the defective clown guarding the gate," he continued on happily now. "Hell, I've got kids who are running away from their families and the families in most cases don't even care where the kids are. I've got people running away from their own money, in order to "find themselves" as they say, so as not to be defined by their wealth. And I have some really stupid ones who think they'll get rich here, and they're really pathetic," he quietly chuckled. "I even have a defecting hockey player from the Czech Republic, who I think has a crush on me, and at least half a dozen who think they *might* be gay but want the opportunity to figure it all out.

"Shit," Conrad said openly laughing now, "I even have at least another six who think that Ted Kosinski, the Unabomber, is a folk hero, and our owner is a guy who still has never made peace with his family; but I have hopes."

"We're some shining example of moral fortitude, eh Pieter?" he snorted. "Hell, next to most of these people, you appear to be the most normal."

"Okay, tough guy;" Pieter said, convinced that he was not going to be falsely charmed by this man, "What about the clown guarding the gate?"

"Clown?" Conrad repeated, forgetting his analogy.

"Yeah you," Pieter challenged. "What is it that he is running away from? I can't believe that you were sent here like some sort of archangel just to guard all of us freaks."

Conrad had not expected such a personal question. After all, this was about Pieter's problem, not his. He settled softly into his chair while he studied the man before him.

"I suppose that's a fair enough question," he conceded. "Since we're trying to be candid with each other."

The wary rancher reached for the pack of cigarettes on the desk and the smoke, exhaled through his nostrils, wreathed his head in a cloud.

"I didn't have far to run," Conrad began, "and when I ran, I ran in the other direction. I ran from a dirt poor ranch house where there never was enough money to feed or clothe five kids. I ran from an alcoholic father that would take turns beating on each of us, my mom included. I thought that I could prove to everybody how tough I was; scare the Old Man away from me. I thought that I could take these legs and just ski away."

Conrad's eyes focused on a point far more distant than the wall, a point that only he could see in the past. "I thought that I could ski down a hill so fast that nothing, or nobody, would ever touch me again."

"Well, that didn't happen," he now shrugged in resignation. "As they say, 'duty called,' and I thought that the Marine Corps was where all the tough guys went, so that's where I went. I was going to be a big hard-ass Marine, full of muscle and brawn; nobody would ever beat me again. The Old Man was going to respect me. He'd lay off the kids and Mom in fear of me. At least that's what I thought; that was my plan."

Conrad exhaled a long stream of smoke into the distance. "Then I ran straight into Vietnam. I ran into the beating of my life, into a beating that made my Old Man's blows look like love taps," his eyes faded painfully into the past as he continued to smoke slowly.

"I wasn't ready," he finally said in quiet resignation. "There were things that I saw that I don't ever want to remember. Things that I did that I don't ever want to recall: things that I won't ever forget, but will always deny ever happened."

"You know, Pieter," he said almost inaudibly now. "I don't think I've ever had a week since returning from that stinking war that I don't wake up without a nightmare. I wake up shaking. I wake up in sweats. I don't think that I've ever had a week that passed without crying over something totally inane."

"One of my baby goats died last week," Conrad whispered secretly. "Big deal. Sometimes they just die. I cried for an hour," he confessed hoarsely, the memory still fresh in his mind's eye. "Everybody sees Conrad like the Rock of frigging Gibraltar standing before them, but Conrad is just full of fragile sand. Mount Bellew, to me, was never running away," he continued. "Mount Bellew, to me, was running back home, where I can lick my wounds and try to stabilize my life again, but it's still running away I guess, because every day I try not to remember."

"The Old Man died before I got out of the Marines," Conrad snapped back from his reverie, "so I never had a chance to kick his ass. I don't think that I ever would have; now I look back and just see him as failed and pathetic. Mom lives with one of my brothers. Things should be different, better. I need to forget, but I can't. I still carry all of the bruises; feel all of the blows."

"So, is that what you wanted for your present, Pieter? To find me?" he said as he angrily flipped the spent butt into a trash can. "Well, there I am, and I'm a friggin' mess."

"That's not exactly what I was looking for," Pieter said quietly, "but it will do."

"Why do you act like that?" Pieter then questioned.

"Like what?" asked Conrad.

"You know, like the Rock of Gibraltar, as you said."

"I guess it's my 'position' around here," Conrad answered, "What people expect from me."

"The position is what you make of it," smiled Pieter. "I heard that once from a great man."

Conrad considered him slowly, a bit shocked at the compliment, and finally said, "You certainly are a piece of work. And now, if you'll let me skip over to my office, I'll find a bottle of Beam which I think I could use a pull on; especially if we are going to continue this conversation any further."

"Pieter?" Conrad asked later, after the Beam had passed between them a few times, "Do you think that you will feel more at home, more accepted, as you put it, in some gay community, some place in a big sophisticated city away from all these cowboys? Some place with no buffalo steak and lots of flan?"

"I do, Conrad," the small blond figure piped up from his place reclining on the couch. "At least I won't stand out so much."

"Well, you're wrong!" Conrad sat up straight with the sudden assurance of insight brought on by enough liquor. "You'd be just another lost and homosexual soul," he lectured. "You'd be in a community full of people just like yourself. You'd lose your uniqueness. Where the hell is the fun in that?"

"I don't get what you are driving at," said Pieter, now pouring them another shot. "I am not doing this for 'fun' as you say."

"Well you *should* be," Conrad emphasized. "Hell, man, we are the weirdest most unique community in the world, as far as I can see. *Everybody* here is different! We celebrate and revel in our own uniqueness. We're like the New Orleans of the new West! It's probably the most common bond that we have between us all! Think about it, man," he babbled on. "For God's sake, even those awful purple jackets of yours…"

"You ordered them," Pieter defended himself.

"Yeah, I know," Conrad conceded, "but I'm colorblind. That's not the point."

"What is the point, then?" slurred Pieter.

"The point is," Conrad stressed, "the kids wear them like a badge of honor. Nobody in this entire business has that color. It says, 'Hey, I'm from Mount Bellew, and I just might be too crazy to screw around with."

"So?" agreed Pieter. "Most of them are."

"You just don't get it," Conrad said now warming to his subject. "You *do* belong here Pieter. You are one of us whether you like it or not!" he said while pounding his fist on the chair. "You see yourself as a misfit, but that's because you can't let go; be yourself; have some fun. That three piece suit act of yours is killing you, man. It's *killing* you. I'd like you a whole lot better if you just came to work in a dress."

"Well, that might be going a little bit too far," Pieter cautioned.

"It's symbolism, Pieter," said Conrad dryly. "What I mean is that these kids will never open up to you, until you open up to them. You're the boss. You've got to make the first move. You're the supposed genius, *you* figure it out."

Conrad abruptly rose to his feet and started for the door. "Party's over Pieter," he declared, "but I'm going to make you a deal. You drop the attitude against this prom. You promise me that for this one time you'll be just Pieter; and then you and I will go to that shindig together. Anybody, anybody at all, that messes with you, and I'll be all over them like a damn bull terrier. I might be an old man full of sand," Conrad puffed up, "but there isn't one man," he stabbed the air with his finger for emphasis, "on this *entire mountain* that I can't kick ass on."

"That's a tough decision, my macho man," laughed Pieter now intrigued. "Easier for you than for me. I'll have to think on it for awhile."

"Okay," conceded Conrad, "but let me know by next week, would you? I'll need to get a tux. I plan to be styling that night," he said with a sly wink as he continued for the door.

"Hey, by the way," the slightly tipsy Conrad turned as he went for the knob, struck by a sudden thought, "if you get some time, why don't we get some lunch together downtown, my friend. I know a great place with the most delicious flan."

"I'd be honored, *my friend*, and I look forward to it," smiled a beaming Pieter.

Ivana Chomutuv was this year's prom chairwoman by popular proclamation: a prom committee of one. As she had previously confessed, she had never been to a prom. She had never been *invited* to a prom, and certainly had never been the distinguished Prom Chairperson. Ivana guarded this honor like a rabid Doberman Pincher, chained to her responsibilities, and no outside input was solicited. She believed in absolute dictatorship.

We simply did like we were told.

The Mount Bellew Cotillion and Ball was her sweet revenge for all those lonely times when she had never been invited to the big party; when she was always ignored on the social scene; when her most elegant moves were danced upon the ice with a whizzing, but cold hockey puck as her partner. She ran her group of volunteers with the efficiency and resolve of the Marines storming Iwo Jima. Nobody could resist her persuasive arm-twisting. Sometimes it was psychological (Do it or I'll break your arm), but then again, sometimes it was very physical (See; now it is broken and that is all of your own fault).

I still carry the wounds proudly.

The food was plentiful, the cheap champagne was free, and the good liquor was sold at discount prices, all courtesy of Hermann and The Management. Tickets barely paid the cost of cleanup and damages.

There was a DJ who would spin music all night long: swing, rap, Motown, and wedding music. There never seemed to be a "theme" at these things and Ivana's selection was more eclectic than most years past in an attempt to cover a span of at least two musical decades without ever having a date.

An institution at the Cotillion was the giant costumed English Beefeater (you know, just like the guy on the gin bottle) who would announce your arrival at the door in a Booming electronically enhanced voice, as though you really were somebody important.

"Ladies and Gentlemen !!! (BOOM ! BOOM ! As his weighted staff pounded the parquet floor) **"Please welcome Mr. Louie Mayfield, 'Earl of Snowboarding,'"** or maybe, **"The Lady Bobbi O'Donnell and her escort...Gus...somebody,"** or, when he really began to forget names, **"This man is...Bob."** (BOOM!)

Even the "bobs" deserved a BOOM!

Dependent upon the crowd's reaction to your arrival you could immediately tell whether you were Mr. Popularity for

293

that season, a complete asshole, or generally still unknown.

Sometimes the fruit was thrown, but that wasn't polite, and often got messy. I took a strawberry dead center in the forehead, but it was certainly well intentioned, well aimed, and possibly, in retrospect, well deserved.

There was a photographer there, too. He took those nice prom pictures with a cloth backdrop that had mountains painted on it. They made you look like you were standing out on a snow covered cliff in freezing weather with a tux on while the wind blew up your date's short cocktail dress, but still you were both smiling like idiots.

Your parents would see this later on and say, "Damn son that must be a good job you have there. You have to get dressed up like that every day?"

Lots of guys took this opportunity to moon the photographer, but he did not seem to care since he had been at these things for a long time and never took it personally. He was a real professional and had probably seen more than a naked butt or two in his career (try www.Mtbellewhotchicks.com for a sample of his work. Very nice.)

Later, after the party, he often took mug shots for the police.

Ivana and the girls (me and Wally, too) put a lot of effort into decorating the ballroom of the local Howard Johnson's and it did not even look like Howard Johnson's anymore! There were flowers everywhere, helium balloons filled the ceiling and there were lots of good fake plants lent to us by the local funeral home. The crepe paper looked festive. I curled it myself. Again, no "theme."

Ivana said, "Use all the colors dufus," and rather than risk further injury, that is what I did.

Her reputation preceded her and, understandably enough, the decorations received an enormous amount of respect and compliments.

I was like a Martha Stewart God (dess). Whatever.

We behaved like civilized human beings, for awhile; and it was fun being sophisticated and classy, for awhile that is.

Then it got boring.

The choice of dress for this auspicious event would best be described as "non-traditional" for a formal affair.

I found myself not believing that I actually worked with some of these women. The transformation that a woman can make to herself is remarkable. It's like, she has all this "stuff," these "tools" to work with, and when she puts her mind to it, Mona Lisa's can be produced from a finger painting set.

Okay, guys comb their hair, brush their teeth and put on a jacket, then they look like a cleaned up guy. But women enter a cocoon in their bathrooms and emerge like golden butterflies; unrecognizable from the worms they once were.

It is very upsetting because when they don't always look this good, you have the feeling that they just aren't trying.

There was cleavage announcing itself everywhere. A word on that if you will; cleavage is one of those things that says, HERE I AM BIG BOY! NOW, WHAT ARE YOU GOING TO DO ABOUT IT! It can be very intimidating—especially for a guy raised with a lot of brothers.

(Imagine that you are innocently walking down the street somewhere, pretty much minding your own business, when you turn the corner and are suddenly confronted by an 800 pound gorilla sitting in the middle of the sidewalk. She apparently wants to play.

Well, your first reaction is quite naturally one of shock to even have encountered this powerful creature; then you become fascinated as you begin to wonder how to exactly deal with it. After all, merely by sitting there it says, "I WILL NOT BE IGNORED!" Staring at it does not seem to be polite but since the gorilla, confident in its own power, really doesn't seem to mind; that is what you do. Anything else would be *dangerous.*

Okay; so big cleavage is kind of like that; wonderful, fascinating, dominating.

Small cleavage? Same thing; smaller gorilla.)

Thick, shiny hair was piled high on top of beautiful tanned faces and set free from ski hats. There were long black stocking legs on women that I had forgotten even had legs, and slinky high heels had magically replaced clunky ski and snow-board boots.

Professional makeup and gold glitter dusted suspiciously browned bodies which sparkled in the reflected light of the disco ball. There were "millions of dollars" in fake jewels being flashed pretentiously about the room and the entire Howard Johnsons seemed suddenly infested with New York-style models. It was as though a hundred Cinderella's had arranged to high-jack a huge pumpkin and they had all finally come to the enchanted ball.

And that was just the females!

I say that because a number of confused guys chose to go in drag, and well, I think I'm pretty normal, as far as sexual preferences go at least, but Damn; some of these guys really looked good!

Of course, some also looked incredibly ugly, but then, that is the way with the real women, too.

Nevermind …

There were black ties and tuxedos, suits and very funky hats, a few tee shirts that were painted to look like tuxes and a few women in formal men's wear with lined-on pencil-thin mustaches. That doesn't do much for me.

An outfit or two could best be described as "clown-like," but hey, I'm not being critical; I usually dress like that.

The thing was, I just wasn't in Mount Bellew anymore! I had somehow blasted off the rock and had ended up in a Hollywood movie.

During the ski season, a true romance or two actually would bloom and prom night was the opportunity for the couple to display their affections in a real public forum. Public love was often evident throughout the night and though I'm not comfortable with that sort of disgusting display; I must admit that I like to watch.

Who you went with to the prom often confirmed rumors that you were going with someone, or squelched rumors that you weren't going with somebody, or started rumors that you were or were not going with someone else; or something to that effect. I'm not good at rumors or any romantic pecking order.

I spent four years of high school in total social confusion while being manipulated by young girls practicing to be old women and I still do not understand any of it to this day.

The dates were not always of the opposite sex either; which then made more rumors. Maybe they were just dating—I don't know—but it adds a whole new modern social twist to things that I'm working on trying to accept.

Finally, some people arrived single and that was okay, because I can relate to that. It seems normal to me. But then still others had two or three dates. However, I think some of those just needed a ride.

It would have been nice to have a date.

I tried, but had no luck. Wally wouldn't go with me. He was one of those guys that the girls just naturally loved like a big teddy bear and he showed up with three fairly strange and obnoxious women. I think he left drunk and alone.

Good.

The Beefeater slammed his heavy staff on the floor **(BOOM!)** and rumbled in his best, deep (James Earl Jones) Darth Vader voice, **"Ladies and Gentlemen, it is my pleasure to announce the arrival of Mr. Pieter Pietrosky, Director of Administration, and Mr. Conrad King, Director of Skiing." (BOOM! BOOM!).**

The announcement rumbled through the hall like a sudden clap of thunder from the sky and people were frozen in their revelry. A few hands, (not planning to be rehired next year) instinctively reached for the melon tray and small grapes were weighed in the palm to gauge velocity and trajectory. Everybody was too fearful of Conrad to even consider hurling the tinniest bit of kiwi in his direction, but the reaction to Pieter's impending arrival had brought about an inadvertent and collective groan.

Conrad and Pieter strode into the sparkling and suddenly stilled room in a shocking arm-in-arm display with wide-open grins that even managed to dwarf Conrad's large, midnight black Stetson hat. He wore his respectability like a fortress surrounding Pieter and any thoughts of mischief were quickly dropped with the fruit in the gathering buzz of the crowd. The gnarly old cowboy was the epitome of cowboy chic and elegance and he creaked into the ballroom like a well-oiled and extremely expensive leather saddle. Black tuxedo and spaghetti tie, topped with a silver and diamond choker were complimented by a shining pair of rattlesnake boots with four inch heels.

Conrad needed the height, for the boots served to put him eye to eye with arguably the most beautiful woman(?) to ever grace the Howard Johnson's Ballroom at Mount Bellew.

Maybe *any* Howard Johnson's for that matter.

Now some guys come in drag just as a spoof, as a fun thing to do. Then again, maybe they were serious and their little charade was just a pathetic cry for help. Anyway, they never pulled it off.

But there was nothing pathetic about Pieter's performance! It was an in your face, bite me, arrogant and glorious display of cross dressing. Pieter had not only come out of the closet, he had brazenly elected to *wear* the closet. Wearing it like no one has ever worn a closet before him. He was quite simply—magnificent!

Pieter had taken Conrad up on his challenge to "just be yourself and you will be accepted." He had donned a mid-length black dress, slit provocatively up the side, and (I must admit) showed the greatest legs. They were accentuated nicely by a pair of short black pumps. His close-cropped blond hair was curled and then framed by a pair of dazzling faux diamond earrings and his pale blue eyes, which were made up to perfection, blazed dominantly from the smooth skin of his face.

Then again, maybe I'm making too much of this...

Okay, I swear...I am not gay! I knew, deep down inside, that it was Pieter. The Beefeater said so, but I was stunned. I and just about every other guy in the place would have been "floored," but the only thing keeping us off the floor were our impending woodies. We found ourselves suddenly "wanting" Pieter.

When Pieter goes drag, the transformation is 110 percent effective. Women were jealous, men were horny, and Pieter was gorgeous. There is this little sane voice in your head that says, "You asshole; it's Pieter…"

Then the other little male voice says, "So what?"

Men are weird.

Did you ever read about the bonobo monkeys of central Zaire? I didn't think so. Why would you?

Anyway, these little chimps live on the equator and are named 'pygmy chimps' because they are, on the average, slightly smaller with slender builds and longer legs than their cousins "common chimps" which range across Africa just north of the equator.

Sometimes, when the bus isn't running, I read National Geographic.

These little buggers are very matriarchal and have an extremely interesting social structure, primarily because they will pretty much screw anything. Unlike common chimps, pygmy chimps assume a wide variety of positions for copulation, including face to face. They're quite inventive and unscrupulous and copulation can be initiated by either sex, not just by the male.

This makes it rather apparent that the Catholic missionaries have failed miserably in their quest to convert *all* of Africa to the Faith. These monkeys are holding out in protest.

The females are sexually receptive for much of the month (God love them) and there are strong bonds between males and females, females and females, and males and males: sometimes all at once! Like I said, they'll pretty much screw anything. I imagine that they throw great jungle parties with lots of bongo music and fresh fruit.

If we get to choose our reincarnation, I'm coming back as a monkey.

What is really fascinating, at least to me, is the fact that their DNA is about 99.3 percent similar to humans, and if I could find out exactly "what" that other 0.7 percent is made of, what drives their insatiable libidos, well, I could mix up a batch in the kitchen, be a very wealthy man, and would quit driving the bus.

Is it only coincidence that the little horny bonobo is the closest relative to man?

I don't think soooooo.

Conrad and Pieter floated through the room like a prince and his princess, making the social rounds at their own personal ball. Everybody wanted to be near them, some of them from respect, but most from curiosity.

The inevitable probes were sent harmlessly forth in Conrad's direction, "So, how long have you two been going together?" or "I like your date, but she doesn't seem to be your type." You know, that sort of stuff.

Conrad deflected them all with an air of joviality and took the inevitable good natured ribbing which he had known would be coming. Only when it got too close to the bone would he growl menacingly, "Don't screw with me tonight, friend, and don't screw with my date or *you'll* be hoping that there is a doctor in this madhouse."

That seemed to scare all of them off and it was not too soon after their arrival that Conrad found himself isolated from Pieter. He was given a few glasses of champagne, then a whole bottle attached itself to his hand. And since Conrad really didn't care for champagne, he began to use it only as a chaser for the bottle of Jim Beam clutched tightly in the other old fist. Soon the tough drinking cowboy found himself in similar rowdy company and the ski stories, ranching stories, and jokes began to get better and bawdier as they lost any semblance of truth.

But Pieter, for his part, for his first time at Mount Bellew, was not isolated from the crowd. He remained like the sun at its center and graciously entertained his new circle of friends. He did not drink much, possibly being leery for the attacks on him that never came.

The women buzzed around him protectively as though he was the Queen Bee himself; exchanging make-up hints, accessorizing tips, and if anyone with any sense was scared of Conrad, then just the thought of crossing these excited women was simply terrifying. They complimented him on his dress and on his hair. They wanted to know where he had gotten it done and later on we endured a complete summer of fashionable "Pan" cuts. They discussed the latest fashion trends and generally treated him as though he was the newest and most popular girl on the block.

Pieter was in heaven. He was suddenly adopted, loved, and having fun with himself.

Eventually, some poor confused kid asked Pieter to dance and the room around them froze in tense anticipation. The guy probably did not know that it was Pieter in disguise, but Pieter accepted with a fine and aloof air while his entourage whooped their approval. Then, more sober individuals asked him to dance, but nothing slow. They were still concerned that he just might magically metamorph back into ogre Pieter if they offended him or worse still, they might get an erection.

The girls asked him to dance. Some of *them* were slow dances. I think that Pieter still has plenty of the old testosterone brewing down there.

I didn't ask him to dance.

I was scared.

Bob Seager's rocking "Hollywood Nights" cranked up the crowd and it was soon followed by a maudlin version of "The Birthday Song": everybody sang.

Metallica preceded a crashing polka tune and everybody danced—even though they didn't know how to polka. They made it up.

Ivana grabbed a microphone and tried to imitate Celine Dion, and everybody booed. She cried; but she cried a lot that night.

Like I said, the music (and emotions) were varied, a regular roller coaster.

Eventually the gravelly voice of Joe Ely ground out a

booming country rock song which I thought was poignant and as he growled *"...the road goes on forever and the party never ends,"* we stomped a celebration through the endless night to the closing season.

The crepe paper eventually lost its curl and came floating down beneath the crush of a thousand feet. Conrad and his crew drank boisterously on while lean athletic bodies steamed and crashed through the air. Helium-enhanced voices reached to the stars with madhouse Mickey Mouse screams as balloons were popped and their contents inhaled.

Pieter and the twirlers seemed to levitate higher and higher above the floor in a whirlwind of spinning jewels and shouts of newfound friends.

And the party raged on and on and on, beating a tribal welcome to the rising dawn.

SUMMER

"What has my life meant so far, and what can it mean in the time left to me?" And now we are coming to the wicked poison dart: "What have I contributed in the great ledger? What am I worth?" And this isn't vanity or ambition. Men seem to be born with a debt they can never repay no matter how hard they try. It piles up ahead of them. Man owes something to man. If he ignores the debt it poisons him, and if he tries to make payments, the debt only increases, and the quality of his gift is the Measure of the Man.

John Steinbeck

SUMMER

*"For the joy of the battles we have fought together and for the
dignity of the battles we have fought between us"*

Paul Choloe

Fine mists of dust swirled in the air like tiny tornados, energized to flight by the dry and constant winds which blew throughout the abandoned parking lots and quiet slopes. Mount Bellew sat disheveled and lonely, a tired and overworked hooker without the inclination to put on her makeup. No customers now. This was a time for the rest that she dearly needed, a time to pull the blanket of warm summer days over her head and hide from the constant hubbub of a seemingly endless winter throng, a time for her to feed her hummingbirds, tend to her wildflowers and bake in the sun.

Bobbi sat in her new office leisurely reviewing the past year's performance, absently contemplating where the coming year would lead them and enjoying the feel of her new responsibilities. Her reverie was startled by a quick rap on the door as a battered felt cowboy hat poked its unannounced head around the corner.

"How's it going, gal?" Conrad asked happily from beneath the brim. "Looks like you're settling in pretty good here," he noted while doing a quick once over on the newly redecorated office. "Got a few minutes to spare for a cup of coffee with an old employee?"

"Just fine, Mr. King," Bobbi said a bit too tautly, her smile parked frozen on her face like a shiny new sports car. "It looks like we have the place all to ourselves for awhile," she indicated the empty spaces around her, "so why not pour yourself a cup and come on in."

Conrad busied himself at the pot. Since he gulped his coffee straight up and black, there really was not much to do, but he wanted to give her time to reassemble the scattered papers on the desk into a neat, new pile before swinging himself into the wooden chair beside her.

"So, how'd we do last year, boss?" he asked cheerfully acknowledging her new position, but also getting close enough to sneak a peek at what she had been working on before his intrusion.

"Slightly better than the worst that we expected," she answered coolly; not giving much of an answer at all and moving the papers out of his sight. She had felt that the relationship between Conrad and Hermann was a little too cozy for her own management style and that he should be reminded that he was an employee around here, not a co-owner.

"How do you think your Ski School operation is going to hold up?" she inquired professionally, trying to switch him onto a more germane topic.

"Well, I know that the basic core will be coming back," Conrad answered, "Most of them quite simply love it and the other ones haven't figured out where else to go for now," he laughed at the thought. "For instance, Ivana will return and I just might ask her to help out as a supervisor next year. She's so naturally bossy that we just as well might make the best of it," he pointed out. "And Mayfield seems to have found a home of sorts. I think that given some time he will turn out to be one of our best instructors."

"I expect that you will want to help out on occasion," Conrad continued with his voice assuming a fatherly and stern tone, "but we need to make one thing clear; Hermann used to flip burgers and pour beer to get him out of this office. He enjoyed that. You enjoy teaching, and that's okay, but the difference is that Hermann was giving away four dollar burgers and you would be giving away forty dollar lessons . I'd appreciate it if you didn't give out any freebies. If you want to feel noble, give your tips to the needy."

Conrad instantly knew that he had been too abrupt and Bobbi stared quietly, a bit stunned, for she was not taking well to this confrontation of her position so early in their relationship.

"You are out of line, Mr. King," she said coolly. "That will be my call to make. We will see how it pans out."

Conrad knew that he had inadvertently stepped out of bounds and moved quickly to make it right again. "Speaking of Pan, Pieter is not coming back, is he?" he questioned lightly hoping to break this new ice and change the subject.

"No, I don't think that we will ever see much of Pieter again," Bobbi said. "I think that, among other things, he realized that he would never really be happy here, but he did find out that he could be happy *somewhere*, if he was just himself. Oddly enough, he found that truth right here." She smiled in recollection of the prom. "That's one guy who owes you a favor," she kidded.

"And one guy who I hope never returns it," Conrad retorted. "If he asks me to be the maid of honor at his wedding, I would have simply no idea what to wear."

That loosened Bobbi up and they both enjoyed a laugh at Conrad's gay mimicry.

"Hey, speaking of favors," he piped up as though remembering why he came, "come on with me for just a minute. I got something to show you."

Conrad rose from his chair and led her outside to his old pickup truck.

"How about Ski Patrol?" he said nonchalantly as they crossed the expanse of the deserted parking lot while the wind whipped dry dust devils around their legs.

"Well, we lost Erik to somewhere out around California, but that's not so bad; ski gods are a dime a dozen in this business and someone else will show up to take his place," Bobbi said confidently. "More important is that we lost Daisy and she will be difficult and very expensive to replace.

"I know," Conrad said sadly shaking his head and thinking of his canine friend. "She was one hell of a great dog."

"Jeez, Conrad," Bobbi chided him while looking around her, "you didn't have to park halfway to town did you? Next time use the spaces next to the office."

"Sorry," he mumbled, a bit distracted with his thoughts, "I thought that the walk together would do us some good right now. Anyway, as far as that avalanche dog goes," he continued, "I guess that we can get another one before the season. I have a friend up Park City way that can get us a loaner. The other one will never be able to handle the work," he added absently.

"Other one? Which other one?" Bobbi asked suspiciously.

The windows were rolled down in the battered and mud splattered truck to allow the breeze in, and as they approached the doors, Conrad gently reached inside, fumbled around a bit to get a secure grip and emerged with a small, black lab puppy which immediately began to lick his face and hands in greeting.

"She's for you," he grinned proudly holding the dog out in Bobbi's direction like a wiggly present.

The young woman, now stunned by the gift, was hesitant to take the pup at first, unsure of its meaning, unsure of where it had come from; but then she eagerly picked the dog from Conrad's offering arms. The puppy was much too small for her age and had a feeling of fragility about her, but her dazzling black eyes danced with life and her fur was silky soft, black as ink.

Bobbi pressed the warm package to her chest and got a happy "yip" in reply. She looked at Conrad who was now beaming at the two of them like a proud father, and questioned him. "Tell me. Is this the same girl that you took away from me—away from Daisy? Is it, Conrad?"

"Yep, I'm happy to say so, gal," he nodded in confirmation. "I know some pretty good vets that can do some mighty fine work. She'll never be quite right," Conrad said in the way of an apology while reaching in to stroke the fine fur, "so if you don't want her, I'll be glad to take her back. She's very sweet," he added as though trying to sell Bobbi on the idea," and I've grown to like her a lot, but if you want her, she's yours. I think that she should belong to you."

Bobbi's dark eyes flicked in confusion between the pup and Conrad, Conrad and the pup. She had lived every day since January thinking that he had destroyed the struggling puppy and now this complicated everything. She had wanted to label the rancher as being "mean," as being a "bad person." She wanted to categorize him and put him securely away in her mind as somebody not to associate with. But now it wasn't so simple. It is never so black and white.

"Why didn't you tell me?" Bobbi said softly to him. "Now I feel so awful for the things I felt about you for so long. Why didn't you tell me that you were working on her?"

"Because you couldn't have handled it," Conrad replied simply while trying not to look at the questioning young woman. "Because if it all turned out bad, and the operations weren't simple," he cautioned, "you would have felt worse."

"That doesn't explain why," Bobbi said sternly, "and it's no real excuse."

Conrad studied the ground before him for answers, scratching with his boots on the dry earth, hoping to find something truthful to offer in the dirt.

"I'm not so sure of the 'why' either—not just yet," he fumbled. "But I seem to want to take all the things that I love and never let them go. I want to take all the things that I hate and never let them happen. I suppose, only recently, I have begun to understand that it just doesn't work that way; that both love and hate come and go of their own accord, but if I open up my heart, I see that the lovely things always come around again and the hateful things never last. In this case," he sighed, "I only know that I feel better for having gone a few steps further to save something this time and return it to a new life."

The glint of Conrad's misty eyes caught her own puzzled

stare and she knew not to press much further.

"It's hard for me sometimes, Bobbi. That's all I want to say for now. Don't ask too many questions, please," he added as to confirm her suspicions, "I'm still working on it."

"Anyway..." Conrad cleared his throat and pretended to survey the purple sky around him as if to break a spell. "The other two characters I worked for around here, Pete and Hermann, well, we used to do a little bit of hunting and fishing together, among other things, and I just wanted to know; do you like to fish?"

"Never did much fishing, Old Man," she said beaming a bright smile at him. "Daddy O'Donnell didn't have much time for that kind of stuff, but if you're willing to try teaching, I think you'll find that I'm willing to start learning."

"You know Bobbi, I think that I'm the one still learning," Conrad mumbled. "Tomorrow maybe?" he asked more brightly.

"Tomorrow definitely," Bobbi said, hugging the lively puppy now squirming in her arms in an effort to get down and explore some recently spotted garbage blowing by.

"Can I bring the dog?" Bobbi asked as she set her down.

"Of course," Conrad laughed. "We don't go anywhere without her. She's one of the Gang now!" he declared.

"Does she have a name yet?" Bobbi quizzed him.

"Yeah" he answered. "I called her 'Hope.'"

EPILOGUE

Come, step upon me: and add your rocks upon mine.
I don't know if these stones are stable
or even if I cross a stream.
I don't know if there is a bank we seek,
Or an endless river of water.

These are the stones which have led me this far.
They are mine, not yours.
They offer a safe haven from the torrent.
Use them if you will.

Please don't blame me if they lead to nowhere.
They have guided me well,
But I have gotten wet in my travels.
I have passed them to you my love.
The journey is entirely in your hands.

Walt Whitman

EPILOGUE

Be content with what you have;
  Rejoice in the way things are.

When you realize there is nothing lacking,
  The whole world belongs to you.

Tao te Ching

D own in the quiet town Hermann Olsen was slowly packing his sparse bags, taking the time to touch, feel, fondle and smell every item that he wished to take with him. Each small thing a story within itself—small things, important things.

He seemed perplexed, a little depressed, that over the course of time he had accumulated so few material goods to call is own. Where were the physical things of dubious value? He never seemed inclined to collect them.

Hermann had fought numerous moral dilemmas concerning the sale of Mount Bellew to large investors over the years before. With his final decision made, he inexplicably found himself to feel tired, just plain tired, but satisfied and content. Like a man after a strenuous workout, he had been put through a battle which had sapped both his physical and mental reserves. Now he needed some time to simply watch the clouds billow over the sea.

When he had arrived here in 1972, the young runaway had stumbled innocently into a dilapidated bar for a beer;

313

struggled with his future as he slept fitfully in a rundown motel, and ultimately bought an abandoned ski hill, in a failing town, using bags full of borrowed money. Not exactly the perfect business formula for unbridled success.

Hermann had entered this alpine world as a story on a blank page, waiting to be written, waiting to fill it with words, pictures, and experiences that were thrown his way: expecting nothing, ready for anything.

Some of the time here had been tragic, some uplifting, some comedic; but the story unfolded as it should have and often, despite his best intentions, despite his desire for nobility, Hermann Olsen had reverted to the frailty and foibles of simply being plain human.

That seemed to be his greatest gift and strength. The display of a childish wide-eyed innocence and naiveté of the world around him. People liked him for his simplicity. They liked him for being sincere and open. They liked him for his ability to fail and smile at himself without bearing grudges or resentment. Hermann never saw the struggle, he only saw it all as "Life."

There were heartbreaking disappointments which he stoically endured; financial worries which he kept to himself; and aching muscles nagging him for rest. All of these conspiring for a chance to offer Hermann numerous sleepless nights. And yet, he persevered, always with the hope that things would get better.

And so there it was. A season—both of time and of life.

Many Seasons had passed before his own time here, which he had never seen. *Were they much like this?* Hermann thought. There were uncountable ones left, when the snows would pile high against the windows, kids would scream in delight, and the laughter of parents would clap in the frozen air. Seasons which he would never see. *Would they be much like this?* Hermann wondered.

Probably; but *this* season was special, because this season was his. Hermann had lived it, he had owned it, and now it defined his life. There was no turning back, no erasers, no regrets. Because now the story had been written. There was no rewind button where he would walk away from old Pete's bar and stride purposefully out of the Mahogany Ridge Club into a different future. He would never be offered a chance to correct the mistakes, because then the future could not be the now, and the present can be the only place to fully live.

Ah, there is a picture of Conrad, Hermann thought, and his hands reached out to gently hold it in the plain wooden frame. It is just the two of them. They are young, buff, dirty and sweating over the trees that they had dropped for the new trails; a lean Hermann captured with his rugged friend.

He'll take that: a small thing of immeasurable value. They look good together—frozen in time. Hermann hides them between his folded shirts and soon they are snuggled securely together in his old black bag.

Gosh, you know, Conrad never seemed to age. He mused. *When I met him he looked as tough and as worn as the oak on the barroom floor. Pretty much the same now, but mellower. Spends more time ranching and less time skiing. Gotten quieter over the years, maybe a little more grouchy; at least with humans. Spends more time giving extensive lectures to his livestock than to his employees. Told me the other day that "The more I find out about people, the more I like my dog". HA!*

Anyway, it is time to move on. All the goodbyes that truly matter have been said and people are moving forward with their lives. They are busy storing their own memories for another day, when they too will have the time and the need for reflection.

Wally is waiting patiently outside to give him a lift to the airport. *This should be an interesting ride,* Hermann thinks a bit fearfully.

Time to let Mount Bellew move into the next generation.

It will be safe now.

Bobbi has the energy and the vision of youth. He, himself, had the opportunity to show her the value of experience; and the Old Man will somehow find a way to put it all together, again.

Hermann remembered that Pete once warned him, "There ain't some half-naked fakir hiding in the mountains up there."

Well, guess Pete was more right than he knew: seems that the old fakir was sitting right at the bar next to him, pretending to chase spiders from the ceiling.

There were good times here. Times, which like food for the soul, would sustain him for many days into his future. Hermann will never regret that day when he first stopped by and took flight from the cage. It's simply time to move on to other things. Strange how many people never realize that.

He remembered a line from a favorite book. The author said, *"The future lay sparkling ahead, and we thought that we would know each other forever."*

Guess not, Hermann reflected. *Times change.*

The thought absently swept the far corners of his mind looking for discarded particles of past remembrances and, finding too many to deal with at this moment, Hermann Olsen shut his battered suitcase on a lifetime of memories. He took a sad, nostalgic look around the small rooms that he had called his home these many years realizing that things can never be the same for him at Mount Bellew again: always different.

And then he slowly shuffled out to meet the waiting car, with a recent copy of *Boating* magazine tucked hopefully under his arm, his lips are softly whistling...

A Season of Hope

With those Changes in Latitudes,
Changes in Attitudes
Nothing remains quite the same.
With all of our running,
And all of our cunning,
If we couldn't laugh,
We would all go insane.

—Jimmy Buffet

So now, much like my former boss Hermann, most of my own stories remain forever frozen in the time/space which I have passed through, and, without the wisdom to see it for what it is, I might often feel regret for the incompleteness and swift passage of my life. I have found that the need to define the story in terms of "I" and "me" has lost its allure with age.

I sit here now, sorting through cartons of photographs which have been squirreled away in dusty shoe boxes. I search for the defining moments of my life. I seek those picture-perfect definitions of family and friends when I was always young, when I was never afraid, when I too was frozen in time.

I want to show the grandkids. I don't want them to think that I made this all up.

I do find some.

I like the photo of the family all together at Christmas. The one in front of the big stone fireplace. Too bad the fire wasn't going though. That would have been nice. It wasn't our fireplace anyway; although I led some people to believe that it was.

There is another; it is of my parents at Sapphire Point. It looks just like them when they were older, but nothing like them when they were young. My Dad was more muscular; my Mom like a movie star.

The shot of my favorite dog playing in the reeds when she was a puppy still makes me smile, although she got sick and we had to put her down. We eventually got another dog and, at least for now, I think that I love this one more.

Things pass, and our memories become selective and vague.

I search my mind to find a story to write for the kids— something they can understand as they grow older. I want it to have a clear beginning and the characters must emerge strong and well-defined. I want my heroes to exist for a specific purpose. I hope that purpose is noble: but sometimes they fail me.

In my imagination, the story will unfold in clearly defined blocks of time and a definitive conclusion will be reached. All of the problems will be resolved. The readers will slowly close the cover, nodding their heads in pensive agreement. They will thank the author for his incredible insight and then search the endless shelves of countless stores for another book which will give them further answers to very large questions.

There is no such story; at least not from me. Sorry.

Somewhere along the edges of many tattered pages, it simply ran out of words.

I continue mining the innumerable shoe boxes in a desperate search to find defining pictures. I need them for my book!

The color must be good, the subjects bright and clear,

their smiles gleaming and happy, their future never-ending. I want to see faces perpetually filled with promise and hope, a sincere love that will carry them through.

There will be no such pictures; simple sketches seem to say it all. They are done in black/white, shades of gray. Soulless people without names seem easier to capture in time. Ideas and concepts can then be easily erased and altered to fit the fashion of Society. Sketches become timeless because they are amorphous.

In retrospect, many of the photographs that passed through my hands seemed so wrong—out of focus, fuzzy, off center. I put them back into the tattered cardboard boxes without bothering to sort them out as I had intended, without bothering to put my life into a chronological order, without bothering to mark my progress through the years.

Once they were all jumbled up again—the old with the new, Christmases and birthdays running together, dead aunts and uncles snuggled tightly with the grandkids, no order to time or Season—I see my life and my story for what it truly is: the pictures only now ideal and complete in every way, captured in perfect harmony by their own vague indistinguishable relationships.

They are mashed together in a stew of jumbled boxes. One being stuck upon the other, a complicated weaving of bright tapestry, a riot of color and life.

They are out of focus, strangely spicy... and *perfect.*

All served up with the recommended condiments: ketchup, toast, and beer.

For after all, as Grandmom indicated, in a whirlwind of change and fashion, you *still* need the basics!

Printed in the United States
141818LV00001BA/152/A

9 781587 364006